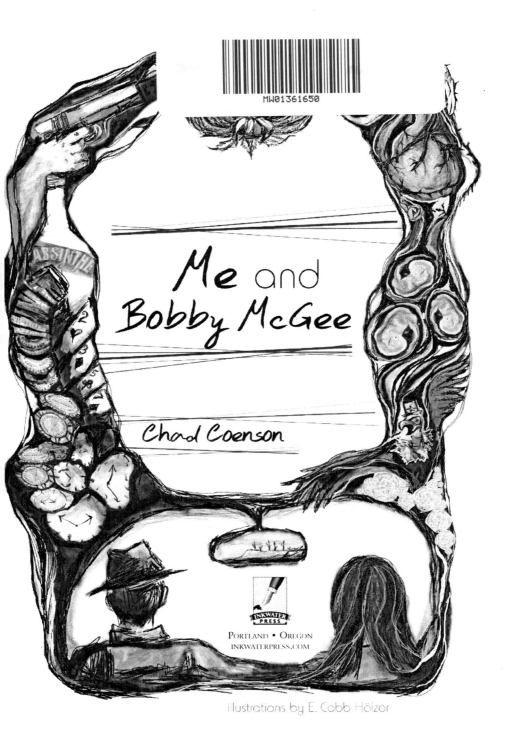

Copyright © 2010 by Chad W. Coenson

Cover Art & Illustrations by E. Cobb Hölzer
Interior design by Masha Shubin
Edited by Linda Franklin

This is a work of fiction. The events described here are imaginary. The settings and characters are fictitious or used in a fictitious manner and do not represent specific places or living or dead people. Any resemblance is entirely coincidental.

All rights reserved. No part of this book may be reproduced or transmitted in any form or by any means whatsoever, including photocopying, recording or by any information storage and retrieval system, without written permission from the publisher and/or author. Contact Inkwater Press at 6750 SW Franklin Street, Suite A, Portland, OR 97223-2542. 503.968.6777

www.inkwaterpress.com

ISBN-13 978-1-59299-488-5
ISBN-10 1-59299-488-1

Publisher: Inkwater Press

Printed in the U.S.A.
All paper is acid free and meets all ANSI standards for archival quality paper.

1 3 5 7 9 10 8 6 4 2

*For my beautiful and wondrous wife Megan;
without her undying love and relentless
tolerance for my unabashed insanity none
of this would have been possible.*

And for Kris for obvious reasons.

Contents

Part One 1
1. The Day After Fat Tuesday 3
2. Stuck in the Middle with You 10
3. Things to Do When You Don't 16
4. Things to Do When You Do 19
5. Retrospect and Disappointment 22
6. Building Relationships, One Failure at a Time 25
7. A Soft Spot on a Hard Rock 29
8. The Undeniable Past and the Relatively
   Forgettable Future 32
9. As They Are Made So Are They Broken 42
10. The Sun Rises in the East and Passes Out in
    the West 46
11. Casa-Notta 51
12. Better Off Than Dead...Maybe 58
13. W.W.J.V.D. 64
14. The Other History 75
15. Destination – Fifty-Two Years Ago 80
16. Places I've Never Been, People I've Never Known 87
17. Walking the Line to Cross the Border 94
18. Swing Low Sour Chariot 100
19. Dusty Path to a Desert Oasis 107
20. I'd Give All of My Tomorrows... 113
21. The Hour That the Ship Comes In 117

22. A Whopper with a Side of Insanity 124
23. Ambitious Sobriety 135
24. Games of Guarantee 144
25. Moving On Up 147
26. Of Mouths and Money 153
27. Coffee is for Closers (Who Can't Drink) 160
28. Forget What You Think 171
29. This Way to Your New Life 180

Part Two 187
30. Seven Years of Luck, Some Good, Some Bad 189
31. Bigger Picture Partners 195
32. The King on the Throne 203
33. Plan for the Worst, Hope for Anything Else 207
34. Why I Hate Public Transportation 211
35. Double-Cross Squared 215
36. Where Do We Go From Here? 222
37. The Inevitable I Told You So 225
38. Memories, Like a Bullet Through My Mind 231
39. A Real Bad Guy 236
40. Send in the Superiors 238
41. The Truth, The Whole Truth, and a Little Extra 242
42. Oh, and One More Thing 249
43. In This Corner, "The Shit." In That Corner,
    "The Fan." 254
44. Which Way Back to Nowhere? 262

Me and Bobby McGee

"Freedom is just another word for nothin' left to lose…"
— Kris Kristofferson

Part One

CHAPTER 1

The Day After Fat Tuesday

Wednesday – I awoke between the breasts of a perfectly inviting stranger. After an awkward moment of silence I offered an ignorant smile, a kiss on the cheek, and then an indifferent farewell. Apparently this is customary in New Orleans the day after Fat Tuesday as she offered the same unaffected grace with no interest in my identity or next destination.

The morning air smelt of lost innocence and bourbon as I wandered the streets trying to trace my steps or more, my stumbles from the preceding evening. Sin is supposed to have been filtered from the body on this day and a renewal of piety is meant to occur. Of course this is Louisiana or more so this is New Orleans, where all the names have tattoos, and the tattoos have faces, and behind those faces, those deprecating glares that falsely advertise sincerity, there is always an ulterior motive. The only trustworthy adversaries left are the shadows, and perhaps the wordless gospel sounding from the cardboard stages of displaced blues musicians; the revelry of Cajun saxophones, the soft inspirations of *the hopeful* and the somber lamentations of *the hopeless*. Either way I suppose it is life in a balance. All actions of *the lost* are counteracted by *the found*, but the lingering question is always, "who is who?"

And amidst these misplaced identities, on that plane of existence in between the scent of day-old jambalaya and ageless voodoo incantations, are those of us who still think we have a purpose. I was relieved when I found I was able to align myself with this order of souls. My purpose: to find a purpose. This is never an easy task, especially for a drunkard son-of-a-bitch like me.

I think that is in fact the central problem with alcohol. When the sun is down you can do anything you want because the rest of the fuck-ups around you don't care, don't notice, or would do the same thing if only they could walk. The morning though is spent contemplating just about everything, uncertain if perhaps you did solve some major social issue or economic world problem last night; and no matter what anyone tells you the charming humor of retrospect is still countered by reason and conscience accountability.

And now the sun was up, there was jazz in the wind, and life had begun again. I think Fat Tuesday is the perfect sequel to New Year's Eve. It's another wonderful excuse to be human. Another time to remember that before there were words, before everything needed to be defined, there was raw, unconscious bliss. And that's comforting because I couldn't recall a moment of the preceding evening.

As I wandered through the French Quarter entertaining my nose and torturing my stomach with the scent of Cajun breakfast, I tried to envision where I'd left my car. I had started this day three nights ago when I first rolled into town. It was four in the morning and the streets were filled

Me and Bobby McGee

with people as was expected. It was instantaneous madness; I had crossed the city limits, which entailed entering a social contract with some manner of spirit in between Lucifer and Dionysius. With a quart of confidence in hand, I dove into the sea of ten-dollar identities and bare-breasted beauties. Beer and bayou-brewed bourbon stole my face and some voodoo gypsy with beads around her waist stole my mind. I'm sure plenty of other stuff happened too but that was about all I could remember, which of course helped me in no way with my only chore.

Everyone I saw on the street had the same look on their face, what I like to call the, "Why the hell did I get up this morning look?" *And I never, ever, ever, do a thing about the weather because the weather never ever does a thing for me.*[1] There is no solace or comfort in that look, just ill will and the smell of vomit and whiskey sweat. And then suddenly a sweet sound grabbed my ears and led me like one of the pied piper's rats. I tripped over some broken cardboard boxes as the sound carried me down the remains of an alley way. It was the sweetest sax I had ever heard. Even the great John Coltrane had never inspired me in such a way. I was blind to the world and used my ears to see and guide me. It was like looking for the end of the rainbow except there was no pot of gold, just an old, toothless bum sitting on the ground with a Styrofoam urn filled to the brim with change. His music pierced through my entire body, all the way to the depths of my soul. It filled my hollow intentions with something a bit more soluble, a reason for being alive. I listened for a while and then dropped a five-dollar bill in the cup. The old man

---

[1] *Alice in Wonderland*, dir. Clyde Geronimi, perf. J. Pat O'Malley, Film, Disney, 1951

winked at me but just kept on playing. My existence was a mirage to him but at least he could buy a bottle of wine or something to warm himself, some blanket of escape.

The music danced around in my head as I walked back to Bourbon Street and it filled me with the desire to do something, to become someone more. It's easy to rationalize emptiness with illusions of grandeur when you're all alone in the world. There was a time when I wanted to be lots of things but somehow along the way my desire for greatness became a daydream of sorts and I settled for this life. This wandering decadence, a wash of sin and deceit; this was my existence.

But who's to say I had to give up on dreams? All I needed was a little taste of wonder and magnificence; then I could make my mark on this world…an enormous, neon mark, big enough to hide the last one I'd made. But first and foremost I needed money. Luckily that was the true reason I had come to this insane asylum city. Yes folks, I'm a gambling man, a Doc Holliday prodigy if you will. I live by the roll of the dice, the flip of the cards, and the gentle caress of lady luck. Some people think the great American gambler is dead and gone, but I'll tell you, it is one hell of a way to live if you play your cards right. But let's call a spade a spade, living this way only leaves you chasing the queen of diamonds and dodging the queen of hearts. But I guess it's only lonely when I'm alone.

Anyway, I needed to score big and the only way I could do that was to find an unsanctioned game. That riverboat shit is for tourists and the stakes are never high enough. Don't get me wrong, a few rounds of blackjack are not unlike good sex, especially when the cards are falling your way. In this particular instance though, I needed enough money to make it to the great western United States, and some tourist attraction was not going to get me there. I needed to find

Me and Bobby McGee

some gritty moonshine-blind Cajuns who had money to lose. The question was of course, *Where do I find them in this strange city?* You can always check the local bars for a game, but when you have a powerful thirst such as the one that has plagued me since I can or cannot remember, it's hard to avoid ending up drunk and in bed with some desperate waitress. With this in mind I forced myself to seek assistance in my quest elsewhere.

On my way to seek assistance elsewhere I stopped in a bar called Elsewhere, to have a drink, to help me think about where I might find this assistance which I did so desperately seek. There's nothing my old friends Jacky D. and the Captain don't have an answer for. Surely with their help I would be able to find a high-stakes game; and for the record I'm not an alcoholic, I'm a seasoned professional.

The bar was dark, cold, and extremely cozy, a place for strangers and the remains of outlaws. The wooden walls bore no nostalgia or photographs, except just behind the bar there was a framed print of Van Gogh's painting of the Absinthe bottle. At first I was aroused by the cultural depth the shithole dive chose to display, but then I began to wonder if perhaps it was not excellent taste in artwork but more an advertisement. I sat down at the bar, which was made of unfinished wood, and got a splinter as soon as I put my hand on the surly thing.

The bartender, a heavy-set gentleman with an obvious glass eye and minimal teeth, waddled over. I could see by the look in his good eye that I wasn't welcome; the glass eye remained indifferent. It seemed as though my penchant for dental hygiene had gotten me on someone's bad side once again. Not only did I have all my teeth, not one of them gold, but I didn't even have a cavity. I could see it in his eye...hell, I could see it in that hideous glass eye; I was everything he hated.

"Play it cool," I thought, "order something or bang your jaw against the counter so a few teeth come out, just don't let him know that you know." I shuffled in my seat a little and cleared my throat. I was about to say something when he beat me to it.

"Whatcha want?" he snarled.

"Um, nice artwork you got there," I responded.

"This ain't no fehggot bar, Suzy. I ain't here to discuss no cult'cha wit'choo."

"Wow, you southern folks really are gentlemen; you're like a walking cliché, my backwoods friend." He looked puzzled but I kept on, hoping I was talking too fast for him to pick up on the insults. "I'll have a pint of the dark stuff and a shot of Absinthe." A smirk crossed his lips and I thought he was going to laugh in my face. Instead he filled a beer glass and then blew the dust off a black bottle and poured me a shot of the green death; liquid Expressionism.

Oh, it chills me how I get myself into these perils. Sometimes I think I'm out of control and wish I had someone to think for me. But I don't. I stand alone in a desert of faces. Like the cracked section of a cheap stained-glass window, no one cares, because no one notices.

CHAPTER 2

Stuck in the Middle with You

I woke up to cold water being thrown in my face again – never a good sign. My head felt like tractors had been having sex in it. In these situations it is always smart to make your hands the first body parts you attempt to move. That way you can tell if you're tied up or not. If you are tied up you know that you're in a hostile situation and that the chances of talking your way out of the problem are much slimmer, and you can bet pink slips that you're going to get some new scars. If your hands are free you know that you've merely gotten too shithoused and you're either getting kicked out of the bar or you're in jail.

Luckily my hands were free and as I gazed around the room I saw no bars or police officers. But I was definitely still inside and not out on the street, and in a different room from the last one I remembered being in. The floor was concrete and the lights were much brighter than those of the Absinthe bar; it was more like some suburban garage. Of course my next thoughts were, "Goddamn it, turn down those lights. I've got a ridiculous hangover right now and I'd really like to sleep it off." Then I began to wonder how the hell I had gotten to this elegant Louisiana garage. Of course, then the guys who'd just woken me up with the cold water decided I'd had enough time to reorient myself with the planet.

They were big fat fuckers. It was like Burger King's version of the Double-Mint twins. They were wearing cheap gray suits and white shirts with those silly little cowboy ties that country singers often sport. Both of them were sweating heavily. It was by far the worst wet t-shirt contest I had ever been to.

"You know why you's here?" Sweaty Fat Guy asked, with Dixie pride in his voice.

"Sure. You guys are the IRS and you're here to personally present me an award for honesty and diligence when filing my taxes. Good to see you fellows." They looked at me perplexed. At least I knew I was dealing with intelligent life forms.

"You's gotta strange attitude foe someone who-dun know where they's at," Big Fat Fucker responded.

"And you've got great taste in suits for a guy with a fourth-grade education," I don't always try to be so charming when I speak to people but I liked these two guys. They were amusing me, until Big Fat Fucker landed a roundhouse kick to the side of my face and Sweaty Fat Guy decided to garnish me with a slimy side of his finest saliva.

"That smart-ass mouth of yas' gonna git ya into moe trouble if ya ain't careful," Big Fat Fucker replied. I could sense he was apologetic for kicking me in the face so I decided to play nice.

"Okay, where am I, fellas?"

"We ain't gon-da tell you's that just yet," Sweaty Fat Guy responded.

"Okay, why am I here?" I rephrased the question, hoping this would be the correct way to start collecting answers.

"You're here because you were gambling with money you didn't have and now you have a significant debt to pay," a voice behind me spoke. A much more articulate and intimidating voice I might add. "You're here because you're a degenerate alcoholic and no one will miss you. You're here because you're a parasite in the heart of evolution. You're here because you are a shitty poker player."

"Look asshole, I am not an alcoholic." It's important to stand up for yourself in situations such as this one. You can't let the guy you've pissed off know you are weak. Weakness is the first step towards impotence and no one respects a guy with a flaccid penis.

"My Mr. Cypher, there's no need to stop being a gentleman," the voice chuckled as it edged closer. I knew soon enough I would see the owner's face. The slow footsteps in my direction made me ponder why I didn't just turn around and look at the guy, but then I thought, "Bad guys are so good at being dramatic, don't ruin the moment, let your life mimic the movies." Seconds later I realized I'd made a terrible mistake when the fucker kicked me in the back of my head.

"It's rude not to look at someone when they're talking to you!" the voice shouted angrily. I still couldn't look at him though because my eyes were shut in nightmarish pain. The back of my head was sore from the kick, the front sore from drinking. When is my life going to add up to something more than excuses for suicidal tendencies and experimental psychology? I needed a beer and a shot of whiskey in the worst way and I figured the only means of getting a taste would be to behave.

Me and Bobby McGee

I swung blindly and hit the bastard in the knee. The twin tubbies were on me instantly. They stretched my arms out and each chose a hand to stand on.

"Why didn't you tie him up?!" The bad guy shouted as he rose to his feet. I could see his face now. He was a simple looking, white-bread, southern type. He wasn't flashy, he wasn't scary, he was just normal. It was like Mr. Rogers trying to be a hard-ass, with the pointy nose and flat demeanor; all he needed was a sweater. He had brown hair, parted to the left, with a few gray patches that so eloquently benchmarked his age. His eyes were glaringly shallow, like deserted tide pools occasionally stirred by rain. I can always gauge the extent of a man's compassion by the depth of his eyes. By the looks of his, I was in deep shit. "You're feisty, Cypher! I like that, it's not just a parlor act to disguise your bad luck," he breathed heavily.

"That's what the drinking is for," I grimaced. "Speaking of which, I could really go for one."

"All in good time," a grin made a cameo on his scornful lips and then he pulled a cigar from his suit. He didn't light it though; he just sniffed it and put it back. My hands were killing me; I wondered when he was going to get these fat bastards to move. "Nothing quite like a Cuban cigar."

"You spend a lot of time there?" I replied, close to tears, and looked up at Sweaty Fat Guy and Big Fat Fucker, "You two should spend some time in Ethiopia." They both spat on me.

"I've never been to Cuba. I get these from Mexico. As long as you know the right places to shop, it's just like being in Havana."

"And by saying, 'just like Havana,' you mean you assume it is just like being in Havana. Not really knowing for sure since you've never really been there, but that's what you meant, right?" I responded rudely. I hate people who make assumptions about places they've never been. It's like saying Greenland is a lush and tropical island or that Hollywood, Florida, is ripe with movie stars.

"You've been to Havana I assume?"

"In my younger years I found myself shipwrecked on that island once or twice."

"That's a fine way to put it," he answered thoughtfully, "business or pleasure?"

"What pleasure can there be without business?"

"You have a strange attitude, Mr. Cypher," he scratched his chin, "You also have a debt to pay."

"Okay hold on a minute. I'll give you the list and you answer one at a time: Who are you? How did I get here? Can you get the poster children for Crisco off of my hands? And how much?" The first two really weren't that important to me but I figured it would give me time to prepare myself for the bad news.

"Boys, I think he'll behave now." They slowly lifted their feet up and the blood that had abandoned my hands for fear of being pulverized into a gaseous state returned in haste to comfort my aching bones.

"Jesus, those guys are fat," I rubbed my hands lovingly. As the pain subsided I was ready to listen to the missing details of my life.

"Well, the food is good around here," he laughed. I laughed a little too and remembered that this guy had just had two of the most obese people I've ever encountered standing on my hands. My giggling eyes returned to their glare of disdain. His laughter deserted him as well and business resumed.

"So tell me, how did we become buddies?" I smiled sarcastically.

"I believe you had one or twelve shots of Absinthe at my Cousin Leo's bar. You told him you were a Hollywood producer looking for a bunch of redneck suckers to play poker with and that you were really sorry he didn't have all of his teeth, and could recommend a fabulous dentist in Malibu."

"I do remember him. You should get him a toothbrush next Christmas," I suggested. "I doubt they have any in Louisiana but I think they sell them in Mexico. You know, just down the street from the cigar shop."

He shook off my comments, "Leo called me and the boys to come out from the back and we sat down to play a little no limit Texas Hold 'Em. You won a few hands until we realized exactly how drunk you were. Then we cleaned you out. You swore you could win it all back, I asked you if you wanted the opportunity to do more than win it back. You asked me exactly what I meant. I told you I could lend you up to a million dollars but no more. Is any of this ringing a bell?"

"Not exactly," I replied, "but it does sound like something I would do."

CHAPTER 3

Things to Do When You Don't

Humidity makes me sweat. Some people sweat from fear or exercise but not me. I never exercise and I ran out of fear some years back, just before I lost my job. You see, I used to work for the worldwide sponsor of fear and paranoia, a nameless government agency with all the group-wide aptitude you could possibly imagine but not a single individual brain. Clichés lie like shopping mall Santas the day before Christmas and safety in numbers is the most strategic one of all. It keeps the masses from regressing to the temperament of primitive beasts. There is no national intelligence as far I'm concerned, just a lot of complex guessing games.

Fucking heat. It always keeps my mind wandering...I can never focus on the problem and I had just found my way into a big one. The illustrious "Bad Guy," who I came to find out was named Monte Weecel, had me in a bind unlike any other. I owed him 1.2 million dollars and had no way to pay. Damn Van Gogh and his overly appealing obsession with mild hallucinogens that taste like black licorice-flavored urine. Find me one person who can resist such an appealing drink, just one sane individual who can shake off the offer of a flame-toasted shot of Absinthe, and I'll get a 9 to 5 job and spend the rest of my life drying out in the pitiless sun.

But anyway, I was deep in debt and Monte gave me two choices. The first was to die, a typical offer which shouldn't count as a choice because I've never heard of anyone choosing it. It shouldn't be called a choice, it should be called, "shitty option number one." Following the first shitty option of course was a second that didn't involve being shot, stabbed, tossed into a river with cinder blocks tied to my feet, and/or eaten by rabid dogs. At least not directly, which was good enough for me, being that despite my past career choices I have always valued *my* life. I am the center of mine own universe, and no sun shines brighter than the two-dimensional glow of self-glorification.

With this in mind the second shitty option was in fact, my only option. It involved running an errand of some type. I was to meet my point of contact in Tucson, Arizona, where he would give me "the goods," and I would then bring them across the border into Mexico. I would be given more details when I arrived in Tucson, but Monte felt this was sufficient for now.

My assumption was of course that, "the goods," were drugs, but who has ever smuggled drugs into Mexico? There's no money in that. It's like bringing whiskey to Ireland. I would have to wait until I met my contact to find out exactly what the deal was.

As you can imagine my first instinct was to agree to the whole thing and then flee the country and never look back. Unfortunately, Monte had accounted for this already. I would have a chaperone of sorts with me the whole way. Well, almost the whole way. I would have to cross the border myself, therefore assuming all of the risk, whatever the risk was to be. The foiling of my plan of escape was disheartening but only at first; then I met my chaperone.

CHAPTER 4
Things to Do When You Do

She was statuesque as any femme fatale should be. She had long flowing brown hair that halted itself a few inches past her shoulders. Her brown eyes matched her hair in a chorus of exquisite simplicity, but their soft shape and intricate gaze made her exotic and penetrating. She could make heads turn like traffic lights and my heart's once evasive palpations seemed too long for capture. I hadn't felt this way about a woman since yesterday and I knew I wasn't going to let this feeling go.

Lucky for me I had many designated and required hours to spend in her company. The wind would blow her alluring scent under my nose and I would allow myself to be seduced by its charms. I would introduce a new and exciting thought into her mind, something intellectual but not showy. We'd talk about it for hours and then realize halfway through that we were in love. Soon she would suggest that we pull over for the evening and I would reciprocate the suggestion with one of my own – a bottle of wine. My choice would impress her and she would comment on my "having good taste." I would respond with an, "I know," and an obvious nod in her direction. The arms of passion would wrap around us both and pull us closer together, and then we would make love until dawn. I would then wake before her, kiss her on the cheek, and slip out before she opened her eyes to live happily ever after in a third world country with a fake passport and a stolen car.

Of course nothing ever happens the way you want it too. As I reached out my hand to offer a greeting she kicked me in the balls.

"You fucking bitch!" I coughed out.

"I just wanted to set a precedent for our relationship in case you were having any thoughts about pulling over for the evening and getting drunk and screwing. This is strictly business," she barked just like the bitch I thought she'd be. I knew from the minute I saw her that she was a stuck-up, plastic whore. She had devil eyes, bad hair, and the signature of fading beauty written in permanent ink across her entire body. It was going to be a long trip and yet I remained optimistic that she would choke on her arrogance and die from the agonizing realization of her own self-worth.

"You fucking bitch," I thought aloud, not meaning to be redundant, "I mean, pleased to meet you too...you fucking bitch!"

"It seems you have a true knack for conversation, Mr. Cypher, please tell me more," she smirked.

"Hey Monte, can I get one of the Weight Watchers' 'before' models to come with me instead?" I said winking and pointing at Big Fat Fucker and Sweaty Fat Guy.

"No Mr. Cypher, I think Miss McGee here will be the perfect company for you on this mission."

"Miss McGee? You mean she's not married? What a

surprise, I thought every guy liked to get sucker kicked in the balls," I shook my head at her, "you fucking bitch."

"Oh, get over it, we have work to do," she smiled as if she greeted everyone in the same manner...she probably did.

"Fine. But not without a proper introduction. I am Keesey Cypher," I said, reaching out my hand. She then landed a second swift kick right in my crotch. I fell to my knees again.

"And I am Bobby McGee. And this, as I told you before," she smirked, "is strictly business. Get up and let's go."

"You fucking bitch!" was my only response.

CHAPTER 5

Retrospect and Disappointment

You know, a lot of times when you think you know… you might. I might have thought my life was going to turn out easy and I'd have died young, died long before all the guilt, self-disappointment, and empty bottles piled up. But it didn't happen that way. I've sipped from the pit of longevity, against my will, and have entered my late thirties a mere mirror of the man I might have been.

I guess what I'm trying to say is there's a lot of things that might have happened and at that time I may or may not have been able to predict accurately what was to come, even though I may have known exactly what was to be. But, in the day's particular instance, I seem to be rather clairvoyant. I had moved my usual maybe or might stance on life to an unfortunate certainty. I knew that the future I could see bending over the horizon was going to suck.

Yes, a cheap-shot taking bitch as my co-pilot on a mission of mystery through the fucking desert and I had to drive. Most likely she would have a gun pointed at me the entire time, and some Gila monster would edge its leisurely ass across the road, I'd slam on the brakes, and the gun would go off. And then, for extra fun, I probably wouldn't die. I'd just be missing an ear and half of my brain. And it wouldn't be the half of the brain that I think with. No, not at all. It would be the half of the brain that controls all of my motor skills and instinctive actions. I would be able to recite Chaucer in my mind word for word, yet I wouldn't be able to begin explaining that I had shit myself. A living mind and a dead body, not really a vegetable, more of a fungus, like psilocybin or athlete's foot.

But maybe I didn't have to worry about it. If she shot me, the bitch would surely leave me out in the desert to be eaten by vultures or worse, maybe Texas locals. I can't be fed to Texans, I prefer Memphis style BBQ sauce.

Yes, it was for certain that this trip was going to be the most fun I've had since I stopped assassinating the country's most feared enemies that you've never heard of. That was the one thing these people didn't know: I liked to kill and had nothing but utter disregard for human life, including my own. I got fired because I killed too many people on a mission that never really existed in the first place. But then again it is all confidential and I deny my own realities.

Have you ever had dreams that seemed reasonable? Dreams that you were sure you could accomplish someday. Not the flying or illusions of supernatural grandeur type of bullshit, but practical dreams. Those are the only types of dreams I have these days, that and the occasional nightmarish flashback to my previous life and my last day of work. But I don't like to think about that unless my mind forces me to. The rest of you is so genuinely vulnerable when you sleep and memory is often as hostile as a scorned woman. But when my dreams are filtered by peace I prefer to gaze upon a house of my own, tucked away somewhere by the shore in Northern California. A place accessible only by some dirt road visible to the invited or watchful eye. A holy place, blessed by solitude and worshiped by forgetfulness. A place to rest until the mighty Pacific finally gives in to its hunger and swallows the West Coast and all its inhabitants. But that would all have to wait.

Through all the quickly fleeting notions of possibility and nervous sarcasm, my gut, which I trust way more than my heart, told me after much deliberation that the car ride I was about to take was going to seriously fuck up my life forever. I took a deep breath and then casually asked my hosts if I could use the restroom before we left.

CHAPTER 6

Building Relationships, One Failure at a Time

Bobby The Bitch. Sounds like a man...a scrawny inmate at some last-stop state prison, probably a child molester or a computer hacker. Either way, I was stuck in a black Cadillac with the "alleged" female version going ninety miles per hour down I-10 somewhere west of Houston. On the bright side I was trying to get to Vegas anyway, at least I'd found a free ride there. But at such a price...the price of my balls...twice.

I'll tell you something, that Texas sky does *something* to you. As the swelling dwindled she didn't look half bad. I kept adjusting the rearview mirror to catch two-second peeps of her cleavage. I know I'm immature, but only in a playful dirty uncle sort of way. And only with women I know are 18 and over...scratch that, only women I think are 18 and over. But whatever, I wasn't wrong about the gun thing. She had one but it was holstered like a billboard sign on the side of her breast. For all I knew she was about to pull it out and cap me, and I deserved one last look at two of nature's most beautiful creations. Not Bobby's in particular either, all the world's breasts are blessed.

I couldn't tell if she was catching me or not. She cranked up the radio so we wouldn't have to communicate verbally. Her choice in music was impressive though. I smiled under my mask of contempt as the sandpaper voice of Bob Dylan belted "One Too Many Mornings." I really was *a thousand miles behind* at this point in my life. But there was no time for catching up now. It wouldn't be long before the years started counting down instead of up. At fifty, I think the clock changes its course like a mutinous ship of fools, and sails backwards over the same sea it battled so long to reach the center of. Slow regression, not painful in mind, glorious and pitiless, and then you're an infant again. And then you're blinked out of existence. Things are funny.

As the song came to a close I felt myself wanting to say something. It had to be something charming and romantically bold in order to break such a thick silence, and maybe catch a hummer on this tedious drive.

"I'm lonely but I hate people," I decided to go with just plain bold. I had to get her attention and I figured profound honesty would create a bond between us. Then I could get close and get that gun off of her. And then, then I could feel her tits without worrying about getting my fingers blown off.

Of course she turned the stereo up louder after I spoke. I didn't quite agree with the gesture and went to turn the stereo down. She responded quickly with yet another silent expression and the gun made its first non-holstered appearance. Fearing that people would nickname me "Stubby" if I kept up my protest, I turned the music up slowly and then interjected, "The car is getting low on gas again; we've got to pull over at the next exit."

"Fine," she replied.
I nodded and chuckled to myself.
"What?" she questioned.
"You couldn't think of a good gesture."
"Huh?"
"A nod would have worked or a thumbs up."
"Honestly, Cypher, what the fuck are you talking about?"
"We've been driving for at least ten hours and you haven't spoken to me once. Why break this vow of silent hatred now, in such an easy instance for a non-spoken response?" I'm so witty, sometimes I wanna make love to myself…sometimes I do.
"Did you think I was playing schoolyard games with you?"
"'Schoolyard games'? What are you, British?"
"You're an asshole, Cypher," she said glancing at the gas gauge. "And why do we need to stop, there is still almost a half tank in the car."
"Because this is west Texas, a land just south of Purgatory that beckons for us to remain for all eternity."
"What does that mean, and why do you talk like a dime-store Shakespeare?" she questioned.
"It means there is one gas station every 200 miles out here and we need to fill up every time we see one or we'll never make it. And the way I talk is at least worth a dollar."
She giggled a little bit and for a second the temperature rose from cold to awkward cool. I could tell that despite her unexplained hatred for me there was some attraction. The question as always presented itself: could I expound on this or would it simply fade with the daily vanishing moon?
I found a Texaco three quarters of a mile later. We pulled into the station just as the weary sun had fully laid itself to rest. That's got to be a lonesome job; the old sun just isn't

as lucky as its rays. As I pumped the gas I realized I had no money to pay for it. I tapped on the glass and Bobby rolled down the window.

"What is it, Cypher?"

"You know, I realize my first name is weird but you could use it once in awhile."

"And call you Keesey?" she smirked, "Were your parents on drugs?"

"Actually yeah, they were. They were San Francisco hippies. The real deal. And they used to like to take acid, and read chapters of *One Flew Over the Cuckoo's Nest* to each other. My mom got pregnant at seventeen and named me after 'the other man,' that assisted in my conception. And my dad added the extra 'e' so I could keep my individuality."

"Why didn't your mother name you after your real father?" she asked.

"My dad's name was Bill. That's far too boring for 1968. I'm lucky they didn't name me Moonbeam Kool-Aid Factory."

She nodded in agreement and shrugged off a smile.

"Well, your name is still terrible."

"Why do you hate me?"

"Why did you knock on the window?"

"I need money for gas."

"Give me the car keys and I'll go inside and pay." I handed her the keys but oddly enough I hadn't even thought about running away. I glanced around and the choking glow of classic neon bar signs caught my eye. It was a Texas dive if I had ever seen one, with a lush, friendly, cheap motel next door. Suddenly my desire became uncontrollable. I needed just one sweet taste for the long road ahead.

CHAPTER 7

A Soft Spot on a Hard Rock

She walked out of the store wearing a pair of cheap sunglasses composed of light blue lenses and old lady frames. The sun had just gone down; what a tacky chick, it suddenly felt like I was trapped in a really bad commercial. Cue the music: she exits the store at sundown with her cheesy sunglasses on and walks up to my car to hand me a Diet Pepsi. If she'd been wearing a bikini, I would have bought a twelve-pack.

She tossed me the keys as she approached and hopped back in the passenger seat. I put the keys in the ignition but I didn't turn the car on; I was trying to think of the best way to ask about taking a load off for the evening and getting loaded.

"The engine is not going to turn itself on Cypher."

"So I've got what some people call a problem," I began, "I have this powerful thirst that I can never seem to quench."

"Well at least you can admit it, that is the first step," she smirked.

"I didn't say I was trying to solve the problem or even

claim it was a problem to begin with. I've spent half of my life thinking I could change the world and all it got me was drunk. These days I just leave well enough alone."

"What the fuck are you talking about?" she barked.

I really hate it when I have to spell it out for people. It was so obvious what I was alluding to. Even an inbred child with half a baboon brain could have drawn the conclusion that I wanted to go to the bar. Either she was as dumb as a televangelist, as they are in fact the only known entity dumber than an inbred child with half a baboon brain, or she shouldn't have worn sunglasses at night.

"I want to go to that bar and have a few drinks," I said pointing to southern decay's favorite shrine, "it's been a long day, I deserve it, and I'm starting to get the shakes."

"Well, I guess we could stop, we're making good time," she answered me. I must say that she caught me by surprise. I thought she would surely make some demeaning comment and then force me to continue on through this wasteland, parched and approaching a seizure. But somewhere in that well-endowed chest beat at least the final remains of a heart. I drove to the bar's parking lot and we got out.

The wooden porch squealed as we stepped onto it. Our weight, plus the savage burn of termites, was too much for the geriatric structure to take. As we entered the bar the damn thing collapsed behind us. It was the grand entrance to the rest of my life.

CHAPTER 8

The Undeniable Past and the Relatively Forgettable Future

"Two more shots of Jack," Bobby shouted to the tattooed Texan behind the bar. He was, without a doubt, the last member of some biker dynasty trying so hard not to die off, never realizing that you can't build an empire from a bunch of smelly guys in leather who talk about chicks in big groups but still have drunken sex with each other. You can build a reputation, or a following, or you can build a bar in a San Francisco, but without women…no dynasty, no empire. You have to accept that you are going to just disappear and your name will be left to no one. And while we are on the subject, it is such a burden anyway, leaving your name to someone. Who would want mine? I've done such a royal job fucking it up there's no reason to give it to someone else; that would just be rude and inconsiderate. By the looks of the bartender, he felt the same way. I like people I can identify with; it gives me fleeting opportunities to justify my immoral and irresponsible existence.

"Keesey," Bobby smiled at me as the bartender put our third round of drinks down, "bottoms up." Just a little booze and she softened right up. We clanged glasses and banged the shots down hard. "I think you're an ugly asshole."

"Don't flatter me, darling. I might hit you over the head with a bottle," I replied. Why did this woman despise me so much? What had I personally done to insult her to such a degree that every word and every phrase that slipped past her lips was derogatory? I had to find out before I had too many sips of social lubricant.

"What did I do to you?"

"Huh?" was her reply.

"Why do you hate me? You don't even know me."

"Why are you being such a pussy? Did I hurt your feelings, sweetie?" she taunted me.

"I have no feelings, but I don't hate people without a reason. Consider my question more for the purposes of psychology...further analysis about the relationships between men and women."

"Well," she thought for a second, "I guess it's not you I hate, more your kind."

"My kind?"

"Yeah, drunken losers that gamble all their money away and don't give a rat's ass about anyone else. My father was..."

"Oh, here we go. I remind you of your deadbeat father who gambled all the family's money away, was drunk and abusive because of it, and probably sexually molested you. Am I right?"

"Actually, my father was a police officer in Biloxi, Mississippi. He used to work the Casino beat. If you've ever been, which I'm sure you have, you know it's rancid with thieves and lowlifes. Anyway, my father used to bust these end-of-the-rope types. Teary-eyed fanatics without a dime to their name, stealing purses from old ladies and coins from the pay phones just to throw it down on one last hand, or one last spin of the wheel, or one last prostitute. Most of them had families that they left on welfare and never had the guts to go back to. My father would sometimes bring them by our house before he took them in to be booked so they could get a good Christian punishment before being given to the system."

"Well, it's always important to separate church and state," I interrupted. Not amused, she continued her story:

"We would handcuff them to the fence in the backyard and cast stones at them for twenty minutes or so, and then my father would cart them off to jail," she paused and glanced up at me. The horrified look on my face made her smile, but only for a second. The grin faded and she proceeded with the story, "One day, when I was about seventeen, my father brought home a paraplegic gambler and as per usual we brought him out to the backyard, but because of his disability, my father, merciful as he was, decided not to handcuff him. As we gathered sharp stones from the ground the crippled gambler reached into a hidden wheelchair pocket that my father had neglected to search during the pat-down. The legless bastard pulled out a gun and shot my father. My mother and I screamed for help but no one heard. He wheeled his way towards us and then shot my mother as well. I thought he was going to shoot me too, but instead he just ran over my foot and scooted toward the gate, and then let himself out..."

"And he got away so you've vowed to hate, and possibly kill, every drunken gambler you meet to avenge your parents' death," I interjected.

"No! He tried to make it down the driveway but it was too steep. He lost control of his wheelchair and then a pickup truck turned him from paralyzed to pulverized. I guess man was never meant to have wheels for legs," she brushed a tear from her eye. At that moment I realized something; Bobby was out of her fucking mind.

"So a drunken gambler killed your parents and that's why you hate my kind," I said to her, nodding with understanding.

"I said 'shot,' not killed," she corrected me, "both of my parents survived, but I was left with this." She took her shoe off and showed me the tire tracks across the center of her foot. She began to cry, "I am a horrible freak and it's all because of you fucking drunken, gambling assholes!" She became hysterical and threw a shot glass at me. It missed and shattered against the wall.

"'Scuse me, Ma'am," the bartender said, "I don't mean tah interrupt' beings that yous a friggin' lunatic and all, but you gonna have to pay for that."

"Of course," she said regaining composure, "I apologize for the outburst." Man, she was crazy. She had tortured people in her backyard as a child, kicked me in the balls a couple of times, picked on the handicapped, had a cop for a father, thrown a shot glass in a public arena while lashing out irrationally, and yet I was still attracted to her, except for one major concern.

"So Bobby," I began, fearing some kind of violent reaction, "are you still a Jesus freak?" She stared at me blankly for an instant, and then a smile broke free across her lips.

"Is that all that you got from that story?" she asked.

"No, but it's the only thing that worries me about you."

"Why? Because you think I won't have sex with you?"

"No, because now that we're talking, I sure as hell don't want to have to listen to you preach," I replied. I have never been big on religion, and it's not because of the needless wars that have been fought over it, or because of the outdated traditions, or even the funny hats that people wear. It's because it seems like the easy way out. Put your faith in some invisible deity, donate some money, and all your sins can be forgiven once a year, or once a week, or once a day depending on which folktales you choose to accept as your belief structure. Yeah, it seems everyone is looking for forgiveness; me, I'm just looking for remorse.

"No, I'm not still religious. After my foot was mutilated I realized there was no God."

"Well, don't feel bad," I comforted her, "it took a lot less for me to realize that there was no God."

"Oh yeah," she responded, "What caused you to lose your faith, Cypher?"

"Humanity."

"Explain how 'humanity' caused you to lose your faith."

"That's easy. God is supposed to be this omnipotent, all-wise, all-knowing, all-powerful, spiritual being." Content with my answer, I turned to order another drink.

"Elaborate!" she demanded.

"What sort of all-wise, all-knowing, all-powerful being would be stupid enough to create such a wretched flock of beast to inherit the earth?" I can never understand why it's not obvious to more people, but I continued nonetheless, "Why would God create a species that would wipe out entire other species? Mostly the most beautiful species, I might add. Why would God, all-wise, make a species that would commit mass genocide willingly for money or patriotism or whatever? A species that would…"

"You were in the CIA or something, weren't you?"

"Okay, wait a second. How am I so predictable?"

"Because that is the only type of person that would

commit mass genocide for money and then be pissed off about it for the whole of their existence," she smiled and gloated with her perfect, Sunday-white teeth.

Is that really what it boils down too? She pegged my whole life in thirty seconds; it was unbelievable. I think I had subconsciously been waiting all day to entertain her with heroic stories from my past, and present myself as a man of mystery and excitement. All fucking day I waited, and she sniffed it out in two sentences. I needed another drink.

"Bartender," I grabbed his attention and he walked over, "Something different this time…how about whatever flavor is the opposite of utter disappointment." He looked confused and then he poured me a shot of some tequila I had never seen or heard of called "Sudor Del Niños – *Blanco Tequila*." I had no idea what that meant so I asked the barkeep.

"It means, 'Sweat of the Children,' burns like hell on the way down and finishes like heaven. It'll gitcha real good and drunk," he told me.

"Strange name, but what the hell, it's the recommendation of the house." I dumped the shot down my throat and felt my liver ignite. It was like drinking gasoline that had been lit on fire, with a throat made of wood. "Holy shit, that burns," I began to cough uncontrollably.

"I told ya it burns like hell, at least ya ain't disappointed," he chuckled. Everyone is a fucking comedian around here. I hate being made fun of, it makes me angry. I thought about killing the asshole, I really did, but more to put fear into Bobby than to repair my already dejected pride. Instead, I grinned at him (as the shot did settle kindly in my stomach and filled me with an odd sort of euphoria), accepted his mildly amusing joke, and resumed my conversation.

"Yes, I was in a nameless subsidiary of the CIA. My job

was to shoot people, and unlike your poor, crippled pal, my job was to shoot people and make sure they were dead. Needless to say, I sometimes had to shoot people twice or even three times, and sometimes I had to shoot the people that may have seen me shoot someone else. And sometimes I had to kill lots of people at once, so I used bigger guns. But then I didn't shoot people, I blew them up instead."

"Sounds like good work, why did you quit?" she asked, sincerely interested in my reply.

"I lost my edge, started drinking too much, and then I made a mistake that cost me everything. After that, I lost my identity, and was forced to walk the Earth drunk, living score to score, and growing more and more heartless day in and day out. And now..." I paused for a second and looked deep into her eyes, "And now I'm in Texas because I have to pay a debt to some guy I don't remember owing money too." I hate feeling sorry for myself but it is the only thing that keeps me going sometimes.

"What was the mistake?" Bobby asked.

"Huh?"

"The mistake you made 'that cost you everything.' What was it?"

"That's classified," I winked at her.

"You're an asshole, Cypher."

"Not so predictable now, am I?" It was my turn to gloat, I had finally gained her interest and now maybe she would cease kicking me in the groin. Maybe now she would find other uses for it. We sat speechless for a few moments. I ordered another round of shots for both of us and some beers on the side. Don't you hate those moments where all you want to do is say the right thing? You flip through your mind's vocabulary looking for the perfect words, the perfect phrase, something poetic, yet firm. You have to make sure the words come out right and once you have them in line, you have to gaze deeply into the woman's eyes and let her know how you feel. Of course, sometimes they beat you to the punch.

"You wanna fuck?" she asked very nonchalantly. I couldn't believe it; I've never had a woman ask me that without wanting to steal my wallet and this one knew I had no money. I think I may have started to pant a little but *that's just the dog in me.*

"Absolutely, I was just thinking that myself when…"

"Well here's the deal," she cut me off, "if you can complete this little task Monte has lined up for you, then you can have me. Until then, get it out of your head."

"What if I promise to complete it and you help me celebrate now?" You can't blame a guy for trying, especially when he's getting drunk next door to a motel.

"Nope, you've got to get it done first. Think of it as proving your sexual worthiness," she kind of laughed to herself after that remark. I had nothing to prove, I was a man with a penis; how much more worthy did I need to be?

"Fine, it's a deal. But I want it writing," I reached for a napkin and asked the bartender for a pen. I scribbled some words out and handed her the napkin. She shook her head and then looked at what I had written:

THIS NAPKIN IS TO BE TREATED AS A LEGAL CONTRACT:

I, the undersigned, do solemnly swear that I will have sex with Keesey Cypher after he completes his mystery errand. I will not only have sex with him but I will enjoy it and take it in the rear if he so desires. May the God that I formerly believed in strike me down if I am lying.

_X_____

"We're crossing out that last part," she said.

"I agree with your revision," I said and then crossed out the line about God.

"Not that part, Keesey," she smirked. I rewrote the contract on another napkin and she signed it. I put it in my jeans and promised myself I would never lose that piece of paper, and never use it to blow my nose. We ordered one more round and I decided to make a toast, or at least my withered version of a toast; a burnt slice of bread.

"Raise to the future," I said and we both lifted our glasses, "drink to the past." We both slammed the drinks down. Bobby wiped her lips and then looked at me oddly.

"Why do you drink to a past you despise?" she was genuinely curious.

I smiled, "Because I'm trying to forget it." And with that we agreed that we were both tired and headed next door to the motel. I wish I could tell you she changed her mind and things turned out good for yours truly, that it was magical and we found true love that night. But this is not a fairy tale. Fairy tales are for fairies, the real world is a lot more complex. We got a room with two double beds and Bobby handcuffed my ankle to my bed so I couldn't run off. Luckily I fell asleep quickly and without dreams to distract me from my rest.

CHAPTER 9

As They Are Made So Are They Broken

The day hit me like a brick...but I think today it was made of limestone, instead of the usual sharp cement. In fact, the usual pain in my head and the confused state of being were in no way present. How long had the bender been going on, I wondered? How many blackouts had there been? I had gotten so used to waking up to fading memories that become ever transparent by the second, and then disappear forever with the day's first flush of the toilet, that the alertness of my short-term memory on this particular day alarmed me. For so long I had been avoiding real human contact, and I don't mean I was a hermit living in a hollowed-out oak tree, eating squirrel meat and poisonous berries day in and day out. I mean, I avoided having connections to anyone or, more so, getting to know anyone, and now I was forging some kind of psychosomatic bond with a woman who would kill me in an instant and probably throw rocks at me before I died. Let he who is without sin cast the first stone, my ass.

In a past life I've pondered my existence as I wiped the dust from my sharpest eye and then gazed into the scope of my rifle. Was I an angel of death, an angel of mercy, or perhaps a demon from the pits of hell? And what is your life worth when you spend your time blinking others out of existence? I guess it depends on the exchange rate. But angel, devil, saint, or sinner, I've never changed sides; I just left the fortress and chose to remain unrefined and invisible. The beautiful existence of false omnipotence retired. But the past is behind us for a reason and each sunrise gives way to new hope and new disappointment, and either way, at least it is reliable.

I began to gather my things when I realized I didn't have anything at all. Bobby had been up for a little while already and had released me from my bedtime bondage while I slept. I had a nasty bruise around my ankle where the handcuffs had been but it was nothing worth complaining over, especially to a woman prone to kicking me in the crotch. I opted for silence and walked into the bathroom. After relieving myself I put some of Bobby's toothpaste on my finger and did my best to clean my teeth. It would have been nice of my captors to have let me grab my travel bag back in New Orleans, although it probably would have taken days to find my car. They could have at least provided me with the bare essentials: toothbrush, deodorant, change of underwear – these people were obviously very inconsiderate and probably cared less for humanity than I did.

"Hey Bobby," I said. She popped her head into the bathroom and I continued, "Can we stop at a store at some point so I can grab some supplies?"

"If you can pay for them," she replied.

"You know I don't have any money."

"Well, then you'll have to wait until you do. Besides,

we'll be in Tucson in seven hours or so and you'll just be a day away from being rid of this whole ordeal."

"But my breath is going to smell like my armpits, and my armpits are going to smell like my ass, and I don't even want to think about what my ass is going to smell like," I whined.

"You smell like booze no matter how hygienically balanced you may try to be," the bitch had a point, "And who are you trying to impress anyway? You've already got your little napkin contract from me," she said.

"Bobby, let me fill you in on something. Contrary to popular belief, I get lots of women. I know you may think I'm just a degenerate gambler with a terminal case of alcoholism that would do anything for a fuck, but I've got news for you," I grinned, "lots of women like a man with secrets." She shook her head and left me alone in the bathroom. I couldn't tell if she was incredulous, offended, or jealous but either way I still didn't have a fucking toothbrush. I've got to learn to avoid mixing pride with charm; it never gets me anywhere.

I finished up in the bathroom and we checked out of the motel. We had a full tank of gas and would probably be able to make it to El Paso without worrying about putting juice in the car. As we got back onto the highway it became apparent to me that Bobby had resumed her temporary vow of silence and was not going to speak to me unless she absolutely had to. Instead of questioning it I decided to play along, and I turned up the radio as loud as I could.

The humble voice of John Fogerty belted the words to "Lodi," and I began to remember what it was like to be a teenager...you know, that day you become disillusioned and realize that all those dreams you had as a child aren't worth a damn. When I was five I thought I was going to be a rock star; when I was fifteen I decided I had no talent and then figured I'd be better off killing people. My hippie parents didn't like the idea at all but they were never into holding me back from achieving my goals. And so reality coaxed my young mind away from bright lights and loud music, and brought me to a pitiless world of two-dimensional friendships, orders and covert assignments; death. And now the aftermath of derailed ambitions and aspirations had taken over. Yes, my adult life was an accurate reflection of that crowning adolescent moment and it seemed that everything I had worked for, which was nothing, wasn't going to pay off in the end. I guess it's comforting to be enlightened, even when you're a pessimist. *I came into town a one night stand, looks like my plans fell through, Oh lord, stuck in Lodi again.*

CHAPTER 10

The Sun Rises in the East and Passes Out in the West

Seven and a half hours and she didn't say a fucking word to me. She left me wandering around in my mind, digging up teenage memories and trying to draw connections between classic rock songs, my insistent self-loathing, and my appetite for violence. I hated her more than ever. You never let a man who has seen the shadowy corridors of this sunny planet think too much without interjecting. If she hadn't had that gun I would have forced her to talk to me. Even when we stopped for gas she just took the keys and went inside to pay. I tried to ask why she didn't just use a credit card, but she wouldn't respond. I figured she had bad credit and then we would have something in common, a conversation starter of sorts, but still nothing. She just wore a blank stare behind those stupid blue lenses all the way to Tucson. We exited the highway at Speedway Ave and she finally spoke.

"Turn right," she said. I was relieved to hear her voice even though I hated her. It was about 6:30 pm Tucson time, which is a strange and rebellious time in the region as Tucson, and all of Arizona for that matter, does not follow daylight savings like the rest of the United States. We were headed toward the mountains when Bobby pointed to a gas station and we turned in. There was a set of payphones on a cement island away from everything else and she needed to make a call to someone. As she went to get out of the car I grabbed her hand, she spun around with a hard right that caught me directly on the cheek bone.

"What the fuck?!" I shouted at her. She was holding her hand in pain and I could see the knuckle of her index finger swelling already.

"You asshole, Cypher, look at what you did to my hand," she growled in pain.

"Well, you shouldn't have hit me then," I grunted back rubbing the side of my face.

"Oh, don't make this my fault," she said, "besides, you can always get one of your many women to take care of you."

"Ha! Is that was this is about?"

"Shut up, Cypher," she paused, "or I'll shoot you."

"You're in love with me, aren't you?" Like a cowboy from the Old West, she whipped that gun out so fast I'd have been dead at high noon for sure. She pressed it against the side of my head and grabbed my chin with her other hand. It was very sensual and I started to get aroused.

"If you ever say that again I *will* kill you," she said.

"You so are," I replied. She cocked the gun and pointed it at my semi-aroused penis and smiled at me wickedly.

"Oh yes, Cypher," she said sarcastically, "you're irresistible to me and if I can't have you..."

"Okay, you're not in love with me and I'll never say it again!" She withdrew the gun and put it back in its lucky little location, right next to her breasts. How come inanimate objects always get the best jobs? How come I can't get a job that entails my hanging out next to a woman's tits all day in order to protect her?

The gun seemed to laugh at me boastfully as her boobs bounced their way over to the payphone. She pulled out a calling card and entered the numbers. I could only make out pieces of her conversation but nothing that gave me any clue as to what my little task was. It seemed that she was just letting someone know that we had arrived; probably Monte. She hung up and then made a second call. This time she spoke in Spanish and I was only catching a word here and there. I kept hearing the word "bebé," which of course means "baby" in English. I was completely confused. She had been sending me signals this whole time and there she was, affectionately calling her Mexican boyfriend *Baby* right in front of me. Will the cruelty of this world ever cease to bless me? She finished up with her *Bebé* and got back in the car.

"You know you could have just told me. I'm not one to impede another man's happiness despite my limited morals," I proclaimed.

"What?" she looked confused.

"Oh, and now you think I'm too dumb to understand Spanish. I was in the CIA, remember? Traveled the world, lots of foreign countries, very little English, shot people of all nationalities."

"Keesey, I honestly have no idea what you are talking about right now."

"I just heard you call somebody *Bebé* on the phone. Obviously you have a boyfriend in Mexico and that is why I am here. To run some errand to help him, you, and Monte, and then be left with nothing but a napkin contract that isn't even notarized!"

Me and Bobby McGee

She looked at me dumbfounded for a minute and then began to giggle, "You think I have an evil Mexican boyfriend that set this whole thing up in conjunction with Monte?" Her giggling turned to full-on hysterical laughter and I became more perplexed each time she gasped for air.

"So you don't have a boyfriend?" She just laughed and shook her head some more, "Well then, what was all that, *bebé* talk about?"

"Sorry, Cypher," she regained her composure, "that's classified."

"Touché," I replied. She was a sneaky bitch, I had to give her that. She used my own favorite line against me and continued to remain ever more mysterious than me, but only by one point. The game was still up for grabs and no psychotic, ex-Jesus freak, tease was going to beat me out. And if she was going to beat me out, at least she didn't have a boyfriend and I would still get a piece, as long as I survived the coming challenge.

"You love me, don't you?" she asked.

"Only when I'm masturbating," I replied. She looked at me disgusted; perhaps she would have been more charmed if I had pulled an axe out and held it against her forehead. I'll never understand women; I guess that's why I like one-night stands or more poetically put, "provisional love." Physical attraction is so much more simplistic and primal. You don't have to watch what you say, or do, or where your eyes wander to. It's only about the sex and that is how I like it. And with that in mind, I had to get laid before I ventured forth on this little mystery task because for all I knew I wasn't going to survive it. If Bobby wasn't going to help me out, then I had to find someone who would.

"So, what now?" I asked.

"Now we wait for the morning to come," she said.

"Are we just going to sit here, I mean, the sun isn't even down yet."

"No, but we've got to lay low," she said, glancing around as if someone could attack us at any minute, "Let's go to Miracle Mile, we can have a drink there."

Miracle Mile is the armpit of the city. It is nothing but cheap fetish strip clubs, transvestite hookers, bikers, and illegal aliens. I figured asking Bobby if we could go to one of the college bars was out of the question, so I just kept my mouth shut and drove. We reached our destination just as the sun began its final descent. I wish I could have gone with it but instead I was walking into a biker bar called Eden. Bobby had put on a jean jacket that she had in the trunk of the car in order to hide the gun. Arizona and Texas are very different places despite their geographical locations. For instance, in Arizona you can't blatantly display a firearm, but in Texas, it is considered stylish. We entered Eden; I was nervous and hot as hell but I wasn't sweating. You don't sweat in Tucson; it evaporates before you have the chance.

CHAPTER 11
Casa-Notta

Fuckin' dry heat. The desert is no place. It's a world of struggle and alchemy, an ancient burial site for hobo sailors and Apache warriors. The ground crawls with fate and the sun cries for its apostles to grovel for mercy. Saguaros, stone people, and blood beneath the dirt, there is no present here and the future is only found in postcards; this is the promised land of ghosts. And on days like today, when faces surround you like a house of mirrors and your soul abandons you for cigarettes and coffee, you can't help but wonder if you may end up buried out here. Because desolation row is an oasis somewhere in the middle of the desert, a truck-stop resort & spa for liars and thieves, and people who still have a conscience. The rest of this biome is reserved for poets, ex-cons, sad-faced fools, and everyone else who fucks the fear out of loneliness.

There is nothing but poison in the vibrations of this kingdom of malice. Poison in the water...in the wind...in the women. Not all of it can kill you though; some of it just induces mild hallucinations and false ambitions. It's a slow, painless process, like alcohol and promiscuity. So as I sit here in this dive-bar paradise called Eden, knocking back shots for charity, scrawling a requiem for salvation, and trying to get laid, I realize there's nothing you can do but pick out your favorite lies from the songs of roadside convicts, and scowl at the supernatural glory of a Tucson sunset. *"How did I get here?"* The most common question a person asks themselves in this climate. And looking around this room, at the dead remains of a lost civilization, I can understand why.

The cursed feeling of anticipation wouldn't leave me alone and not a woman in the bar wanted anything to do with me. Bobby sat beside me silently, sipping on a beer. It seemed as though the coming of tomorrow in some way frightened her as well, but why? I had to figure all of it out, I had to know what I was getting into, I had to get Bobby in bed, and goddamn it, I had to escape this trepidation. It was not like me to cower at the possibility of death, but the lack of information, coupled with the ambiguity of the task, had gotten to me. In fact, it had gotten to me so much that I hadn't even thought about drinking…it was time I started. I ordered two double shots of Jack Daniel's and slammed one down hard. Bobby reached for the other and I grabbed her hand with glaring conviction.

"I'm paying for it," she said.

"Well then order another one. That's my chaser," I explained.

"You think that's a good idea?" she asked.

"I don't understand what you're asking," I replied.

"Well," she turned her whole body toward me as she spoke, "You have a big day tomorrow. You may need your wits. Are you sure you want the distraction of a hangover?"

"Well, that's a great fucking question, Bobby. I guess if I

knew what I had to do exactly tomorrow, I could better judge my actions for this evening."

"You're scared aren't you, Mr. CIA assassin?" she took pleasure in my pain to such a degree that I couldn't help but fall in love with her. The fact that I could vanish into the dust and she wouldn't so much as flinch made my heart race. We had such similar minds; I knew if the situation was reversed, I wouldn't flinch for her either. The ever indefinite *"They"* say that true love is hard to find. I think that is because everyone is looking for flowers and ballads and long walks on the beach, and that shit only exists in the movies that your lousy date drags you to.

The way I see it, if you can find one key thing that you have in common, you may be able to build from there. Bobby and I had two. The first was that we were both lonely whether or not we wanted to admit it (and for the record, I have never been lonely, I'm just better off alone). The second was sheer disregard for the lives of others. It was like a match made in Purgatory, two lost souls headed nowhere, waiting for nothing; it was beautiful and pitiful all at once.

"I'm not scared, I'm anxious. I want to know what this is all about."

"You'll find out tomorrow. Just try to take it easy on the booze tonight," she replied.

"That is the first compassionate thing you've said to me. I'm moved," I said and then slammed the other shot down.

"Look, Keesey," she said with a strange seriousness in her voice, "a lot of people are counting on you tomorrow and if things go wrong, well..." she hesitated.

"Well, what?"

"I'll never see you again and you'll never be able to cash in on that little contract of ours." I knew she was in love with me. I couldn't say it aloud because she would shoot me in the penis, but I knew it nonetheless. Of course, then I caught the eye of the waitress, and found a new type of love to focus on. Not true love, like what Bobby and I had going, but that *provisional love* I was talking about earlier.

She was tending to the five tables that Eden had. She wasn't flashy, but she was plainly beautiful. She had curly blonde hair that halted about an inch above her shoulders. The shape of her eyes, the cut of her lips, the valley that was her cleavage were all so inviting. All my worries were put on hold as she bent over to pick up a pen that she had dropped. As she stood upright again, she shot a wink in my direction and I began to stand up.

"Where are you going, Cypher?" Bobby asked. I didn't respond though, I just kept on walking over towards the waitress. She kept glancing at me and then turning away as if she wasn't glancing at me. I looked back at Bobby and smiled, she responded by crossing her arms and rubbing the handle of the gun inside her jean jacket. What was she going to do, shoot me in front of everyone and risk blowing this whole adventure for life in jail? She was nuts but she wasn't stupid. I continued to walk towards the waitress and as I approached my destination I realized I didn't know what I was going to say. Go for the gamble, as always, just open your mouth and hope you get lucky.

"You know, that woman over there is thinking about shooting me because of you," I said.

"That's too bad," she combed my body with her eyes, "you'd be no use to me dead." You know, I'm not an arrogant man by any means but I…let's just say, that despite my "loner label," I do mingle quite well with the ladies. I began to think deeper on the subject and was reminded that I had started this whole nightmare between two very nice breasts, and had since let Bobby make me feel like less of a man. I'd even pondered the notion of love. A sickness crept into my stomach but only for a moment...The whiskey hadn't sat well and it came up faster than I could control.

The waitress dry heaved as I finished vomiting on her and sure enough kicked me hard in the balls. Now a man in my situation can only assess his plot in life in two ways. Optimistically, I was probably infertile by now and would never have to worry about being anyone's father, or at least anyone's father to my knowledge. The converse was I had been kicked in the balls three times in these past two days and I was starting to bruise. And it seemed the darker my bruises turned, the more Bobby's eyes shined with piercing white light. She loved watching me suffer at the hands of another woman; I could tell. I limped back over to the bar where she waited, quietly smiling and sipping on a beer.

"How did it go?" she asked.

"Don't patronize me," I said and then flagged down the bartender, "I need a glass of ice and a shot of Jack." The bartender nodded and brought me my request. Finally I had found a bartender who knew his place; he was silent and polite. If I had been his supervisor I would have given him a raise. Of course, as soon as I finished my shot and put the glass of ice in between my legs for comfort, I was rushed by two large men in all black. These steroid-filled bouncers had obviously been tipped off by the vomit-covered waitress and were here to help with any first aid I required.

I hit the ground with a thud as they tossed me out of the bar. Bobby paid the tab and then slowly walked outside to join me. I was counting my new scratches as she stood over me, still smiling. I couldn't stand to look at her. I was just waiting for her to bust into one of those kindergarten recess chants, "Nah, Nah, Nah, Nah, Nah, Keesey gets no pussy." But she didn't. Instead she helped me to my feet and kissed me on the cheek.

"What was that for?" I asked.

"Because you make me laugh," she answered.

"Now what?"

"Now we find a hotel to sleep in before you draw any more attention to us."

"Draw attention to us? We're just faces in the crowd. No one knows who we are or what we're up to. Hell I don't even know what we're…" I stopped in the middle of my thought as the look in Bobby's eyes changed my mind mid-sentence. At the risk of sounding redundant, I asked myself again what type of shit I had gotten into. I had lost a few hands of poker and now I was somehow involved with low-profile types who didn't want to be seen in public. Damn, this was just like the old days again; it seemed I was finally starting to enjoy myself. I stood there dumbfounded as I thought about tomorrow's possibilities, and stopped worrying about women.

"Come on, Keesey, we should go now," Bobby whispered with urgency in her voice. We both hopped in the car; this time she drove. I sat there like a kid on Christmas Eve fantasizing about what Santa was going to bring this year: Was I going to get to use automatic weapons? Was I delivering a bomb to some un-expecting sucker? Was I going to get to disguise myself as a Mexican in order to off somebody? I would name myself Juan Villalopez and wear one of those long Clint Eastwood trench coats with a shotgun underneath it.

"Where are we going?" I said with a bit of Latino in my vernacular.

"Don't worry about that, Keesey."

"Please," I said sternly, "call me Juan Villalopez." She didn't respond, she just looked at me awkwardly and mouthed the name silently while shaking her head. I leaned back in the seat and kept daydreaming about my new identity, and the adventures he and I would have. I recognized that it was slightly psychotic, the way I was feeling, but in such a comforting way that sleep overtook me before Bobby stopped the car.

CHAPTER 12

Better Off Than Dead...Maybe

Morning. I *knew* it was coming. It always sneaks up on me but today, today I beat the sunrise. Deep within my sleep-built nirvana, amidst new false identities and Brazilian waxes, the gleeful voice of anxiety and anticipation chipped away at my eyelids until they opened. The voice repeated only one phrase as it tapped through my fantasies, *Today is the day*. And I must say, it was a rather impressive phrase to say so many times repetitively because when I say it over and over, it gets jumbled in my jaw. But regardless of the many analytical distractions that surrounded me it was true; it was "the day."

I looked around at my surroundings and saw that I was still in the car but alone. I wasn't handcuffed this time around and thus I found myself with two options. The first was to enter the small house I was parked in front of. The second was to make a run for it. I looked about the scattered desert and saw nothing but vast nothingness in all directions. I would die of thirst before I made it anywhere, I was sure of that. And as my reasoning began to work harder with each morning breath, I realized it was likely the reason I had been left out here unattended and unshackled. Furthermore, last night's inspiring possibilities had left me more excited for the task than anything and had caused me to move from my former stance of reluctance to one of eager participation despite the evasive nature of the thing. With this in mind I decided that heading into the house for breakfast and perhaps a long-awaited, detailed briefing of this mission would be the best option to exercise. Of course, when I opened the car door an obnoxiously loud alarm sounded and lights from within the house immediately flashed on.

I didn't move. I even held my breath so as not to create any further panic. The door to the house opened and three dark figures made their way towards the car. I could tell that the one in front was Bobby holding her gun; the two that followed were unrecognizable to me. On the other hand, I did recognize that they were holding large machine guns, M-16s to be precise. I figured it would be best to nullify the situation as quickly as I could, so I spoke.

"It's cool," I began, "I just woke up and thought I would come inside for some cornflakes, maybe a muffin or something."

"Put your hands where I can see them, Cypher!" Bobby said firmly. I stuck my hands out of the car door with my palms open so they could see I wasn't doing anything hostile. She ran over and handcuffed me immediately, "Trying to escape, are you? I should have known."

"Bobby, relax. I just woke up and wanted to get out of the car," I explained.

"What were you going to do?" she asked as the machine gunners joined her side. They were both large Mexican fellows in tattered desert camouflage. In the poor lighting of the dawn they looked like the third world's version of a comic book G.I. Joe.

"What was I going to do?" I replied, "Well, for starters, probably take a piss. It's been a good twelve or so hours since I did that. I thought I would follow that with a few minutes of scratching myself and then move on to finding something to eat in the house. Next I would probably..."

"Enough of the smart-ass commentary, I'm in no mood today," Bobby interjected.

"Your moods change with the fucking tides," I mumbled almost incoherently.

"What was that?" she snapped at me. The big Mexicans remained silent.

"Just clearing my throat," I smiled sheepishly. She glared at me and then unlocked the handcuffs. I was going to make a comment but I decided I would be better off keeping my mouth shut. She motioned for me to follow her so I did. The big Mexicans followed behind me, still silent, and still holding M-16s.

The inside of the house was dull and very empty. I could tell no one lived here on a regular basis; it was more of a transient resting place for those who knew it existed. The floors were all hardwood and the walls were all white. I could see doors leading to two bedrooms and a bathroom. There was a small kitchen and a table with four chairs as well as a large black sofa in the main area. There was no television, there were no pictures on the walls; this house *was* Purgatory's waiting room.

I used the bathroom and scratched myself for a few minutes. Then I sat down at the kitchen table. Bobby was in one of the bedrooms so it was just the machine gunners and me.

"Nice place, is it yours?" I asked one of them. He just

stared at me and so I addressed the other guy, "Have you ever thought about putting a TV in this place to help avoid awkward conversation?" His stare was even stronger than the first guy's, so I decided to twiddle my thumbs until Bobby came back. When she finally sat down to join us, she placed a cell phone in the middle of the table. I thought we were going to play some form of "Russian Roulette" or even an awkward version of "Spin the Bottle," but instead we all just sat there silently.

A good twenty minutes went by and no one said a word until the phone rang and Bobby answered it without haste. She didn't do much talking; she just gave one-word answers and nodded her head a lot. The conversation ended and she hung up the phone. She took a deep breath and then looked at me for a moment before she began to speak.

"Okay, Keesey, here's the deal," she started. I was ripe with anticipation; finally the mystery of this fucking errand would be unveiled. "In about thirty minutes a van will arrive here. At that time you are to drive it across the Mexican border. You will be given this cell phone and once we see that you have successfully made it across we will call you with further instructions."

"What is going to be in the van?" I asked.

"That is none of your fucking business," she answered, "and that brings me to the next part of the instructions…"

"What if the cell phone doesn't get service? Which carrier are you guys on anyways?" I inquired glancing around at each individual in the room, "hopefully not Verizotel Cingusprint, I had a bad experience with those guys. I couldn't get coverage in my own home for a while and I called customer service but it was…"

"Keesey!" Bobby yelled, "Shut up!" I gulped and took

her advice, she was probably on the rag and I didn't want to upset her even more. I nodded and she proceeded.

"Thank you. Now this part is important so listen. When the van arrives you are to enter through the driver-side door only. You are to remain at the wheel at all times, and you are not permitted to enter the cargo portion of the van for any reason. The back section of the van will be sealed off and soundproofed, and there will only be one key that can access it."

"Will I have possession of that key?"

"Of course not, that belongs to the owner of the cargo. When you reach your drop-off point he will take the van from you and do what he chooses with it."

"What about me?" I wondered aloud.

"You will be taken care of."

"What if I get stopped at the border and they want to look in the van? Shouldn't I at least know what I am carrying so that I can..."

"You'll have to use your wits for that situation" was her only reply. So that was that. I was a half an hour away from the meat of this nightmare and I still didn't know what I was doing exactly and why it was so important. The thing that puzzled me most was the soundproofing of the van. Were they afraid I would catch the inanimate objects in the middle of some sort of top-secret conversation? Then I began to think maybe I wasn't transporting inanimate objects; maybe I was transporting people. But who would want to sneak people into Mexico? I could understand a few immigrants wanting a ride if I was going the other way but the only people I could think of that would need to be snuck into Mexico were ex-cons. Of course, after I snuck them in they would probably try to cut my throat and then I would probably end up killing them all, and then these bastards would say I'm in even deeper debt because I killed their cargo. And then I would probably have to do something even crazier, like ride a giant iguana bareback with no pants on just for Monte and Bobby's sick, personal amusement. They would probably record the whole thing and then put it on the internet so I could be gawked at by all the world's most twisted perverts. I had seen stuff like that on the internet before and I sure as hell wasn't going to be a part of it. I had to get things cleared up immediately.

"I know what you people are up to," I proclaimed.

"Oh, really?" Bobby sneered, "Enlighten us, Keesey."

"You're having me sneak convicts into Mexico," I stated. She looked at me blankly. At first I thought it was because of my intelligence; I soon realized it was because of my stupidity.

"You know I can't figure you out," Bobby said, "sometimes I think you are smart and even kind of witty and then other times, like this time for example, you're as dumb as they get. I told you before I hate criminal types, why would I be helping them get their freedom?" She had me there, so I conceded with a nod and shut my mouth.

All I had now was time, and even that seemed to be ready to betray and confuse the hell out of me. These minutes were made up of sixty-five seconds, and they kept throwing me off as I watched the clock. Sometimes the numbers counted down, sometimes up, sometimes sideways. I was waiting for the clocks to melt and swallow me into some Dali painting; I would be forever the mark of a twisted brush. And just as this fate seemed ever more appropriate and the colors all seemed to balance each other, I heard a motor outside. The clocks went sane; my time had come.

CHAPTER 13

W.W.J.V.D

I approached the border after about twenty-five minutes of driving. My gracious hosts, including Bobby, had followed me for most of it and then got off at the last exit before the border. From the moment my ass had become acquainted with the worn upholstery of the big boat with wheels, my nerves had been twitching in a seizure-like frenzy. The van itself was enormous, one of those family-camper-like vehicles, but with an industrial twang to it. A guy named Bentzel had delivered it. I'm not sure if that was his first or his last name but either way, he should have gotten it changed a long time ago or had people call him something else. I mean honestly, who introduces themselves as Bentzel? It sounded like some sort of crooked writing utensil or a name for funny-looking genitals. It was comforting to know that no matter what happened to me when I attempted to cross the border at least my name wasn't Bentzel.

But distractions are just the scenery on the way to insanity. I had no idea what I was carrying, no idea what would come up if the cops ran my license, and no reason for

Me and Bobby McGee

being in Mexico. Not to mention, I was in an extremely large vehicle for a single individual to be driving. It was going to be interesting to say the very least.

You know that feeling you get right when the roller-coaster begins. The repetitive, lisping jerk with the microphone finally hits the switch, the gears rumble like clouds of rusted thunder, and your body jolts and begins to produce adrenaline. You start to climb up the hill knowing that some enormously steep drop is awaiting you on the other side and the anticipation builds like an orgasm and just before they let you go, a pause, a moment to reflect and perhaps even repent your sins before the big plunge, and finally the relief after it's over. Well friends, that same feeling, that same exact pause, is what crossing the border with illegal goods feels like, except on this ride they can cut the tracks out from under you, pull you off the fucking thing altogether, and leave you to sit and pathetically reminisce about what it feels like to be moving at top speeds, surrounded only by the open air. They leave you to sit until you lose your soul and forget why you came in the first place. They leave you to sit until the open air becomes a myth.

I didn't want to go to prison, I had to think fast. I rolled down the window and cut the radio as I pulled up to the border. A bucktoothed cop with a thick, black mustache and slicked-back hair half grinned as I pulled up. He had on those goddamn reflector-lens sunglasses that only desert cops wear. I've always hated having to look at my own reflection while I fed a cop a load of bullshit. I can't lie to myself and all those bastards know it. *Sink or swim*? I suppose is the cliché, but the real question was, What would Juan Villalopez do?

"Morning, officer," I said as I brought the van to a halt.

"What's your purpose for going to Mexico?"

"Relaxation," I replied only half lying, "have a couple cervezas, prostitution is virtually legal, I'll probably get a hooker or two."

"How long do you plan on staying?" the officer asked. I could tell he was glaring at me in disgust from underneath his reflector lenses. I had just ruined the fantasy for him. Now he knew he wasn't the first guy to sleep with all the whores in Mexico. Someone had vocalized it and now his fantasy was forever destroyed. Yep, the pig bastard would finally have to go for that doctor's appointment. Of course, he may have just been disgusted by the fact that I wanted to sleep with prostitutes but either way, it was amusing to watch him squirm in that chair.

"I'm probably just going to stay for a day or two. You know, until I run out of money and awaken from a drunken slumber. Pretty much like every other American that goes down to the border towns, Sir."

"Funny guy," the pig grunted, "what do you need such a big van for?"

"On my way back I'm going to pick up a few migrant workers and try and sneak them into the US. I then plan to have them work on my opal farm for very low wages and shelter," the shit that comes out of my mouth sometimes.

"Who do you think you're talking to, pal?" the cop only spoke in questions.

"Look officer, I'm sorry," I knew I was going to be fucked so I figured why not just go for it, "its early, I'm in a bad mood. My wife just dumped me and took the kids. She also took my Jeep and left me with this ridiculous van. I just want to blow off some steam in your wonderful country." The cop stood silent for a moment and then shook his head and smiled a little.

Me and Bobby McGee

"Try not to be so rude to people you don't know," he said as he waved me through.

"Long live motherfucking Juan!" is all I could think in my head, so much so that I almost yelled it aloud. I had done it, I was going to be free very shortly and I would never have to deal with girls named Bobby, rich guys named Monte, or anyone named Bentzel ever again. It was a glorious moment in the life of Keesey Cypher, the brains behind the great Juan Villalopez.

My moment of revelry was ended abruptly by the ringing of the cell phone. I picked it up without haste.

"Cypher here."

"Cypher, this is Bentzel," the scratchy, nasally, tone-deaf voice of Bentzel poured through the phone like vomit, "Excellent job. Now it's time for phase two."

"Wait a second, Bentzel. I don't respect you and I'm sure as shit not taking orders from you. Put Bobby on the phone."

"You will listen to me, Cypher," he croaked, "or I will…"

"You will what? Get your ass kicked when I get back? Probably. Put Bobby on the phone." I could hear some rustling and a bit of whispering but then her voice came through.

"Keesey," she said, "why won't you talk to Bentzel?"

"I just can't talk to a guy who introduces himself with a name that stupid."

"There are a lot of people with stupid names out there, Keesey," she replied like some grammar school guidance counselor.

"Yeah, but Bentzel takes the fucking cake. Anyway, I've got that little contract in my pocket, what do you want me to do next?"

"Take your third left off the main road. Go about 20 miles and you will come to an old statue of the Virgin Mary that seems to be oddly placed. A man named Koetay will be waiting for you. He will direct you to your destination and when you get there he will give you something in return. Do not ask questions, bring what he gives you straight back across the border and then take the second exit off the highway. I will contact you when you get there."

"How will you know I'm there?" I said, already knowing the answer.

"You're being watched."

"I figured. I just always wanted to hear someone actually say it to me. Now my life has completely mimicked bad cinema. Thanks, Bobby, buy some condoms." I hung up before she could yell at me.

Driving in Mexico is like playing basketball with a square-shaped ball. You know what you are supposed to do but the old techniques don't work the way they should. You've got to learn again and adjust to your environment. Needless to say I averted disaster at least four times on my way to that third left.

The road led me out of town and into a sort of desert countryside. There wasn't much around, just some small dwellings and crippled Mom-and-Pop shops. I came to a crossroad some twenty miles down the road and there on the corner was an oddly placed statue of the Virgin Mary. A man sat with his legs crossed next to the statue. He had tan skin and fiery green eyes. His black hair was tied back in a ponytail and some gray whiskers danced amongst his nightshade beard. He wore jeans and a dusty shirt, but he didn't look poor, just comfortable. I rolled down the window.

"You Koetay?"

"Depends," he replied with a mild Mexican accent.

"Depends on what?"

"Depends on who you are."

"I'm Juan Villalopez."

"Then I'm not Koetay."

"What if I said my name was Cypher?"

"Then I *may* change my mind," Koetay winked at me.

"What if we agree that my name is Cypher, but only on that side of the border?" I proposed, pointing north.

"I'd say take a left here, Señor Villalopez," he replied as he climbed into the van. I think Koetay was the first person I actually kind of liked in a long time. We talked about life in Mexico, and fishing, and about how stupid the name Bentzel was. I think we drove about seven miles before we came to a large farm. There were acres and acres of thick green grass. It was unlike anything I had seen in the middle of the desert before. Some horses ran around in the distance as we pulled up to a large colonial-style home. There were large white pillars in the front and a cobblestone path leading to the entrance. It was like being in a scene from *Gone With the Wind* except I was somewhere outside of Nogales, Mexico, instead of confederacy-ruled Georgia.

Koetay and I drove around to the back of the house. There was a swimming pool with three separate guesthouses nestled around it, and I began to wonder exactly how many people lived in this palace. There was also a large silver dome off in the distance. I wasn't quite sure what it was for but I figured I didn't know my host well enough to ask yet. Beyond the dome I could see a point where the grass stopped and the desert began again. I couldn't see beyond that as my eyesight isn't that good.

"Where do you want me to stop?" I asked Koetay.

"At the nursery. It's coming up."

"Aha!" I exclaimed, "The nursery is it. What do you

guys grow? Marijuana? Peyote? Is that what I'm supposed to do, pick up some pot plants and bring them back across the border?" I couldn't believe I had to go through all this trouble for some lousy dope. Why couldn't these jokers just grow it themselves instead of importing it from Mexico? And why pot of all drugs? It smells the most and has got to be the hardest to drive across the border. I was sure the goddamn dogs would smell me coming from a mile away. It definitely explained why they had gone through all the trouble of making the van super-sealed and even soundproof.

"I'm a little disappointed," I told Koetay. He looked at me puzzled. "I thought this job was going to be something more exciting than drug running. I used to be an assassin and I thought there would at least be a little carnage."

"What do you do now, Mr. Villalopez?" he asked.

"Huh?"

"You said you 'used to be an assassin'; what do you do now?"

"Oh," I grinned, "I'm a drunk."

"Me too," replied Koetay, "Are you as fortunate as I am?" I glanced around at his impressive house and immense property.

"No, not quite. I like to gamble almost as much as I like to drink."

"A noble life but there is not really a consistent flow of income, would you agree?"

"Yeah, you know, win some, lose some."

"Is that how you like to live your life? Win some, lose some?"

"Hey, I didn't know this was a Gamblers Anonymous meeting. How far are we?"

"Just making conversation," said Koetay, "Pull over here, this is the nursery." It wasn't what I pictured at all. It was a large, white, enclosed structure that looked more like a small hospital rather than a plant nursery. I was even more confused when four white women in nurse uniforms came out to greet us. The nurses were in their early twenties and I began to wonder if I was in some *Candid Camera*–style porno film.

I stopped the van and we both got out. The nurses walked over to us and took a knee as if they were bowing to royalty in the Dark Ages. The shit was getting stranger by the minute. The doors of the nursery were closed and the windows had a dark tint to them. I wondered if they only grew indoor plants but even so, why they would go through such trouble to keep the sunlight out baffled me. Of course, I had never taken any horticulture classes and I preferred cocaine to marijuana…it goes better with alcohol. I figured I could make assumptions all day but Koetay seemed like a decent enough guy so I decided to just ask him what was going on.

"What do you grow in here and who are these chicks? You got some kinky fetishes or what?" Koetay chuckled a little, put his arm on my shoulder, and then walked me toward the main entrance of the nursery. I thought I heard someone crying inside but it could have just been a coyote dying in the distance.

"Welcome to Mother Mary's Nursery of Semi-Immaculate Conception," Koetay announced to me. I remember thinking only one thing, *What the fuck is this guy talking about?*

"Koetay," I began, "can I be frank with you for a minute?"
"Absolutely," he replied.
"What the fuck are you talking about?" I asked as politely as I could, "Semi-Immaculate Conception, what does that mean?"

"It means the babies in this nursery have appeared here

without a mother, rather than a mother becoming impregnated by the Holy One while she is still a virgin."

"How did they get here then?" And as I asked the question the answer hit me faster than the sunlight reflecting off the van. Koetay started to laugh hysterically as he realized my realization.

"The people you are working for told you nothing?" he questioned, still giggling, "And you still went through with it? You've got balls, amigo."

"I kind of had to. I owe the guy who sent me on this mission a million dollars."

"Win some, lose some?" Koetay joked.

"Yes, how witty of you," I smiled sarcastically, "but let's take a step back here. What the fuck is going on?"

"Okay, okay. I know you are confused but perhaps this will help clear things up," Koetay led me back to the van. He snapped his fingers as we walked and the four nurses who were still kneeling on the ground stood up and followed behind us, still not saying a word. As we approached the back of the van Koetay reached down his shirt and pulled out a long silver chain that he had draped around his neck. At the end of the chain was a key. He inserted it in the backdoor of the van and unlocked it. I could lie and say I was prepared for what came next but I won't bother.

As the door swung slowly open I saw the horror that was my cargo. Packed tightly in the van were about thirty small wooden cradles. They were stacked up on top of each other like bunk beds but with less space between them. There was a large military oxygen filter in the corner that had been providing the inhabitants of the cradles with the necessary air they needed to make the journey. Koetay snapped his fingers and the nurses all reached into the van to pull out a piece of "cargo." Koetay nodded at one of the nurses and she brought the cradle over to me. Inside was a small, blonde-haired, blue-eyed, white baby that must have been right around three to four months old. The child was strapped to the cradle so as not to move around during the shipping and even had a little milk-dispensing contraption in close proximity to its mouth. It was not unlike one of those water dispensers a pet rodent has except it had a rubber nipple on the end.

My first instinct was to be appalled, but soon my utter lack of compassion kicked in and my stance of terror moved to one of curiosity. I wanted to know what Koetay was doing with all these babies. Was he a cannibal or a pedophile? I also wanted to know how much he was paying for these things. Did he get them at a premium or was he paying list price? Was there a price break if he bought in bulk? I also wanted a drink and I wondered if Koetay had any of that good Mexican tequila. But before I could choose the first question to ask, Koetay read my mind.

"You look rather confused, Mr. Cypher, I mean, Mr. Villalopez. Let us have a drink while my servants unload the cargo," he said.

"Koetay, what do you do for a living?"

"My friend, I do a lot of things, but my primary business is tequila," he reached around his back and pulled a liter bottle from his pants. He tossed me the bottle and I looked down at the label. It read, "Sudor Del Niños Blanco Tequila – Reserva Especial."

CHAPTER 14

The Other History

"Sounds like a great investment to me, how much do you pay for the little fuckers?" I laughed at the question. I couldn't believe the story I'd just heard. I had been living as a member of the kinless underground, immersed in a social mutiny for the better half of my life and this wholly inhumane operation had gone undisclosed to me. And even after I left the CIA, which I'll note is known to all assassins as the Center for Intelligent Adjustments, or more defined:

> *- (verb): changing things that could affect our country negatively by exterminating the people that are doing them.*

Even after I departed ways with that monster and aligned with a new order of beasts (alcohol and wandering), I hadn't heard of an underground group stealing white babies en masse and then selling them into Mexico in a sort of modern-day slave trade. But I suppose karma is a bitch and you have to be able to take what you dish. Yep, as it's said, "You reap what you sow and you shit out what you eat the night before." It was hard to believe that this whole thing had slipped under everyone's noses for years, fifty-two years to be exact, but the details made it all seemingly possible.

Koetay told me that fifty-two years ago the tequila farmers or, *agaveros,* as they are properly called, formed a union. Prior to doing this their lives had not differed much over the years, laboring hard and living just above the poverty line. They were awarded with little of the financial success that the rich CEOs of the commercial producers were endowed. The corporate bastards took all the money and did none of the work; they were rich relatives of Spanish nobles whose families had been given land grants from the King of Spain two hundred years earlier. They had enough money to build large bottling plants, and the blue agave grew on their inherited land, so they had all the power. It seemed that overall the small region in southwestern Mexico where tequila was produced at the time received almost all of its income from the coveted liquor though its average population still remained poor. But one day a white man from Fuget, Kentucky, came to visit the region.

Koetay told the story, "When Dan Bristol first came to visit I was not even one year old. My father and the other elders of the villages had to deal with many loud-mouth braggarts from the North who came down to coax them into investing in all manners of get rich quick schemes; that is how the region learned to speak English. They always played on the fact that we did not make much money as tequila farmers and the only way to ever take the power away from the corporations was to have more money than them. We never bought into it because we knew that the blue agave only grew in certain soil, in a particular climate, and that all of the proper land was owned and controlled by the large manufacturers; but there was something different about Bristol. He didn't have that used car salesman, slicked-back hair look to him. He didn't wear a suit and tie and was never condescending when he spoke. He told us he had a way for us all to become millionaires if we believed in investing not only our money, but our time."

Koetay explained how word of a white man with the true cure for poverty spread across the region and one night the heads of each agavero family assembled at a secret meeting in the hills where Bristol outlined his plan in detail. Bristol explained that his brother had developed a way to speed up the growth cycle of blue agave. Blue agave is of course the only source for true tequila; everything else on the shelf is really just mescal. Sadly enough, many of the commercial brands that claim the name are in fact only fifty-one percent blue agave, and that is why some tequila tastes like spoiled gasoline and some tequila tastes like it costs two hundred dollars a bottle. The problem with blue agave is that it takes eight to twelve years to become a ripe *piña* (it is called a piña because of its semblance to a large pineapple). Furthermore, tequila is also regulated by the Mexican government and certain standards must be met before it can truly wear the name, one of those being the location where the blue agave is grown. With time and the government against them, the agaveros were never able to open their own distilleries.

With all this in mind, Bristol explained to Koetay's father and the other agaveros that his brother was a horticulturist with a minor in genetics who had been experimenting with blue agave and had found a way to cultivate the plants in a lab by using black-lights, sand, fertilizer, and battery acid. The four elements combined with blue agave seeds created a ripe piña in six months. It all sounded farfetched and unbelievable to Koetay's ancestors as they were a simple people who knew little of science and technology, but Bristol had with him the proof. In a five-foot silver dome with an upward rising hatch Bristol had a perfectly ripe piña.

At first the elders thought there was some kind of witchcraft at work. Until this very moment the soil of the region had been the only spot on the planet where blue agave could thrive, a small blessing from God to the people of the desert. Now white men from Kentucky had shown up with a genetically engineered piña in a silver container that could forever alter their way of life. It was easy to see why they thought some sort of demon or evil spirit was afoot. Bristol assured the people that there were no dark forces surrounding the miracle; it was simply the product of a lot of experimentation and an insatiable love for fine tequilas.

Koetay explained that the initial excitement and wonder vanished quickly as the pessimistic people felt the corporate manufacturers would soon steal the miracle and be able to control all the blue agave and would no longer have use for the poor farmers of the region. It seemed the people would not listen to Bristol at all; they dispersed and left him where he stood. Koetay's father walked slower than the rest and Bristol soon ran after him. He was eager to grab the ear of anyone who would listen.

Me and Bobby McGee

(**Author's note: in order to better explain the interaction between Koetay's father and Bristol we will now enter into a time warp which will allow you, the reader, to actually hear their conversation. The author recognizes that by creating this time warp I have in fact advanced technology far beyond its scientific limits. Please send one dollar to the address on the back of the book to pay your admission for this ride or I may leave you somewhere in the past under the rule of Richard Nixon for all eternity. Thank you for your compliance and of course, your continued attention.)

CHAPTER 15

Destination – Fifty-Two Years Ago

"Excuse me," the scruffy southern voice of Dan Bristol called out to the silhouette he chased. The village elder kept on walking as if he did not hear the call behind him. The sweet oblivion of detachment seemed to be a common moral stance in the tequila region. Bristol knew he would have to stand in front of the elder if he wanted the man's attention. As he continued his pursuit he caught his foot in a snake hole and hit the ground with a skidding thud. Bristol had had better days visiting the local dentist in Fuget, Kentucky. The dentist had of course gotten his degree through the mail and believed that Novocain was "for pussies."

Bristol wiped the dust from his eyes and began to stand up. He noticed the elder standing over him scratching his head with a curious smirk on his face. Bristol thought the man would extend his hand to help him up, but he did not. The elder just stood there scratching his head until Bristol got to his feet.

"Well, thanks for the help up," Bristol said shaking his head. He waited for the old man to reply but he said nothing.

"Why won't anyone listen to me around here? This discovery could change yer lives forever." Still the old man stood in silence.

"Damn it, do you people even understand what I am saying to you?" Bristol was frustrated, the old man could tell, but still he held his tongue.

"Apparently my words are wasted and this, this is a waste of time," Bristol turned to walk away and gather his belongings.

"Did you have a nice trip?" the old man said, giggling.

"What was that?" Bristol spun around.

"I asked if you had a nice trip. Heh heh."

"Are you the local comedian?"

"No. I'm Julio."

"Well Julio, I'm Dan, nice to meet you."

"I suppose."

"Julio, did you listen to me speak tonight and did you see the miracle I have brought for you?"

"Mr. Bristol, your creation is as large as your divinity complex, but we do not have the power, the money, or the resources to assemble our own bottling plants."

"I have a solution for all that as well if you'd just hear me out. You see, my brother is the scientist, I am a businessman," Bristol grinned at Julio's puzzlement, "I can see yer confused, but curiosity was my intention. You see back home I decided to educate myself well, I read a few books about a lot of things. I read about Mexico, I read about business, I drank a lot of tequila in between, and then I read about investments. I did a bit of time for running dope to jazz musicians and got the shit kicked out of me by a bunch of asshole cops in jail. And all I did to pass the time was read about religion, and how I wasn't ever gonna believe in it. And after I finished that, I read about slave trade, and it made me bitter. I could not believe such a thing could occur and me being from the south, I seen a lot of bad things happen to a lot of people for no particular reason. And then I read about sin and revenge, and in the end, when my spoon gave all that soup a spin, I masturbated to money and the madness I'd begin."

"I think you're insane," Julio replied, "but I am curious."

"Okay, so here's the thing. I'd be lying if I said that I just got the idea to come down here and talk to the village. What that means is that I have this whole thing planned out and the resources lined up, but you've got to do a few things for me."

"I don't even know what this is and you're already trying to get me to buy in? Either this is some other quasi-divine miracle larger than the last or you are on Mescalito," Julio answered.

"What if I said I will give you free labor to help you build yer bottling plant, yer very own silver-dome greenhouse filled with blue agave, and not only will the workers help you but they will do all of the work for you and live here and you, you get to sit on yer ass all day and do, well, whatever it is you like to do."

The old man stood silent for a moment still not quite getting exactly where the madman's ramblings were going and then sighed, "I like to drink tequila and fuck my wife." Bristol laughed and the old man did too. They shared a moment of bonding at the crack of time. Tectonic plates billions of stones beneath the surface were shifting and with an aggravated sort of smile, the tide changed to a new low, a better and more inventive sort of deceit for the players of *Humanity;* all it really takes is one crooked sperm. And now Julio was tired of ambiguity and wanted details, Bristol could tell.

"What if I were to tell you I will personally bring a crew down to help with the construction aspects, but the blue agave, which only takes six months to ripen let me remind you, and all things associated with the making of tequila including bottling, will be handled by yer very own white slaves. That way you won't have to pay anyone to work yer plant. All you've got to do is help me sell them en masse down here."

"The tequila?"

"No," Bristol giggled deviously, "the white slaves."

"There is no way the people can afford such a thing. A slave must cost a million US dollars; the people will have died ten lifetimes before they can afford that."

"No, that's not true. I can get you a good deal because they are babies now, all white babies I might add," Bristol winked at Julio, "Well, they are almost all babies, except for the five-year-olds I have ready for you. I think that is about the right age for them to start working in the factory and it won't cost you a dime. All you've got to do is feed them and give them shelter. These white babies won't even know they were ever anything but slaves; that way you can avoid them trying to escape. It's like, um, a caste system, you know what that is?"

"When you are born into your plot in life, or perhaps 'pre-destined' may be the simplest way to define it," replied Julio.

"Yer a pretty smart guy, aren't you, Julio?"

"I too have educated myself."

"So enough formalities then, here's the gig. We build a nursery down here where we can keep the babies as you work to market and sell them to the people. I'll give them to you at $10,000 a piece to start; with all the money you and the other people in the village will be making on the tequila, it won't be hard to afford them."

"How will the others make money, you said this was a gift for me?" Julio asked.

"Well, Julio, I don't know what it is about you but you seem like a man that would care about his own. That being said, here's how I see it and feel free to jump in at anytime if you have a differing opinion. Since I will be helping you construct the first greenhouse and bottling plant and the slaves will help raise the tequila, you are covered for probably one year, but you will make so much money that soon you will want to expand. When you do this you should employ the people of the village to help you. Have them take over yer tequila operations and pay them good wages so they can realize their dream as well. At this time you can repurpose yer slaves to other activities like doing the household chores or maybe landscaping or picking fruit in yer orchards or whatever other investments you decide to make. You will have so much money because not only will you be distilling and bottling 100% blue agave tequila in record time, you will also be making money on the white babies you sell. As I said before, I will give them to you for $10,000 so that you can mark them up to at least twenty or thirty thousand. I'm sure a white slave is worth as much as a new car and with the wages you will be paying the people they will be able to afford such things. After they purchase a slave and let it grow old enough to work, they will no longer have to work in yer plant, they can send their slave to work and collect their wages for them. Soon they will have enough to buy a second and third slave and eventually they will have enough manpower to run their own small tequila bottling businesses which will produce nothing but the finest, most expensive, rare, pure blue agave nectar there is. Soon the whole region will be rich, the corporate imitation tequilas will fall, and due justice will be served upon the Caucasian population of the United States of America."

"So you wish to get revenge on the US for the slave trade of the past by selling its own newborns as slaves?" Julio scratched his chin.

"Absolutely, but only white babies; I figure no one will really have much sympathy that way and we can avoid any sort of Human Rights protests and other unwanted forms of attention."

"I can see you have given this some thought," Julio smiled while nodding pensively.

"My friend, someone once told me there are only two things that drive businessmen, money and glory. With this, we get both. Will you help me get this rolling or what?" Bristol all but begged.

"How will you get all of these…these white babies?" Julio asked.

"That is the easy part. I've been robbing homes and hospitals for months, and orphanages for a year. Plus, I've got prostitutes in twenty-six states waiting to get pregnant and sell me their kids. I've got channels set up, like I told you, this isn't something that just came to me, I've been working on this for years now and I wanted to come down here with a solid proposal so you'd know I wasn't bullshitting you. Come with me, I'll show you something." Bristol motioned for Julio to come; the shock only temporary, Julio was eager to move as they had been standing in the same spot for quite some time now and his legs had begun to hurt.

Back where they had held the meeting Bristol had a large white van parked. He went and unlocked the back doors and climbed in. The loud racket of chains rattling against the steel floor of the van sent a shiver down Julio's spine.

Bristol appeared again holding a chain that connected five small, blonde-haired, blue-eyed, white children; they looked like miniature felons in a highway-side formation. "This is what I call an incentive," boasted Bristol, "There are five more where these came from and a host of infants if you'll help me with this endeavor."

"This is going to take a lot of time," said Julio.

"My friend, this is why they call it an investment."

CHAPTER 16

Places I've Never Been, People I've Never Known

"So that is how it all began," Koetay explained to me, "and Bristol was right, it did take some time, about three years before the explosion of fine tequilas and the beginning of the end for many of the corporate facilities. The first thing my father did after the initial agreement with Bristol was move to this location and away from the tequila region. He knew that the corporate fat cats had no idea blue agave could be grown anywhere else and that this would give him some time to get set up. He informed the other agaveros that they too would need to move eventually but not just yet. He had plenty of temporary workers to employ until the time was right and then he would help them all realize a dream as well. Sure enough, Bristol was a man of his word, and my father's greenhouse and the bottling plant were constructed," Koetay pointed to the silver dome.

"Same structure fifty-some odd years later, pretty amazing," I said to ensure that I would be further indulged.

"Yep, works like a charm. And the best part is, everything went down exactly as Bristol said it would after it was all built and production began. Money started rolling in and soon the tequila we were making was being distributed all over North America. The ability to produce so much blue agave tequila would have flooded the market so we began to distribute it all over the world. With plenty of work to be done and new markets to conquer, the agaveros migrated north and came to work for my father, and the slaves were put to work on other projects."

"Like what?" I asked.

"Well, they built this house for one."

"A bunch of five-year-olds built this place?" I said trying to sound only slightly shocked.

"Of course not, don't be silly," he replied.

"I thought it was pretty unbelievable…"

"Yes, yes. You forgot that three years had passed. They were eight years old at the time and when construction was completed they were nearly eleven. They did a good job though; the place has never had any real problems."

"Wow, sounds a lot better than some crooked contractor."

"Yes, and it didn't cost us a dime for the labor; in fact I think we made money," Koetay chuckled.

"That is fucking bizarre," I shook my head and thought for a moment, "so the tequila business is good, how is the white-baby-slave-trade going?"

"Honestly, it has made me filthy rich. I think everyone in the *Expanded Tequila Region* has at least one, but we have a vast amount of customers all over Mexico."

"No shit?"

"Well, it started off as a means for helping the agaveros but once word got out, it became the latest fad in many strategically selected areas of Mexico where vacationers and the like never travel. The rich began to buy them first and soon everyone who could afford them started to buy in. In fact, many of the day-to-day jobs in the non–tourist-friendly areas of Mexico are done by white slaves and their masters keep their wages."

"No fucking way. How come all I hear about is how impoverished people are down here?"

"Two reasons. The first being simple; that it is what we want you to think. Thus we keep our sales regulated to the areas where foreign tourists seeking only the comforts of drunken stupidity and unadulterated promiscuity wouldn't dare tread. Secrecy is essential because if your government ever got wind of this, it would soon be the end of the whole thing. The 'trade' has been going on far too long for us to let that happen."

"That makes sense," I nodded, "So what is the other reason?"

"The second reason is that your media is not the most accurate and is far too focused on important American affairs such as slandering your chief political figures and discussing upcoming celebrity birthdays to bother researching the activities of the many non-commercialized areas of Mexico," Koetay winked at me.

"I agree with you there but man, this is just fucking insane. So how many shipments come in a month?"

"Twice a month we receive thirty or so infants. Sometimes we have buyers lined up, sometimes we don't – hence the nursery," Koetay nodded in that direction, "either way, they move pretty fast, so fast in fact, that we typically pay for multiple shipments far in advance. Many Mexican people have more money than they let on." Koetay continued to tell me about the inner workings of the whole operation, where it was routed from, how many people were involved, and other significant details that I didn't pay any attention to. I couldn't focus. All I could think about was my moral stance on the whole thing. Here I was in the midst of the biggest scandal to hit the US since Watergate and I had no idea how to get permanently involved and make some dollars on it. I could threaten to spill the beans but you don't make friends through fear. You have to earn friends through kindness; then you teach them to fear you. Plus, I didn't want to get shot. Not today, not with so much opportunity in front of me. I had to be strategic.

So maybe I'm sick and a little too detached from reality but if you had nothing to lose, could you risk not winning at all? I guess I've just been kicked in the balls one too many times and I can't think straight anymore. But to cross that border and demand a meeting with the head of the organization…well shit, I thought they at least owed that to me, you know, for my troubles. I resolved that I would wrap my hands around Bobby's throat and demand it and if she said, "no," I'd kill her right there. Of course, I'd probably just end up getting kicked in the balls again. The loser's ever evolving poetic justice, a ritual of foolishness.

"So that is how I came to know this life; what do you think?" Koetay asked.

"What do I think about what?"

"Ha ha, do not patronize me. You know what," he said with some annoyance in his voice. I stared at him blankly until he looked at me confused, "You do not find any of this astounding? You have forgotten the story I have told you already?"

"Oh no, it's not that. I'm just thinking about how to make it bigger and better."

"Hmmm…a visionary are you?" Koetay asked.

"Nope," I said, "just a drunk."

"Well, at least you are not a liar, Señor Villalopez."

I proceeded to discuss with Koetay my desperate interest in becoming a full-time part of the whole thing. I thought I could continue to be a driver, at least to start, but that doesn't mix with my lifestyle very well, kind of like tequila and Jägermeister, it has got to be one or the other. I decided I needed a more high level position, sales and marketing perhaps. Koetay said he would put in a good word but it would have to travel by messenger boy, which takes a very long time and sometimes does not arrive at all. Koetay had no traceable conversation with the US headquarters; word traveled either by said messenger boy or through the Mexican border patrol. They had been involved for years and for their cut of the money they would pass on messages to "North-Land" employees that drove down into Mexico to courier news, money, or whatever back to the Las Vegas hub.

That was why the border cop had just let me cruise through. I asked Koetay why the only other option was messenger boy, he told me they couldn't risk having license plates, "very traceable" were his exact words. Koetay was a very paranoid guy, no mail from the US came to the hacienda, nothing at all, except for the babies. The bottom line to all of this, if I was going to get in on the action, I would have do things for myself. It was about that time that I realized it was also about time to get going; the delivery was made and now I had to deal with the fucking US border patrol, not quite as friendly as my Mexican police cohorts.

The plus side was I had finally found some direction in life and I had to act on it while it was burning inside of me.

That sweet taste of wonder renewed like the sensual taste of a virgin's...daiquiri. No need to be rude, I'd have to learn to be professional if I was going to be the greatest *Old American Slave Trade Co.* sales representative to walk the planet. Not that that is the official name of the organization...cough... yet, but doesn't it sound like an old-timey trustworthy organization. Like *the Great American Railroad Company* or *the United States Coast Guard*, they never fuck up. I wondered how deep into Central and South America this thing could go, at least to northern Chile and the tip of Argentina. It was possible and it was dangerous. Needless to say I was up for it. And I can sell anyone, hell, I could sell crack to an asshole. Yep, it was time to go.

"Koetay, my friend, I think I have to leave."

"So soon? You have had little to drink of my fine tequila."

"There will be plenty of time for that," I answered with sincerity, "but there is one thing I need to ask you before I go."

"What's that?"

"Those hot little nurses back there, they're your slaves?"

"Yes, they are MY SLAVES," he said with conviction.

"Just asking, I've always had this crazy fetish about..."

"You are truly a sick man, Señor Villalopez," Koetay shook his head, "I hope to see you again soon." We shared a smile, shook hands, and I headed toward the van. As I walked around the back of it I noticed something I hadn't noticed before. The van didn't have any license plates on it. As fear scaled my spine, Koetay grabbed my shoulder from behind.

"You almost forgot this," he said. I grabbed the briefcase he was holding in his hand and thanked God that Koetay was an honest man. If I had come back without the money they would have killed me on the spot, no questions asked.

"How much is in here?" I asked.
"Three million US dollars."
"And the missing license plates on the van?"
"Very traceable."

CHAPTER 17

Walking the Line to Cross the Border

Do you ever just stop and realize that nothing is ever what it seems? I just think about all these people, Monte, Bobby, Bentzel...Cypher. All these dime-store names that really only gather their minimal value from some irrelevant niche context. They are only famous within their own circles. Like the top-producing broker at some Wall Street firm or the employee of the month at Wal-Mart; if you're in the circle, they're legendary. But when you sit back, outside of that two-dimensional line that really just runs you around, you realize they're all just figments of perception. Almost everyone is and that's not necessarily a bad thing.

Isn't it nice to have your own little world with that special someone or to bear witness to those incredible glimpses of life that you can never describe to anyone with words? Those moments of perfection that only happen when you're all alone and no one else is watching, that shit poets live for. I think about the fact that a bunch of talking heads and black and white print are my only sources for information on current events. I don't trust people who can smile while they talk about wars and car crashes and celebrity birthdays. And the only part of the newspaper that interests me is what's between those lines of print. That blank, gray, recycled paper, the things they're not telling you...the things they're not telling me anymore either.

I think about how people thought the world was flat and that the sun revolved around the earth – the ever powerful ego of mankind. To think the source of life on this planet revolved around us is just so terribly human. There were monstrous dragons and gods amongst the masses and women who liked to fuck were burned as witches. And still to this day we wonder if they all exist in some form or another. You may see ghosts or talk to the dead and your dog may one day decide to give you orders to kill. You may dress up like Superman and think you can fly; you may think you can fly for three bucks a hit, and no matter which way the compass points you can always look to the stars for direction. I guess my point is the world is only how we perceive it to be, and there's a lot you can miss when you only have two eyes.

And to that point, I was hoping the fucking cops would miss the fact that I didn't have any license plates on the van, not to mention that I was carrying three million dollars with me. Yes, hopefully they would perceive me to be a simple traveler on his way home to the good old US of A. As I pulled up to the checkpoint I knew it was going to be a mess. I had to think fast to get back home, bye-bye Mexico, what would Keesey Cypher do aside from trying to kill these assholes with their own guns? Just play it cool like I always do and hope they don't smell the shit in my pants.

"Good afternoon sir, how was your trip?" said the cop with overt cockiness. A young punk rookie with something to prove; the sun reflected off his blond hair and singed my retinas as his senior officers watched eagerly like starving vultures in a circle jerk. Was the kid truly one of them they wondered? *Names that only mean something in niche context.* I knew the cop was a rookie because he didn't have a mustache yet, that was something you had to earn. It is a symbol of one's dedication to the force, and only after intense hazing that ultimately finishes with a gangbang in the locker room does a new recruit become a full-fledged mustache aficionado, better known to the public as a police officer. I could tell this pretty boy couldn't wait to be sodomized, maybe if he fucked me over now it would be his turn come shift change. I can read these assholes like children's books, you just look at the pictures and you can get the basic plot.

"It was a nice trip, really is a lovely country," I said with polite sarcasm.

"How long have you been in Mexico for?"

"Just down here for the day, headed back home to Tucson now."

"You just went down alone for the day? You got friends in Mexico or something?"

"No," I said, "actually I know a good marriage counselor in Nogales, she helps me when things aren't going my way back at that ranch; know what I mean?'

"No I don't sir, please elaborate," the cop looked to his buddies for approval as he raised his voice. They all rubbed their crotches and winked at him; I was in deep shit.

"Hey, haven't you ever heard the expression 'what happens in Mexico stays in Mexico'? I don't really think it's your business or your jurisdiction for that matter. So why don't you just let me go home smelling like cheap perfume so my wife can curse me and I can beat the kids, okay pal?" The bastard's lip curled up and I could tell he wasn't pleased with my response. I figured if I could just get him really angry without breaking the law he wouldn't notice my missing license plates.

"Oh, you're a fucking smart-ass aren't you? Better watch it," he said with his asshole obviously beginning to pucker with pleasant anticipation, "Why do you need this big van for going down to Mexico by yourself?" I could tell he thought he had me.

"Frankly, this piece of shit van is the best automobile my yearly salary allows me to afford. I know it is not the most stylish vehicle but it gets me around. If you like it, I'll gladly trade with you. I got it at one of those police auctions anyways, only three grand. It was like a tax refund for all those salaries I've paid over the years." The cop sort of growled, glared at me, and then punched the side of the van. He startled me but at the cost of a couple broken fingers. He tried to hide the pain but I could tell he was crying inside.

"Get the hell out of here, asshole! Go find Jesus, before you burn in hell for your sins!" he screamed, the pain expanding.

"Go find a doctor before you grow that mustache, kid; it's hard to stand on all fours with a broken hand," I exploded into laughter as I sped off, man I hate cops. As I approached the first exit off the highway the cell phone rang for the first time in hours. I kept hoping it was the local hospital calling to tell me a bunch of dip-shits were run over by an eighteen-wheeler and mine was the only number found in their phone. I've got to stop dreaming though; it distracts me from reality's bitterness. I clicked the answer button on the cursed contraption and held it to my ear but I didn't say a word. After a few seconds Bobby's voice came through the phone.

"Hello," she sounded annoyed.

"Are you trying to order Chinese food because this is the wrong number."

"Keesey, you're such an ass. Did you have a nice trip, bring me back any souvenirs?" She was so greedy, so money hungry, she cared nothing for my well-being at all. I loved her more than ever, if only out of spite.

"Yes, I'm fine and the cops weren't a problem despite the dodgy van with missing license plates. And yes, I've got something for you, and with that in mind, I've got something else for you too, Bobby," I said devilishly.

"Just pull off at the next exit, go down three lights and park in the front lot of the first hotel you see on the right-hand side. There will be a car waiting for you there. Bring your cargo with you and then leave the keys and the cell phone on the seat of the van. If anything unexpected happens, well, you know."

"Wow, Bobby, I'm excited to see you too," I snapped as I hung up the phone and tossed it with unnecessary force onto the passenger seat. The bitch didn't care about me at all, and why should I care about what she cares about? I wanted to be a part of the organization and they say you shouldn't dip your pen in the company ink. It could create friction in the workplace that could eventually lead to lawsuits and high profile pay-offs. How does a man choose between business and pleasure when they're both so often the same entity?

"Fuck it, I should just let the world work itself out," I thought to myself as I pulled up to the hotel. A black Cadillac was waiting with its engine running and suddenly the thought occurred to me that this could be more than a cliché gangster car, it could be a high-class hearse. There was absolutely no reason why they couldn't just kill me and move on. Now that they had their money I had seemingly depreciated in value.

Visions of my own death began to creep into my mind; of course then I remembered that I had just resolved to let the world work itself out. I grabbed the briefcase and hopped out of the van. I threw the keys on the seat and headed for the Cadillac. There were two men I didn't recognize in the front seat. I climbed into the back and the driver stomped on the gas before I could shut the door. I guess some people are just in a hurry.

"Who are you guys?" I asked.
"Just shut up," the tough-guy driver replied.
"Where are we going?"
"Nowhere," the passenger answered.
"Ha ha ha," I laughed aloud.
"What's so funny?" the passenger questioned.
"Nothing really," I said, "that's just the only place I ever go these days."

CHAPTER 18

Swing Low Sour Chariot

As the hours rolled by I gazed out the window wondering exactly when and for that matter where we were going to stop. The driver wouldn't give me any info but the bastard sure did like to talk; the passenger sat silently. I soon learned that he did not work directly for Bobby or Monte and had only heard the names in passing. It was apparent to me that these guys were just someone's street thugs, not privy to all the inner workings of the organization. Their primary function was muscle work, when someone had to be collected or disposed of, that's when they were called in. I asked which category I fell into and the driver, an asshole aptly named Jersey John, replied, "a little bit of both." I hate when stupid people try to be cute in times of serious strife, it only further amplifies their inability to cope with the rest of the world's superior intelligence; the envious look of the minnow in a room full of sharks. It's just like poker, if you can't spot the sucker in the first fifteen minutes it's probably you. That's one of the oldest rules of gambling. As I glanced back and forth between the two heads, I wondered who the sucker was in this car.

You know, I'm not the world's angriest man and certainly not the world's most violent. I have my moments where fits of rage rip through me in uncontrollable tremors of red light, illuminating paths to places of my mind no foot of pondering should ever have wandered down. The cracks. The caverns below the frontal lobe, the outlines never meant for conscious probing. You see I've had my moments but that's all mostly behind me now. I had certainly maintained a positive outlook and relatively mild demeanor during this most recent adventure despite the ratio of good to evil. Certainly. Except for of course when I snapped the neck of the motherfucker in the passenger seat of the Cadillac; I didn't get to find out his name. I figured that would be an easy move; these guys weren't trained in anything. They're used to shaking down sixty-year-old convenience store clerks in Newark. Fucking jokers, they didn't even see it coming and what's the driver going to do? Try and wrestle with me and watch the road at the same time? Even *he* wasn't stupid enough for that…well, I took my chances.

Anyway, it was a peaceful death, very humane for a murder. Only a simple countdown to ten like a space shuttle launch into hell. Pressure applied deeply through the skin, down through to the bone and vocal cords with one hand. The other hand palms the bastard's head like a basketball, fingers digging into his temple for added effect. When you hear a cracking sound you know it's working, three, two, one strong rip with both hands, loud snap and he should now be looking you square in the eyes, bleeding from the mouth and nose.

I had almost gotten the unknown guy's head all the way

around; the car seat made it difficult but not impossible. He still bled from his nose and mouth though and as his head hit the dashboard it knocked some teeth out and even more blood was spilt. The driver had probably pissed his pants and I could tell by the look in his eyes I now had control of the situation. Of course control of the situation doesn't mean you have won the battle, it's more a question of offense and defense. I was now on offense, but that didn't stop Jersey John from trying to draw his gun in one last defensive effort. With his guard down I hit him square in the nose and then reached for the wheel as he squealed in pain. He was a bleeder. The interior of the car quickly became a crimson shade of mistakes. Not only were we speeding down the highway to an undisclosed destination with minimum control, but we had a dead guy in the passenger seat, a bloody Mafia-type in the front seat, and a criminal who had recently committed murder and aggravated assault in the back seat. As if things couldn't get any worse Jersey John explained to me through a mist of tears and blood that he was a hemophiliac.

"And if you don't get me to a hospital soon I could die."

"Stop crying you little pussy. Does this car have cruise control?" I asked compassionately.

"Yes," Jersey John whimpered.

"Okay, put it on and watch the fucking road for a minute while I get this piece of meat in the back seat."

"Shannon."

"Huh?" I looked at him confused.

"His name was Shannon."

"A hemophiliac and a boy named Shannon; they must be running low on bad guys in this world."

"Just at the entry level, everyone wants to jump right into middle management. Too many thugs go to college these days; no one is just born into it anymore, well, except for Shannon and me." Jersey John's eyes rolled off into a reminiscent nirvana, a sigh for the good old days. I kind of felt for the guy until I realized his eyes rolled back because he was running low on blood and getting woozy.

"All right, John, stay with me," I said as I grabbed Shannon underneath the shoulders and pulled him into the back seat. "Okay, now I want you to slide over to the passenger seat and I'll take the wheel. Then if you'll cooperate and tell me what I want to know, I'll drop you off at a hospital. Sound fair?"

"Sure," he answered.

"Actually that was a rhetorical question, John. I don't give a fuck what you think, move over now," it's important to be polite in any circumstances, that way you can get people to listen to you. As John moved over I hopped into the front and grabbed the wheel. I reached over into his jacket and slyly snatched his gun as well. He had lost a lot of blood and couldn't react fast enough to stop me and besides, obedience comes with ease amidst the foggy yearning for mercy.

"I need a doctor," Jersey John moaned.

"I need a drink," I sighed, "Want to stop at a bar?"

"Please take me to a hospital you crazy fuck," he pleaded.

"Hey now, no need to stop being polite, I just want a couple of answers. You do that and all will be well, understand?"

"Okay, what...what do you want to know?" he said, finally recognizing his defeat.

"Where are we going?"

"Las Vegas."

"Why?"

"Because that is where headquarters is."

"And where exactly in Las Vegas are we headed?"

"The Bogota Casino off of Tropicana," he answered. I was puzzled. I had spent many nights in all corners of that rotten city, been in every casino from the high roller hangouts to the senior citizen five-cent slot houses, on and off the strip. Every run-down motel lobby, every dive bar with video poker, anywhere you could lay down a bet. Hell, you can bet on the longevity of your life if you can post enough dough. Vegas and I have always had a special relationship.

"There's no Bogota Casino in Las Vegas."

"Sure there is, opened five years ago, one of the hottest joints in town. Call information on my cell phone if you don't believe me; now please take me to a doctor." I grabbed his cell phone and dialed 411. As I waited for the operator to pick up the line, John spotted a hospital sign indicating that he could get the medical attention he needed at the next exit. As I pulled off I could see some relief wash over his defeated eyes. What a miserable creature, forever sheltered and pitiful at the mercy of its small mind. Of course he didn't like it when I took a left at the end of the ramp instead of a right towards the hospital.

"What are you doing?!" he howled, "The hospital is right there!" I didn't say a thing. I hung up the phone and I looked straight ahead. I looked straight ahead and my blood turned cold, to a temperature that sympathy cannot survive in. I recalled all the sinful temptations that had first led me down this ever-darkening path, the way of a man who can kill another. Walking, and awaiting some sort of big bang that will leave my sense of compassion forever extinct. It's a wandering madness, an ordained lack of control, or perhaps, in some fleeting instances, a sort of primitive pity.

People piss me off for the most part. Too self-serving to be polite, too rich to have time to care, too poor to stop complaining, too stupid to drive, too annoying, fat, thin, pretty, ugly, too drunk…and all fucking insane, every last one of us. It's because we have no grip on existence, no definitive purpose to guide us towards anything besides working for money to buy things that may last or may not, to go places that we may remember or may forget about altogether because of some disease that erases our memories. We trade our time for paper, and our lives for distraction; it's a recipe for unified lost agreement. A safety in the knowledge that no one knows anything for real except the things a bunch of other "somebodies" wrote down a really long time ago. A language invented by us to tell the stories about the things we're afraid to question or unable to leave to their natural ambiguity. People treat living like a job and that makes payday the day you die; you are rewarded with God's own 401(k) plan, a place in heaven, behind the pearly gates, up in the clouds, with the angels…and that giant from "Jack and the Beanstalk." I heard there was a big land dispute up there because God wanted to set up this resort for all the good people and the giant had been living there for a while, so God gave him the right to govern himself as long as he agreed to live in the shittiest clouds around. He became a drunk and built a casino and now all the little dead people's souls head out to his reservation to gamble. No, it's true I swear, haven't you read the EVEN NEWER TESTAMENT?

Religious insanity aside, I'll tell you, there are a lot of things that piss me off about people, and that's why I learned to kill them. And amidst my moment of reflection, as I listened to the last few pints of life pour out of John like the tranquil waters of a cannibal's own Zen fountain, I grew a heart as well. I decided it *would* be a good idea to take John and Shannon to the hospital, because that is where the morgue is typically. Some people call it murder, I call it Darwinian problem solving.

Upon second thought, though, I decided it would be best to find a nice spot in the middle of the desert to leave both him and Shannon, the cops could take whatever meat the vultures didn't want to the morgue and besides, I could use the carpool lane if I hit traffic. I made a U-turn and headed for the highway, I let out a victory howl as I shot down the ramp. I was up on them now, I knew my destination, I had time to plan my next move, and I had finally gotten to kill somebody – all in all the day had worked out better than I'd planned.

The sun gazed down with infinite indifference as I pulled a cigarette and lighter from the corpse's pocket. As I lit up and rolled my window down, the ultraviolet rays warmed my face like a woman's golden locks dangling on the peripherals of my smile. In that moment I realized that when you're bound to a meager existence, it's important to live as large as possible. *Viva Las Vegas.*

CHAPTER 19

Dusty Path to a Desert Oasis

"Operator, how may I help you?"

"Yes, can I have the Bogota Casino in Las Vegas please?" I was sure she would come back without a listing but I've never been paid to think.

"Connecting you now, sir, have a nice day," and like that, things got stranger. I was about three hours from Las Vegas when I finally remembered to check up on John's story. I had left the bodies in a ravine outside of Flagstaff; no one would find them unless the authorities got involved and went searching. Otherwise it would be some unfortunate hiker who stumbled upon John and Shannon's remains, either way I had washed my hands of it and continued onward. On the sixth ring the phone was finally answered.

"Bogota Casino, how can I be of service to you?"

I thought for a second and then replied, "Yes, my good man, can I have Bobby McGee please?" a Cheshire smile tore across my face; I knew I had her cornered. I heard the guy typing on the other end.

"I'll put you through to that room, sir, have a nice day." Anticipation swelled within my cerebrum as I waited for her to pick up the phone. My only worry was what I would say to her after she had just recently tried to have me killed. Then I recalled the fact that it was me who instigated the little bloodbath in the car, those goons were probably just giving me a ride. Problem is I don't like being left in the dark; I used to get "PCS information." PCS is a military term for: *Privileged-Classified-Secret*. It is the most secure information there is and it is shared with only certain individuals and those individuals are in fact the only people who even know there is such a thing as PCS, remember that before you go asking your everyday solider or police detective if such a thing even exists. In fact, PCS is so intensely classified that it doesn't even exist. Get me? My point is that if I previously had access to information that doesn't even exist, there is no fucking reason some jackass from Jersey can't tell me where the fuck we are going. It was a valid point and I was sure I could explain it to Bobby and whoever the big boss was. Conclusive thought leads to forward ideas and brighter futures. As I resolved my stance on the forthcoming issues she answered the phone.

"Hello."

"Hello darling, I'm on my way to collect what's due," such a charming fellow I am, upfront, honest, and passionate.

"How the fuck did you get another cell phone?" she snarled.

"You know those two guys that were sent to pick me up?"

"Yes," she replied.

"Well it's a good a thing they weren't close personal friends of yours. They won't be joining us at the casino I didn't know existed."

"My god!" she exclaimed, "You've never heard of the

Bogota?" The thing I loved about Bobby was her sense of compassion; it was roughly equivalent to my own except with a sweeter smell and tits. "Where were you before you came to New Orleans, Keesey, the sewer?" She was such a spiteful bitch but she did have a slight sense of clairvoyance.

"It was only for like a week and I can explain that later. Anyway, those guys are dead and I'm on my way there. And Bobby when I get there…"

"You want to fuck me, I know," she sighed.

"That's a given, baby. What I want is to speak to the boss."

"Not tonight, he'll be pissed you killed his nephew and he may go berserk," she said.

"I can handle him. I just killed two guys without even getting scratched." How could she not recognize my strength and skills, my wit and my power, the silhouette of the alpha male.

"You killed a hemophiliac and a boy named Shannon, big deal, Cypher. Besides, 'the boss' is into PCP and he gets *wet* every night after 9 pm," she paused and sighed, "And at other random points throughout the day. You're better off waiting until he has his senses back in the morning."

"The guy is into PCP? I didn't know you could still get that shit."

"Yep, he is a blessed individual indeed. He has such a taste for the rare, the exotic, the dangerous, and the forbidden. He's a complex individual, spawned from a long line of complex individuals. He's a psycho and a drug addict, but he's a complex individual most certainly." I wondered if she was ever going to shut up.

"I get it, Bobby. Which one was the boss's nephew? Jersey John?"

"No, the boss isn't from Jersey and neither is anyone in

his family. They're southerners, couldn't you hear Shannon Bristol's accent?" she questioned me.

"Um, well, I didn't really give him much of a chance to talk. They wouldn't tell me where we were going, they were just being smart asses and frankly, I don't like being left in the dark or made fun of and so..."

"You're whining to me now, Cypher," she pointed out with a snooty tone.

"Hold on a sec, I just realized you said Shannon Bristol."

"Yeah, so?"

"Is that Dan Bristol's nephew?" I asked.

"Of course."

"Dan Bristol still runs this operation? How old is he?" She told me he was ninety-two years old. I couldn't believe a guy who did PCP every night lived to ninety-two years and was still capable of running such a syndicate; the world is a fucked-up place. Bobby explained that Shannon was Dan's closest kin next to his brother Trent. Trent was almost ninety-seven years old, catatonic, and would most likely die before Dan so Shannon was the obvious choice to take over the family business. She also told me that the only reason that Shannon had come along was to talk to me about possible job openings within the organization. Having completed my task with little to no difficulty and zero casualties it seemed I was a perfect fit. The type of street-smart, tough guy that could really add value to what Bobby called "the New Wave Slave Trade."

I asked her how come Jersey John referred to Shannon like he was just a fellow lowly thug. She explained that Shannon did not want people outside of his close circle to know who he was or that he was virtually running the whole operation while Dan "PC-pissed" his remaining years away.

Me and Bobby McGee

Apparently he hung out with the street muscle because he liked to watch them kill people who had wronged the family. Karma or irony, I'll let you be the judge.

Regardless, the guy sounded like a weirdo to me so I didn't really care. Plus I figured it would be like an ancient civilization or even a dictatorship where you whack the guy in charge and then you get to take over. Little did I know... and little do I still know, in fact, I know almost nothing, but that is beside the point. One must always take into consideration that assumption and stupidity are very close allies. In fact I think assumption may have been born from stupidity's inbreeding. Therefore, if you assume things, be pleasantly surprised if you are correct but prepare to be stupid. I myself would soon find out exactly how stupid I was.

Bobby told me to meet her at the Orleans Casino off the strip; she said she felt most at home there. I didn't care what she thought though, because I knew that the Orleans had the hottest cocktail waitresses in all of Las Vegas, even at four in the morning when only the degenerates were left pumping their last few bucks into nickel slot machines to ride out the free drinks before dawn hit; even then the waitresses at the Orleans were beautiful. I figured I could romp with Bobby for a bit, let her pass out and then go find myself a sexy casino staff member for dessert. Plus it seemed like forever since I'd had a drink; that was certainly on the to-do list as well. I agreed to meet there and hung up the phone.

A mass of pleasantries danced wildly around inside my head as I sped down the road. The utter darkness of land wasted by radiation poisoning is forever seductive to the tired eye. Your head bows out with each beat of your heart and you catch only ancillary glances of the road in front of you. It doesn't matter what the hour is, as long as the sun is down in Nevada, you must fight the desolate desert's dust for your right to stay awake. Lucky for me, I had plenty to look forward to and there was no way I was going to succumb to the night.

CHAPTER 20

I'd Give All of My Tomorrows...

"Holy shit!" I screamed as I barely dodged a semi. I rubbed my eyes and took a minute to survey my surroundings. Just over the horizon lights shot up to the sky like a bunch of "born-agains" trying to find Jesus. But Vegas is no heaven, it's more like Mecca to me if only because it's tangible. It is the gambler's holy city, a place where you are only judged if you're being judgmental. I make a pilgrimage here every chance I get; apparently I hadn't been in over five years though, as I had never heard of the Bogota Casino.

I got off at the exit for the Orleans shortly after and soon arrived at the hotel. I grabbed my cargo and took a chance that Bobby was already checked in; I was correct. It seemed the cards had already begun to fall my way. The lady at the help desk told me she had left a key and a note for me. I thanked her as she handed the items over and then I unfolded the note. It read:

CYPHER –

It has been a while since I've been laid and I could really use a piece; hurry up!

–Bob

Life was getting better every minute. All I needed was a quick glimpse at an Orleans waitress and I would be ready to go see Miss McGee.

I decided to walk to the elevator by way of the casino. The flashing lights and sounds of slot machines started to make me salivate; as I passed the tables a bit of drool found its way out of my mouth. She was beautiful. Tan-colored, wearing a hint of leather, and cloaked in soft green velvet, she was the ever-sexy single-deck blackjack table. Lucky for me I didn't have any money to blow and though the briefcase in my hand taunted me incessantly, I had not forgotten that owing money to its owners had gotten me into this whole mess to begin with; my balls still ached from that particular memory. I saw a sign for the elevator and headed in that direction. In my haste I almost bumped into a beautiful blonde holding a tray of drinks. Black fishnet stockings and a sexy little miniskirt, perfect plastic tits, and a pretty face; Bobby would have to wait.

"Sorry about that," I said, "I don't know where my head is at."

"That's okay," she smiled, "most assholes don't even take the time to say they're sorry."

"Ouch. I'm automatically an asshole? You don't even know me."

"I know enough," she said.

"You know assumption is stupidity's closest ally," I love when my inner monologues translate to real life conversation.

"Look buddy, I can see that you're a decent-looking guy and under normal circumstances, I might be interested. But I also see that you are some kind of bisexual freak show about to go take a shot in the ass, so if you don't mind I have to deliver these drinks," she said and started in the other direction.

"What the hell are you talking about?" I called out behind her. She turned around and gave me the evil eye.

"Don't keep Bob waiting, sounds like he may give you a reach-around," she laughed and then walked off. It was at that moment I realized I was still holding the note Bobby had left for me. It was in plain view and the waitress had glanced at it when I started talking to her. It was either the worst coincidence ever, or maybe someone was guiding me in the right direction. And there most certainly was, his name was Bill, he was a bellboy at the hotel and he showed me to the elevator.

I got to Bobby's room and knocked on the door. She was slow to answer but when she did my heart started pounding. She wore a black lace baby-doll top, it was see-through and her perfect breasts bounced softly beneath their seductive veil. She smelt of exquisite lotions and perfumes and wore a black thong; her bare bikini line offered hints of a Brazilian wax. She wore black high heels and I...well, I almost lost it before I even entered the room for starters. Luckily the dark powers of Las Vegas were on my side and I was able to maintain my manly composure. She grabbed my hand, led me into the room, and closed the door behind us. As we journeyed into howling oblivion the sign out front taunted the rest of the hotel, just a peek would have helped to satisfy their curiosity but alas it read "DO NOT DISTURB." (**Author's note: Tough shit, perverts, go buy a Danielle Steele novel.)

CHAPTER 21

The Hour That the Ship Comes In

I fell in love with Bobby for real the minute I saw her in that lingerie. It's funny how some people can hold that sort of thing so sacred. For me it's just a casual affair, because I know I'll fuck it up somehow, I always do. It's a demented, relentless, ongoing routine. I think passion may be my worst enemy, being that our relationship thus far has been based around deception…or maybe not. Perhaps love is founded on both pain and pleasure; agonizing defeat, deceit, and unyielding reinvigoration. The murmurs and echoing vibrations that are the anecdotes of my heart tell me nothing more of myself, only that romance and lust are my deities, careless love my formal religion, and sex my sanctuary. It may be best to wear roses around my neck to show my undying devotion to the faith.

I say this because the rose has always symbolized the essence of love for me. Of course that may sound cliché being that the rose has embodied this meaning forever…but why? I see now that it is because of its two faces; the lush, intricate beauty of the blossom and the thin, thorn-ridden stem that lags behind. What we fail to realize in order to delude ourselves is in truth, the stem grows before the blossom though our eyes are immediately drawn to the latter; this is just like love. The primal instincts of the mind instill the thorns in the hearts of both men and women, the elements we discover only in intimacy. But upon first encounters, first impressions, and immediate chemistry, the flower, in all its glory, is what we see. There is no thought of the infinite repercussions, good or bad, that may come from this newfound connection. Only the moment, and perhaps the five-second orgasm that follows – the epilogue to a perfect evening – hold any sort of significance.

The rose; it is red like the blood that flows, that binds. It is the color of love, but in converse, it is the color of wrath, of anger, of pain, of lies. The rose is nature's metaphor for the most pristine of human comedies – the romantic relationship. And so I cling tight to it, pressing my lips to the blossom with closed eyes and embracing the stem, allowing the thorns to penetrate my soul, leaving more holes in my heart, and increasing the will to submit to emptiness. A sadistic dream this want for fulfillment; a primitive, unformulated act of self mutilation. And you know what? I wouldn't have it any other way because it sure beats jerking off.

Las Vegas at dawn is a world removed. The tips of the mountains against the sky accentuate the pastel colors of reawakening, but how does a colony of insomniacs react to that? In a city that never sleeps does time even exist? The empty eye sockets of all-night losers repel the rays of the vampire sun like crucifixes in hopes that the demigod idols composed of glass and neon will instruct them in the proper rituals of morning. Call girl pamphlets coast by on a tobacco-stained breeze advertising redemption for the disciples of loneliness. And those of us that still have a soul are left to be enchanted by greed and converse informally with the devil. But then again, "Sin City" is not for the righteous. It is a parallel universe where the wicked are exalted and numerous vices only make for a more respectable moral stance. There is no prayer for innocence, no clause in a contract of heresy; only the translucent dreams of the vain remain pure and unchanged by this electronic purgatory, this rest home for fallen saints and dead presidents.

"Have you ever tasted blood on a Sunday?" That was the first thing Bobby said to me when she woke up and gleefully opened the briefcase full of money. I thought about it, trying to extract a meaning, but all I found was a comfortable silence that endured for a few moments until she shut the case and latched one ring of her ever useful handcuffs to the handle. Then she smiled and kissed my cheek, "Better than I could have imagined," she whispered as she turned her back on me.

My primal instinct boasted to my conscience, "Victory yet again! Why don't you retire?" I gave myself a rewarding scratch and walked to the bathroom to get washed up. Bobby was making a phone call to someone but I didn't bother to eavesdrop; things were different between us. She trusted me; that was a good thing. I don't trust anyone so I remained pretty much the same, but either way, things were still different between *us*.

As the soap ran off my face and down the drain I felt fully cleansed, as if I had washed off the latest lowest point in my life and begun anew. My face didn't haunt the mirror with ill-endeavored sleep. Even my restless shadow seemed to follow me boastfully from task to task with the knowledge that each moment could lead to that infamous *better tomorrow*. The lack of satisfaction with my overall *life experience* has always been one of the primary contributors to my inability to give a damn about other people; my own personal alumni booster, discontent. It was as if this whole adventure had been the medication I had needed for my self-diagnosed attention deficit disorder; my dismissive focus and intrepid stance of bored existence. Each step had a purpose, in fact, I remember there was a time when I was simply searching for purpose…but that was days ago, now I had sex on tap and a business venture to sink my teeth into. No time to worry about making a mark on the world, the soup of the day for the next few years was going to have to be "secrecy." How's that saying go? "Loose lips sink ships." I prefer "Big fuckin' mouths fuck shit up," but then again, I never paid much attention in English class.

"What the hell are you doing, Keesey?" Bobby popped her head into the bathroom, "how long have you been staring in the mirror for? You're not that pretty," she giggled. What the hell had I done to this woman you may ask. Let's just call it "The Big O," man's only true spell over a woman. You can have all the money and good looks and fame and power, but if you can't satisfy her needs and quench that thirst inside, she's going to search out an oasis. I was glad to have her under my spell though; she was the woman of my dreams. I had lusted for her and hated her in the same instant, the moment I met her, and now all of those audacious emotions had commenced a truce and love was born in a redundant symphony. It's just one of those things that is hard to stop thinking about, especially when you're sober. Falling in and out of love is a lot simpler when you're drunk all the time, you can do it three or four times in a night if you feel up to it and it's awfully easy to forget about someone when you don't know their name to begin with. I knew I would have to get used to the feeling and fast or I'd never be able to think straight, and I needed too, Bobby had made that very clear.

"We're going to see Dan Bristol today, Keesey. I have to warn you the guy is a little bit nuts. You see he likes to do…"

"I know, PCP, you told me, anyway when are we leaving?"

"As soon as you put some pants on," she smiled. I took the hint and finished getting ready. Bobby called down to the front desk and asked them to bring her car around to the front. Upon exiting the room, Bobby left the keycards on the dresser indicating that we would not be returning; she then grabbed the briefcase and latched the idle ring of the handcuffs to her wrist. As we entered the elevator a strangely horrifying and overtly peculiar notion dawned on me. Giving into my own dread I asked Bobby if Bristol would be jacked up on PCP when we got there.

"Doubtful, but you never know," she replied looking down at her watch, "that's why I wanted to get there so early." I smirked at her comment and for the first time in hours fear scaled my spine at an astounding pace. I had whacked the boss's right hand man without reason, sure, but what was most frightening was that I had killed a southerner's kin; he'd probably take a shotgun to my head and make me into vittles for the slave babies. One thing I've found in life is that it's hard to get a job when you've fucked with someone's family. Like when I was a kid, I was bagging groceries at the local market to make some extra cash. The owner of the store had the hottest daughter, man, was she gorgeous. Long story short, one day I ran the family's cat over with my bike and the next day he fired me, because of a stupid animal. I got him back though, I was secretly banging his daughter the whole time; I guess the irony is that he fired me over the wrong pussy. The point of the story is that that was just a stupid cat; this was a southern crazy-man's kin. I suppose there is no rest for the wicked for their stamina is as endless as their trail of woe.

The blending of sunlight and neon blinded me temporarily as we got into Bobby's car, a silver DeLorean. Impressive and cheesy all at once; I'm not much of a car guy but there is a thing or two I've picked up along the way, I had to know her reasoning behind this machine. It was all too obvious, but I still had to push the issue.

"Nice car," I commented as she pulled out of the hotel parking lot. She nodded and smiled, too involved in her left-hand turn to make casual chit chat. "You know they stopped making these, a person would have to go out of their way to get one and probably spend some hefty dough. Plus, this thing will crunch up like a tin can if you wreck it. Gotta be a pretty good driver to handle something like that, so what inspired you to get it?"

"Well Keesey, the truth is I can travel back in time with it, like in that movie…"

"I knew it! You're such a weird chick."

"You didn't let me finish. What I meant is that it's like traveling back in time every time I get into to it. Back to the first time I, myself, ever shot somebody."

"Why does this car make you think of that?" I asked genuinely curious.

"Because I took this car from the fucker after I shot him. It was just two years ago, low-life gamblin' piece of shit, got this car off money he didn't earn. Found out about the whole operation while he was playing roulette at the Bogota, I guess someone forgot to change frequencies on their walkie-talkie and he overheard an internal conversation. He demanded to speak to the casino's owner and, long story short, tried to blackmail Bristol. Dan gave him a bunch of money and this car so he would be easy to track down. Conversely, Dan had purchased this car several years earlier because he did in fact think he would be able to travel through time with it. After several attempts and extensive hospital bills he gave that up, but that's another story. Anyway, the guy split for New Orleans like a jackass and Monte and I were tapped. I caught him just north of Austin, Texas. We drove this car deep into the desert and I put a bullet in him, and then left him there for the vultures and Texas locals to fight over and feast upon. So you see, Keesey, that's why this car is like a time machine," her eyes drifted and she sighed in memory, "I do like that movie though," she smiled as she flipped on the stereo and Huey Lewis belted through the speakers at an unbearable volume, which is in fact the only volume I think he is ever played at, *"Don't take money, don't take fame, don't need no credit card to ride this train."*

"You're crazy, Bobby, I think I love you."

"What was that," she said as she lowered the volume.

"Never mind, it wasn't important," there are some things you can't say twice in the same minute and for me that was one of them. Plus I didn't feel like getting into a romantic, potentially catastrophic conversation when I was on the way to meet what could in fact be my angel-dusted doom.

CHAPTER 22

A Whopper with a Side of Insanity

It turned out the Bogota wasn't exactly on the strip, it was just east of the Palms but you could certainly see it from the south end of "Sinner's heaven." It was a golden tower that seemed to battle the sun for its place in the sky. There was no building in itself more radiant and enviable in all Las Vegas than that of the Bogota. Set in front of the golden tower was an enormous golden ship that contained the casino. The casino claimed that the true "Bogota" was a merchant ship that carried precious jewels and spices from foreign lands and that is where the design came from. I'd buy it if I didn't know the truth. The Bogota, in its golden glory, symbolized every innate social institution we as good God-fearing Americans are supposed to avoid. Greed, power, overindulgence, vanity, jealousy, dictatorship, and citizen supremacy – needless to say I fell in love yet again. It was a monument of defiance, built by the secret society of, "get back at whitey," a southerner's fool's gold, molded by a compassionately insane intellect. I for one felt right at home as soon as we parked the car. There may be a heaven and there may be a hell but when I die I'll probably just end up in Vegas, serving cocktails to saints and criminals at the Bogota pool bar for all eternity.

Senseless fantasies are a great means to distract oneself from fear, but flashing lights, green felt, and free drinks are what dreams are made of. As we walked across the casino floor I wondered if Bobby would let me play a few hands to take the edge off. I thought about asking but then I remembered who I was. Instead, I let her walk slightly ahead of me and then I slyly sat down at a blackjack table. She was too absorbed in her own adrenaline to notice; the safe delivery of the briefcase and perhaps a bit of concern for my safety seemed to preoccupy her mind though the latter was likely my own wishful thinking.

I'll tell you something folks, I'm not gay, but when my ass hit that leather it felt fucking good. I scooted from side to side and made myself comfortable. Before I could begin to reach for my money a sexy brunette waitress was already taking my drink order. I ordered a double Gentleman Jack on the rocks; you should always order liquor straight in Vegas, they can't water it down as much. She scooted off and I reached for my wallet and to my remindful surprise, I still had nothing. Like a baby bird with broken wings, I walked sadly towards the rest of my life removed from the rest of the flock as they flew unbound towards their dreams.

On the bright side of things I caught up with Bobby before she even noticed I was gone. I pinched her ass just to let her know I was there and she smiled back at me. We exited the casino and followed the signs to the *Midas Tower*. My feet were sweating and my nerves made it hard to walk on the golden marble floors of the *Midas Tower Lobby*. We got into the elevator and Bobby pulled out a key, which was predictably golden, and put it in a hole next to the penthouse button. As she turned it, the doors slammed and the elevator began its ascent up Bristol's *Midas Tower*. Bobby could tell I was a little uneasy and she stood close to me.

"You know, Keesey," she began, "I was real proud of you back there in the casino. I thought for sure you were going to beg me to give you some money to play roulette."

"Bobby, we've got important things to do, I would never do that in such tense circumstances." And the truth was I wasn't lying to her, I fucking hate roulette. I could swear on my life that there was no way she would ever catch me begging for money to play that infernal game. People say there is a system to it, some kind of mathematical hokey pokey, I say bullshit. It's a suckers' game unless you were born lucky. I try not to go within ten feet of that stupid wheel unless I'm feeling masochistic and even then, there are much better ways to hurt myself.

The elevator stopped at the penthouse and the doors opened casually. Bobby instructed me to take off my shoes immediately as the carpet was made entirely of silk. And it was; it was made entirely of red, white, and blue silk. It felt amazing beneath my toes, so much so that the rest of the room seemed obsolete. My sense of touch had overcome all others and I closed my eyes in silent celebration knowing that if Bristol didn't kill me I too could one day have a carpet made of silk. We arrived at some oversized oak doors in the center of the room and Bobby banged aggressively on one of them. A strange buzzing filled the room seconds after she knocked; it was eerie but recognizable, a sound I had surely heard before. At that moment I realized the lenses of nearly a hundred surveillance cameras were focusing on us. I knew PCP could make you paranoid but this was borderline unnecessary and therefore it made me sweat even more.

The cameras locked in their position and were apparently satisfied with our appearance because the doors began to open very slowly. As the room on the other side was revealed I was filled with a whole new sense of shock. All of the walls were made of soft golden rubber and the floor was made of patriotic foam that matched the previous room's silk. An enormous window made of thick bulletproof glass was the backdrop to the office of the infamous Dan Bristol. I noticed there were additional doors on each side of the room; I could only imagine what kind of nonsense they kept hidden. There was also a large steel safe that Bobby immediately unlocked, revealing the fact that she had done it many times over. She then unlatched the cuffs and placed the briefcase in the affluent belly of the safe just as our host appeared to greet us.

Dan had a fucked-up looking lip. That was the first thing I noticed about him as he stared at us through bloodshot eyes. It looked as if something or someone had chewed most of it off. He had wild white hair that moved as erratically as he did. He was twitchy, and ugly, and old, but seemingly in good shape. He didn't look frail like most ninety-some-things; you could tell he had some living left to do. It was as if the chaos he had created was still not satisfying and with his full plan for revenge not yet complete, his lip hanging on by a thread, his face wrinkled from stress, his skin wrinkled from fear, I could tell that the race had many miles left, but the marathon was most certainly near completion. The only competition left was time even if Bristol thought he would live forever; I call it *the Castro Complex*.

I'll admit something about Dan Bristol, the guy fuckin' scared me. He sprung to his feet, light as a feather as he glided across the foam floor like a trailer park Jesus. And though he scared me, I was amused by the Bristol creature; its lack of predictability made it a rather charming acquaintance, more a pet than a friend, but could it be tamed? As my mind raced Dan got real close, all the way in my face; it reminded me of Europe.

"So yer the man who killed my kin," were the first words out of the old man's mouth. When your nightmares begin to become more real than your dreams, it usually means death is knocking. I knew that any minute those side doors would swing open and his rabid pack of hounds would devour me like country kibble. Believe me, if I had eaten that morning I would've shit my pants.

"I didn't exactly know he was your kin, Mr. Bristol," I replied. Bobby dug her elbow into my side but I continued, "It was really just an accident, I thought they were going to kill me."

"And what indication did they give you, that made you think they were gonna kill you?" Dan asked breathing hard through the many holes in his face. As far as I know, there comes a time in every man's life when he just has to tell the truth and fess up to his mistakes without making excuses, but rest assured when it's life or death none of that shit matters.

"In all honesty, Mr. Bristol, the guy from Jersey told me that they were going to bury me in the desert somewhere. I assumed that meant that they were going to kill me. Had I known that the other individual was your kin, I would have perhaps judged the situation differently, but you've got balls, what would you have done, Dan?" I winked at him and Bobby squeezed my arm hard. Suddenly Dan's bloodshot eyes became galactic black; his pupils swelled and conquered his irises. Hollow and endless he grabbed hold of my shoulders.

"And why the fuck did you bring these goddamn spider monkeys in here with you?! You kill my kin and then bring me spider monkeys?! What do you think this is, a zoo?! Don't you know you can't keep monkeys in an aquarium?!" Dan yelled, genuinely convinced that I had brought him spider monkeys.

"Sir, I don't see any spider monkeys but whatever is upsetting you I'll..." I began.

"The spider monkey or, 'mono titi,' as our Costa Rican friends may call them, are a rare breed of germs. They exist solely in the poison of a black widow that has fucked any manner of primate. They are noted by their giant asses and eight tails; why have you brought these fucking things in here?!" Bristol screamed. The guy was out of his wits, I could tell that much, but only a truly psychotic human being could have thought up the whole white-baby-slave-trade in the first place; I guess in many ways I wasn't surprised that Bristol saw an invisible spider's ass juice that resembled a pack of eight-tailed monkeys hovering all around me. For a second I thought I saw them too but then I remembered that I wasn't a raving lunatic, I was a mild-mannered, unemployed, government-sanctioned serial killer so I was at least one up on him.

"Dan, I don't know what to tell you, I'm sorry I killed your kin, but it was an accident. If there is a way I can work it off to help ease your pain I'll gladly do it, other than that, I'd just as soon be on my way; the spider monkeys are getting restless," I figured I might as well level with the guy, the only thing I had to lose was my life. He stared at me long and hard, long enough for me to see the distant sunrise of sanity somewhere deep within those once brilliant eyes.

"Skeptical circumstances surround the separation of sinister from sophisticated. So salvage yer sarcasm while speech is still satisfactory. Soon yer sanctuary will be as unforgiving as my own and the reckless abandonment of honor will only lead you down a glorious path to failure, maybe not in your lifetime, but we're all just laying bricks on top of glass foundations. Watching the time, as if the minutes meant something, as if tomorrow was a better day and you could still wish upon a star. But in complete darkness, nothing sparkles, there are no wishes, no dreams, only a sought after perfection that remains hidden despite yer achievements. The relentless grasp of dissatisfaction clenched around yer parched throat, the thirst of tangible desperation and predictable consequence. I guess what I'm asking you, Mr. Cypher, is this: is enough really ever enough?" And suddenly his eyes became engaging and forthright. I could tell that my answer would certainly decide my fate. It was made even clearer when Bristol pulled a golden gun from his belt and told me that he would shoot me if I answered incorrectly.

I thought about it for a while but still had no clue what the fuck he was talking about. I figured I might as well take a guess and see where it gets me, "Only when it's spelled correctly?" I replied in a nervously inquisitive tone. Bristol stared at me blankly; his eyes almost crossed after a minute or so, then he scratched his head and cleared his throat.

"Excuse me," Dan said and then paused, "I beg yer pardon; I don't remember what we were talking about. Anyhow, I guess I'm no man to be pointin' fingers at anyone anyways, 'specially someone like you." For the first time the guy seemed human. He actually reached out his hand for me to shake; cautious though I was, I shook it. "What's a matter, boy? Yer a big bad killer ain't you? Don't be a pussy! Shake my hand," Dan chuckled. He was right, I was being a pussy. I gripped his hand firmly and shook it. "That's more like it," Dan bolstered, "you can tell if a man knows how to grip a gun by his hand shake. Judging by that which I have just received, I reckon that you know how to grip lots of different types of guns," Dan nodded, his eyes ever engaging me, causing me to nod in agreement, "I can tell you've killed lots of people and that yer not afraid to fight, probably broken just as many laws as you done something righteous. A hired outlaw, cold-blooded killer, drunken sumbitch, and yet you've only got one or two issues I'd consider real vices. Impressive, ain't you? See, I know you ain't had a drink in days, and I don't mean a sip here or there, a drink to you means a blackout. And now don't be embarrassed, I too like to walk the line, perhaps by a different manner of poison, but hell, that's why we live in America, freedom of choice despite prohibition. But there is no narcotic, no substance, no pussy perhaps, that gives a man like you a rush like laying money on that line, is there Mister Cypher? You been in my casino not more than five minutes and you was itching to make a bet. I saw you at that table with my security cameras." He pulled a remote control of some sort out of his back pocket and clicked a few buttons as he pointed it at the wall. The wall opened up to what must have been fifty different television screens. "This is my private viewing area. Perhaps someday, I'll show you the real 'security cave,' as I like to call it. Needless to say, I saw you. You were on that game like it was morphine day at the methadone clinic. Yer a sick bastard and you need some help."

I didn't know what to say. First off, this guy was still

fucking nuts. And now, in a PCP haze he tells me that I have a problem. I turned to look at Bobby for some sort of guidance, and soon wished I hadn't. The instant I turned, a familiar, crushing pain rushed up my hips; the bitch had put her foot in my crotch again. I fell to my knees in abashed agony, a repetitive suffering I had known all too well since I had met Bobby. No man should be kicked in the balls this much. I resolved that I would have to tie her toes up like she was some ancient Asian concubine. This would make it difficult for her to balance so she could no longer deliver such damage to my genitals…on all accounts, the bitch was back.

"You're a liar, Keesey! I really believed that you made it through without gambling. You told me you didn't play! How can I even try to trust you?" she whined. I wanted to tell her to go to hell, that I didn't actually play because I didn't have any money, I wanted to tell her she was a fucking dumb bitch and that I never wanted her to come near me again. I wanted to, but I couldn't. No, as much as I wanted to I could not say a word to her because the pain was so excruciating that I could barely breathe, let alone tell Bobby to fuck off.

A few moments must have passed, or the blackout felt like eternity. This time she had really hurt me, that sharp toe went straight through my sack and into my heart. She was supposed to be my woman, stand by her man and such. And on top of that, if I am to be "her man," shouldn't that area be her most protected and treasured, not her personal soccer training machine. As the pain dissipated a bit I looked up at Bristol, he was staring down with what seemed like pity in his dementia-stained eyes.

"Damn woman, I didn't tell you to do that. What the fuck is wrong with you? I'm here to help the boy. You better apologize to our friend Mr. Cypher here. You gonna want that thing working later, darlin'," Bristol scolded her. I started to like the guy and he looked back down at me with a peculiar smile. "Let me ask you something, Mr. Cypher. If you was gonna buy some expensive product from somebody, would you rather buy it from a man whose eyes you can trust or a man who talks a good game?" Bristol was a smart guy; he had lots of interesting questions, kind of how I'd picture a conversation with Doctor Seuss. *Always talking you in different turns and directions, and casually cruising through puzzling intersections, at times he was witty, at times quite confusing, and all the while, I wished I was boozing.* But needless to say, he was smart and I liked the guy, it wasn't your normal everyday bullshitting between people. "How are you?" "The weather is this," "Where are you from?" It was meaningful in some way, as if he really meant it.

"Well, Dan, I must say, if the game the guy talked was good enough and he had a solid track record, I'd probably go with the latter," I said being sincere.

"Always leaning towards 'the game,' exactly yer problem," Bristol looked at my face coldly and then grinned, "Mr. Cypher, if you were to work for me what vision do you have for the organization? What role do you see yer-self playing? And please don't tell me you want to shoot people; I've got plenty of thugs already."

"Well Dan, it's funny that you ask me that because I've been thinking about this since I found out exactly what it is your organization does," I began.

"And who did you find this out from?" Bristol asked.

"From Koetay," I replied.

"Aha, a very credible source," Bristol winked, "but I don't have a clue of who that is." I looked at him confused for a moment. He winked at me again, "Proceed." *What a fucking weirdo*, I thought to myself and then began to tell him about my ideas for global expansion of the business.

CHAPTER 23

Ambitious Sobriety

"We can get this going deep into South America and maybe even do some trading with the Asians. Some of them are still into slave trade as it is. We used to bust those ships open when I was with the CIA. You'd find all kinds of crazy shit, whole families, but never babies. The idea that the child is born into slavery and has no idea of a life outside of it is what makes this unique and what I think makes the whole operation work. Therefore we've got to consider some kind of solid marketing strategy. We've got to make the whole revenge aspect of this be a proprietary reward that only this organization knows about. Bitter revenge only sells in the movies, we need to make this look like the 'in thing to do.'" I was on a roll but I could tell Dan didn't like the last portion, "What's the matter, Dan?"

"The revenge on White America is what I feel is the key component in getting people to move on the goods. I think we should drive that message home, Mr. Cypher," he chimed in. People never want to have their ideas manipulated by outside opinion; it's understandable and sometimes it's hard to surrender and admit that someone has a better idea than you. The trick is then to spin it so that everyone is happy.

"Dan, let's look at our target market for a moment. Most of these countries hate the US as it is so we can make it a subtle point that speaks very loudly to the ears of those who agree with the revenge aspect. Those that may not want to purchase on that angle and can simply afford to have slaves will be more interested in quality and cost of goods, not to mention return on their investment. Revenge on its own will not interest these people, though I do see your point as I admit that I am strangely comfortable with selling these babies into slavery primarily because I know that they are all white. But I digress; we all know that when a person is after quality, nothing speaks louder than a hip, in-your-face marketing campaign with celebrity spokespeople and bright, flashing colors! That is all in due time of course," I was getting overtly excited as both heads nodded in agreement. "But think about it. We go into Africa and sell these babies to the rich. We sell them to the nobles of India; we sell them to the king of Timbuktu. The business in Mexico is a righteous cause and it has helped many and we will continue that partnership, but we need to be thinking outside the box, Dan. Of course the trickiest part will be keeping this a secret from the US government."

"Leave that part to me, Mr. Cypher," Dan grinned with fiery eyes, "there are secrets that even the keepers of secrets don't know about. There are agencies of intelligence that know more than the CIA or any other government-sponsored system will ever know." I could tell that he was serious about this and wanted me to have some kind of reaction.

"Okay, yeah," I said. It didn't seem to suffice though as he glared at me hard.

"You think you know everything don't you?" he said slowly, "You think that fast flapping tongue of yers and detached attitude makes you invincible and all knowledgeable?"

"You said it, not me, pal," I replied.

"Still a smart-ass," Dan snarled, "Well let me tell you something, Mr. Cypher, I like a lot of yer ideas and for the most part, you and I are on the same page. And when you say you can do this, I believe you…"

"Well, thanks Dan, I…"

"Shut yer goddamn mouth, I ain't finished yet!" he snapped. I obeyed him and he began again, "As I was saying. I believe you, but I don't trust you. You talk a good game and that helps, but I don't trust yer eyes."

I looked at him sharply, trying to make his pupils bleed with my razor stare. I was kind of insulted, extremely confused, and my balls were still sore. I almost wished he'd just shoot me and stop fucking with my head. It was exhausting talking to Bristol, and all the while Bobby just stood in the background, never once looking in my direction, and come to think about it, never apologizing for that last cheap shot. But there was no time to let my thoughts wander off, I had to get through this, I had to see where my life was going.

"Well, Dan, maybe it's because I don't trust your fucking eyes either," I said very sincerely. Bristol seemed shocked for an instant and then he smiled.

"And rightfully so," Dan replied, "I guess you don't know me very well and I guess I haven't been completely honest with you anyways."

"Oh shit," I thought, "all I need is more truth." Sometimes ignorance really is bliss, and as cliché as that sounds, I could have really used a lobotomy. I was tired of knowing people's past and what was behind the smoke and mirrors. Hanging out with these people was like reading a "how-to" book of magic; it spoiled the existence of surprise in the world because you know how every trick is done. Bristol was going to tell me that I was actually on an alien spaceship headed for the planet Vagina (pronounced VAH-GUY-NAY) and they had been using this whole mission as an elaborate distraction while they probed my anus with a giant bear trap. Unfortunately, someone had forgotten to put the safety on it and it had snapped shut inside of me destroying all of my internal organs. I therefore had only seconds to live before I would pass on and become food for their giant space pigs. I had to admit to myself that it wouldn't surprise me.

"What, Dan, what haven't you told me? I know about the bear trap," I proclaimed.

"Are you out of yer mind, Mr. Cypher?" Bristol asked but didn't wait for me to answer, "The truth is this, we have been after you for quite some time. You move very quickly and it is hard to keep tabs on you. We know everything about you though; yer habits, yer fears, yer vices, yer addictions, the things that make you tick and the things that make you run." I looked at him puzzled, not sure exactly what he was getting at. "Don't look at me as if this is confusing or new to you. Haven't you done this to others before in yer previous line of work? Caught them unaware after following them for years?"

My stomach curled into an unfamiliar type of knot; I felt violated, like some horny teenager had been peeping in my window. How could I have been so careless? How long had these bastards been following me around for? And more importantly, for how long had I been stupider than I thought I was?

"I don't get it. Why were you following me, and how did I not know about it?" I asked rather politely.

"Mr. Cypher, which part do you reckon I answer first? Never mind what you think actually, I'll answer the first part first, in a proper sort of manner so to speak. We've been following you because yer a cold-blooded sumbitch with nothing to lose. A washed-out government experiment, a byproduct of the justice system that has been twice digested and shit out the wrong hole," it seemed Dan often rambled when he was excited about something. I wanted to punch the fucker in the face because despite his amusing style, he was really pissing me off. I think perhaps it was his honesty that bothered me the most.

"Wow, Dan. Thanks for the abundance of compliments; I'm sure sold on me. It sounds like I'm a real prize to be sought. In fact, could you be a little more insulting so I can muster up the guts to break you?!" I was on edge, "You redneck asshole, I respect you and all but you ought to watch your tongue a bit." The old man stopped and looked at me hard, it hurt my eyes a little and I wanted to flinch but then he cracked a smile and shook his head as he began to speak again.

"As I was saying, a lowlife waste of air, with the temperament of a rodeo bull who has had his nuts tied off for thirty years; a bloodhound by trade but a killer by instinct. The kind of man who has edges on both sides, a social razor blade, seen or unseen, but always in control..." Dan hesitated and looked at me. I wondered what he was about to say and gave him a nod of approval to move forward. He nodded back and began again, "always in control, except when he's drinking. Only problem I see with that, Keesey, is that you like to drink a lot. But you ain't afraid to gamble, and though I gather that it brings you more woes than benefits, ultimately it's a good thing. It's certainly a sickness but it's the best disease you can have if you treat it right. But you don't. All you gamble with is money these days. It's not yer style boy; you need to gamble with yer life to be happy. What does money get you anyway? You buy shit with it and then you have to buy more shit that's better, you know, to keep up with all yer two-dimensional rich friends. Or let's say you buy yerself a fancy house and a nice car. Then you have to pay for the electricity and water and for furniture and electronics and prostitutes and drugs and fixing expensive-ass-car problems and all that other shit, and pretty soon, you need more money. It's a never ending struggle but the problem with all that shit is that when you are lying on yer deathbed and that's all you've got, well, then that's exactly what it is; a bunch of shit. And if that's all it is, and if that's all you have, then son, that's exactly all that yer life means." As Dan finished I scratched my head, what he had said made a lot of sense to me. I had no time for worldly possessions and other junk. Where would I put it? I hadn't had a real home for so long that I'd become accustomed to hanging my hat on the side of the highway. I truly had nothing to lose, except my life of course, and I was willing to bet that I could hold onto that for a while. Besides, I didn't have anything better to do. They had still taken all of my money and…then it dawned on me. If this whole thing was a setup, was I really indebted to these people or had they lied to me about that too?

"That makes sense to me, Mr. Bristol, and I admit that I've got nothing better to do anyways so I would love a chance to expand this organization and make us both rich. Well, make me rich and you richer," I said.

"That is very good of you to say that, Mr. Cypher. I look forward to welcoming you to the family and no hard feelings about this whole debacle. That being said, there is…" Bristol tried to finish but I cut him off.

"You know I was just about to ask you one more question and I'd like you to be honest. If you've been after me this whole time, stalking me, waiting to make your move, was the whole deal back in New Orleans bullshit? I mean, did I really lose a million dollars or did you guys just drug me and tell me that?" I knew I had the fucker now. He was going to be in my debt for this one because the bottom line was that all they had to do was ask me and I would have offered my services. If they knew so much about me, then they knew I was unemployed and searching for some kind of relevant existence.

"The truth there, Mr. Cypher, is sad to tell," Bristol replied.

"I knew it! I just want you to admit it and then I'll let it go," I crossed my fingers behind my back.

"The truth is we did drug you, Keesey, but the sad reality is that you did lose all of that money. You've got a big mouth and a-pair-of-balls to match but you are a liability to yer-self, and even more so when yer drunk. As I was saying, I would truly love to welcome you aboard but one of two things has gotta happen. Either you sober up, which I know you can do if you want to, or I check you into an AA program for a month or so and then, when you get out, we can get to work."

"I don't have a drinking problem, Dan," I smiled, "it's a drinking solution."

"But it solves nothing," he said.

"This lecture coming from the PCP user?"

"I don't use PCP as a solution to my problems; I just think it's fun. What is it going to be, Keesey?"

"Do I have a third option?"

"Of course," Dan grinned insanely, "I could shoot you in the face?"

I thought about it. Self-induced sobriety, group therapy, or casual death? It was hard to determine which one was the worst fate. I quickly narrowed it down to two of the shitty options as there was no way in hell I was going to sit around and listen to a bunch of whiney winos cry about their problem with alcohol and how it has ruined their lives, while some ex-alcoholic counselor who molests little children on the side tells me that Jesus is the solution. And while we're on the subject, Jesus used to turn water into wine. Not exactly the best role model for a recovering alcoholic but for some reason they always push it on you. I know from personal experience because the CIA tried to get me into a program as well. It lasted about two days and then I told the counselor that I could do a neat trick just like Jesus. When she asked what that was, I said I could turn whiskey into piss and then I whipped out my dick and urinated all over the floor. Needless to say I wasn't asked to return to those meetings.

But the past is the past; I was at a new crossroad now and had to choose either death or sobriety. I knew this awful day would come sooner or later. I knew sooner or later my blissful, miserable existence would be compromised by some "greener pastures" counter-offer and I would be forced to make a decision. On the one hand, I could see myself having a bright and prosperous future selling white American children to foreign lands. On the other, death would assure me that I would never have to go through any of this shit again. It's a sad day when a man can't decide what his life is worth, when he has become so jaded and irresponsible that the thought of not having to think anymore seems to make the most sense. Of course, no one knows what happens when we die. With my luck I would spend eternity working in some heavenly Wal-Mart greeting asshole trailer-trash angels and wishing I was still alive. But who am I kidding, I would never make it to heaven and I'm not a big fan of extremely hot climates.

"Dan, after weighing all the possibilities, I've made my choice. It was an awfully tough decision, I might add."

"What, choosing either self-induced sobriety or AA?" Dan asked.

"No. Choosing either death or sobriety," I smirked and for the first time I saw some fear in Dan's eyes. Maybe not fear of me, but fear for what he had gotten himself into, "but after much deliberation, I choose to stay off the booze." Dan was delighted by my choice. He came over and patted me on the back and asked me to sit back down so we could come up with a business plan. It was all becoming very real, this new plot in life, but my expectations were still limited by paranoia. How long would it be until the whole thing was shut down and we were all crucified? How long until it all goes to hell? It was useless trying to answer these questions and Dan was eager to engage me and get things rolling again. Bobby's scorn seemed to dissipate a bit but I knew I could never make her happy. I would have to quit one thing after another: gambling, drinking, and eventually life, for that would be the only way to satisfy her need for control. But there was no time for personal relationships, narcissistic love affairs, and/or attempted suicide; those things would have to wait around for a rainy day. It was time for Bristol and me to get down to business. All I needed was a drink…of water.

CHAPTER 24

Games of Guarantee

Bristol, though a psychopath in many ways, was a kindhearted soul to the very few people he liked. Most of humanity, though, was no better than a, "goddamn piece of gum stuck to yer shoe," in his eyes. The most annoying of trivial consequences, gum on the shoe, kind of an interesting perspective to have on the world. I thought perhaps one day I would be lucky enough to share in such an obtuse opinion of the Earth's most ungrateful pollution, that of course being people. For now I would be content having killed a few and probably having to a kill a few more, but I wondered how I could deal with such a task without drinking? I remember there was a time when that was possible, but unfortunately there was no time to reminisce about the youthful days of yesteryear, there was a more important matter to attend to. Though it was not a matter of business that kept my wandering thoughts enslaved, it was a matter of the heart…and of the balls.

Dan said I had been through a lot and I could knock off for the rest of the day. He even gave me a thousand dollars in chips for the Bogota casino as long as I promised not to

Me and Bobby McGee

drink while I gambled. He also gave me the key to the presidential master suite and assured me it was the one room he didn't have a camera in. That would be the only place that I would be on my honor not to get sauced. He was really forcing me to stick to my resignation of alcohol but I figured it would be worth the money in the end. Besides, Dan couldn't live forever and by the looks of him, my separation from the blunder tonic was only temporary. And as if I didn't have enough problems already, there was Bobby.

I was unsure what to say to her so we didn't talk all the way through the elevator ride down to the casino floor. This is probably the only thing that helped me get to gambling before going to the room. Had she been speaking to me she probably would have asked me to let her off of the elevator but her stubbornness had forced my companionship. I knew I needed to come up with something sweet to say to break the ice; I thought hard about how I could really get her attention.

"You know, Bobby," I began, "you're a real fucking bitch, my balls are killing me and I could really use a drink. Which way is the bar?" The red blood vessels in her eyes slithered across her irises and engulfed them in wrath. Her pupils were lucky enough to survive the attack as she realized I was purposely trying to get a rise out of her. Isn't it wonderful when you know you can pull something like that off? When you can say everything that you truly feel and due to the circumstances, the other person will take it as a joke, or sarcasm, or a means of getting their attention (mental note: next toast, drink to circumstance). I was awfully lucky that that notion registered in her mind or my testes would have surely been tested for endurance yet again. As far as I was concerned I had won my first bet in the casino and winning your first bet usually means you're in for a good run.

"So now that I have your attention, what's the deal with us?" I had decided to go all in. She hesitated before she spoke and I could tell she was really thinking hard about her answer to the question, probing her mind for an insincere response that would hopefully help her true feelings elude my mind. The sinister streak in women is obvious and sexy; it's based around charms and lies and only hurts a man in retrospect. Of course the day it starts hurting, it never stops. But in the moment, it is soothing, the spell of Aphrodite, with oh-so-wicked repercussions.

"I'm sorry Keesey, I overreacted," she looked at me with Cerberus puppy dog eyes, "I still want to be with you and I hope we can work this out." I was a bit confused by this particular response, especially its tone of sincerity. I thought for sure she hated me and that this was surely the sudden end to our even more sudden love affair. Of course, I haven't been paid to think in years and even then I didn't have to think that often. Either way everything was coming up Cypher and I was eager to overindulge in the subtle magic of this strange but perfect day.

"Well," I smiled, "then I accept your apology, but you have to come play a few hands of blackjack with me." She agreed without putting up a fight and we headed to the first $100 table I could find. People have often told me that I'm a fool for carrying limited cash and playing high-stakes games of chance and perhaps, in other situations, they may have been right, but today I was betting with someone else's money.

CHAPTER 25

Moving On Up

It was surely a day to be reckoned with. Only a select few gamblers, and I think the last was probably Doc Holliday, have achieved such an accomplishment in a single day. Not only had my life been taken completely out of the shitter by people I thought were my enemies but were actually my friends, not only had I entered into my first potentially meaningful relationship with a beautiful woman that no man had ever tamed, not only was I a new, semi-permanent resident of glorious Las Vegas, my favorite city in the world, on top of it all, I couldn't lose. If cards were ever like tantric sex, it was on this day of reckoning. I went all in at every table I played and never lost a dime. I must have bankrolled nearly five hundred grand in less than two hours and the funny part was there was nothing they could offer me that I didn't already have. No master suite and free buffet, no rounds of golf or extra days to stay. I was a part of the casino, one of the large flashing bulbs, arranged perfectly, in a power grid paradise lost.

Bobby had been surprisingly pleasant company through

it all. She would kiss the chips as I put them down and offer cute advice. It was probably the most pleasant time we had spent together. Laughing mostly, except for about forty-five minutes or so spent in silent resentment. And to be honest, it was mostly me resenting her when I realized she was having so much fun because her Diet Coke had whiskey in it though mine was merely fake sugar and caffeine. It was childish and as soon as the bets got bigger and the winning continued I was over it. "If only I could win like this all the time, then I'd never need a drink," I thought to myself. In the back of my mind I knew that Bristol had figured the same. I knew the game was rigged but I didn't care. If I really needed to get tossed I could buy plenty of drugs with this money. I promised I wouldn't drink, I didn't say I wouldn't get wildly fucked up out of my mind on cocaine and DMT, and pop whip-its out of balloons until I passed out on the toilet…I made a mental note so I'd remember the plan and then continued to enjoy the winning. My head was clear, my pockets were full, and I had a business to run. It seemed like just yesterday I was sleeping with strangers in between back-alley games of Texas hold 'em and bottles of bourbon. The high life made it easy to focus on more important things, like more money and maybe even a little bit of power, just a taste to keep corruption entertained so it wouldn't desert me altogether; you never know when you can use such an ally.

Having weighed in the chips and taken the cash in $100 bills, I figured it was time to check out the room. There I would spread the money all over the bed and roll around in it like a pig in shit, metaphorically speaking…maybe. Either way, it was going to be nice to be rich, I had made an entire town's yearly salary in a day, imagine what I could make tomorrow, with more coffee and more time. But then

Me and Bobby McGee

I remembered business would start tomorrow. There would be limited time for games but the wagers would be no less enticing. Instead of money, I was to bet my freedom and my life on my ability to sell white babies to foreigners. It was a short stack of chips to play and the stakes were just my type.

The elevator opened up at the hotel's seventy-seventh floor, doubly lucky, Bobby and I walked to the room, which happened to be room number 7711. I was surrounded by positive omens and it helped keep my confidence high. The real shit would be starting in less than twenty-four hours and it was imperative that I maintain a positive outlook, like a true go-getter, an entrepreneur, an American dreamer. I was truly following in the steps of some of the country's finest forefathers, a newly invigorated part of a proud old tradition of greed and crimes against humanity. For shame but forward we go.

I opened the door to the room and we entered. As if surprises were not common already, I was completely taken back. Apparently the presidential master suite was meant to live up to its name. The room was very patriotic; there were portraits of the first fifteen presidents placed throughout the room ending with James Buchanan over the bed all framed in gold. I thought that was an odd choice, wasn't Lincoln the sixteenth president? He was a much more well-recognized figure and frankly I would have felt greater comfort with old honest Abe looking over us. Then it hit me, Lincoln was not a friend of the slave trade and thus, he and all his successors were omitted from the wall. There was some sense to this but in a way I thought Dan had it ass backwards; if the whole plan was to take revenge on White America for the African slave trade, why would he pay homage to the leaders that had blessed it? I would have to ask him that at some point if only to hear his crazy reply.

Beyond the creepy portraits of dead politicians the room was exquisite. Fit for a king, or a president for that matter. The floor was made of marble tile with expensive rugs placed perfectly throughout what must've been 1500 square feet of room to roam in. There was a master bedroom, two bathrooms, a dining room, a full kitchen, and the main lounge area, which had a 60-inch flat screen TV on the wall. There was also a fully functioning wet bar, though the cabinet that held the booze had a gold-plated lock on it. The constant taunting of obstacles that prevented me from drinking had begun to make me immune to the desire. After all, there are only so many times you can have your face rubbed in shit before you realize you ought not to stick your head in the toilet and if I were to honestly quantify it, I had been bobbing for apples in a port-a-john for far too long. I think part of the issue was that it had been years since I was sober enough to identify the problem and now that I was, it was all I could think about.

With that in mind I had to find something else to think about quickly. People that ponder their own problems too often end up redundant and boring. The first rule of life is that it is not going to be easy and the second is only you can effect change. By focusing on your challenges and then waiting around, apathetically, for change you become a reliable source for consistent complaints. Unfortunately, there is not an incredibly large social market for complaints and those that surround you eventually tire of your trouble and woe. Not because they don't sympathize but more because it reminds them of their own problems and unfulfilling plot in life. And perhaps that is what perpetuates our existence,

Me and Bobby McGee

a relentless lack of satisfaction with the undying chance that tomorrow may at least shed light on an individual's purpose. It's really a miserable reality when you break it down but as it's been spoken, "misery deserves company," so rather than admit our loss and failure as terrestrials of this planet, we choose to spill our seed, welcoming others to the nightmare with love and affection, thus preparing them inadequately for the world beyond.

Notions like these make me wonder if Dan's white slave babies really had it that bad. They were, in fact, the exception to the rule. They had no sense of satisfaction as dictated by the boundaries of society. Instead, they were born into a purpose: *servitude*. And though such a thing is meager and uninviting by today's standards, perhaps when the limits of your existence are made clear in the beginning, satisfaction is more easily achieved. Like a dog who wants only for a pat on the head from his master and a warm place to sleep, these slave children, by birth, mitigate the challenges of relevant, modern society. They are not instructed in the science of material desire, but more commanded by order and narrowed perception. Maybe we would have all been better off without "pot-of-gold at the end of the rainbow" stories; maybe then we would be more modest with our own desires, knowing that no matter how far and long the quest may be, all that waits at the spectrum's end is a puddle of muddy rainwater, blessed vainly by the sun, with the glory of temporary magnificence. But then again, who am I to protest dreams?

Either way, pondering relevance often creates an excellent diversion from dealing with your demons and can even assist in justifying your more-than-potential actions. And perhaps that was really what was eating away at me, the subconscious notion of morality. The fact that I had formerly been paid to kill people and was now going to be paid to sell people had forced me to step back and consider my dysfunctional relationship with humanity. Now that I had done so, I could move forward with a clear conscience; I even felt better about the whole thing.

"Keesey, stop staring at that lock!" Bobby exclaimed. Having been lost in thought, it seemed I had not redirected my gaze from the wet bar and despite her rude way of showing me, it seemed Bobby was generally concerned with my well-being.

"Sorry Bobby, I was just thinking about..."

"Having a drink?" she snarled.

"No, not at all," I replied, boastful in my response, "I was actually trying to justify my future and past."

"Something so unjust can never be justified; you'll be lost in thought for years," she laughed. I wasn't sure if the remark was meant to be playful or derogatory but figured it didn't really matter anyway. My verbal battles with Bobby had become a tiresome motif, more a series of endurance tests than logical arguments, and I was far from in the mood for a new one. The fact was that she was a woman and I was the growing larva of a new man. All I needed to complete the transformation was a few hours of primal lust and some worry-free sleep. I approached her without hesitation and she fell into my arms without protest. It seemed we were both in agreement; sex is the perfect tool for avoiding conversation.

CHAPTER 26

Of Mouths and Money

"Wake the fuck up!" screamed the telephone in its alien language. The bitter clock read 7:00 am and a new day, filled with ripe possibilities, was upon us. The savage ringing forced my reflexes into motion before I could re-orient myself with the planet and I grabbed the phone, placed it to my ear, and drifted slowly back to sleep. Within seconds my slumber was displaced by Bristol's southern hospitality.

"Wake the fuck up!" Bristol howled, "This is yer wake up call, it's time to get to work."

"Why are you up so early?" I asked.

"Up early? Boy, I haven't been to sleep yet. I feel it is important to stay awake for at least 66 hours before any important meeting. That way the devil gets his due and all. You should try it sometime." Bristol never ceased to amaze me. Just when I thought the guy was a human being he turned back into some absent-minded mutant, a minister of lunacy, trying to poison my mind with the self-destructive traditions of his street-corner religion. Tempting as it was, I had no interest in conventional insanity; I've always preferred a far different variety. The kind they use drugs to cure, not to induce.

"Send me a memo. Anyway, what's the deal, Dan?"

"Meet me in the conference room at 8:00 am, we have a meeting with some potential clients and I want to see how you do."

"Clients?" the bastard certainly knew how to get my attention, "But I don't have anything prepared!"

"You'll do fine, hurry yer ass up and come alone."

"Wait, Dan, two questions that must be answered."

"Quickly, boy, but one at a time!" he shouted.

"Who are we meeting with?"

"The People's Republic of Bramapudha."

"The who's what?"

"It's a chain of small islands in the South Pacific. Their main exports are gold, diamonds, and opal. This business has been extremely lucrative for the country, as you can imagine, but many have perished in the perilous mines. As the population has dwindled to an alarming nine hundred Bramapoos, they are eager to salvage the lives of their people. There is just one thing though, Cypher…"

"As to be expected."

"Despite their greedy nature the Bramapoos are a very moral people. If they question how our product is, umm, manufactured, yer gonna need to think of a good story. We'll be dead in the water if you tell them our assembly line is comprised of hookers and thieves; I hope you've got a hell of a poker face, kid. What's yer other question?"

"Where the hell is the conference room?"

"Push the button in the elevator that says 'CR' and then scan yer room key in the panel to the left. Anything else?" I heard the last part in a fading whisper as I had already begun to hang up the phone. A power shower and a piss later I was ready to go. I suspected Dan had equipped me with an appropriate wardrobe and when I opened the closet doors it was confirmed. There were clothes for all occasions but the present called for a suit. I went with solid black, gold shirt, no tie. I learned a long time ago that people of the islands rarely wear ties. It's often considered a sign of arrogance and recognized as an immediate mark of the outsider. This was my turf but I wanted them to feel at home. I kissed Bobby's lips quickly and made my way to the conference room.

The elevator doors opened directly into the room. A large film screen was mounted on the wall in front of me while the other walls were simply windows that overlooked the strip. To my right there was a table filled with fruits and cheeses and to my left a full bar. A polished granite table accompanied by twelve throne-like chairs was the room's centerpiece. One of the chairs was occupied by Bristol; across the table from him sat three men dressed in white suits and pink ties, their faces painted with the colors of war and their long black hair tied in pony tails that shot upward from the center of their heads. My first thought was that someone had cloned the Miami Vice guys, given them peyote, and left them to play *Lord of the Flies* on some deserted island. But I guess when you splice ancient island mysticism with pure treasure, free trade routes, the stock market, and the crippling influence of stale American television, you get the Bramapoos.

They were certainly a polite people as they bowed slightly before shaking my hand, each greeting me with the word, "Spam," which is apparently a word that has many meanings in the Bramapoos' language including: "hello," "goodbye," and "shitty canned meat." Wanting to learn their customs quickly as they were, to the date, my largest account, I returned their obscure greeting.

"Spam, gentlemen, and thank you sincerely for making the trip. I'm Keesey Cypher; may I ask your names?"

"We have no names," replied the Bramapoo hereon referred to as Uno.

"If you don't mind me asking, why no names?"

"In Bramapudha only gods and saints have names. If you take a name you better die as one or the other."

"Or else?" I asked truly interested in hearing more about their culture.

"Exactly!" they replied in unison.

"Hmm, clearly it is a noble life you gentlemen lead, and we'd be honored to assist you in any way we can. So tell me, what can I interest you in?" A typical mistake salespeople make is assuming that they know what the customer is looking for and then launching into some endless sales pitch that involves very little breathing but typically a good amount of yawning from the other side of the table. The truth be told, most of the time you do know what the customer is after but something about them telling you makes the client feel self-important, like you're more of a trusted advisor than some prick out to make a buck. By assuming too much you set yourself up for crushing failure and ultimate rejection. You pigeonhole yourself into one thought or idea and the customer labels you as a simple product pusher, not a solution provider. Anyone can sell product but solving problems takes a master of the art.

Post CIA I had a little stint as a privately employed assassin, or "hit-man," as the movies call it. People think anyone with balls enough to kill can do this job but the reality is, if you want the big clients you have to sell yourself.

It's true, any idiot in the world can hold a gun and fire it at people but only a professional can do it without leaving a trace. If you don't have credibility and the ability to understand the delicacy of a situation, you'll end up shooting scumbag, cheating husbands for chump change the rest of your life. This, as you can imagine, is not nearly as lucrative as blowing out the brains of scumbag, cheating business executives and politicians. The good news was that the experience had prepared me for this moment and very little had changed since I was still dealing in an illegal product rather than something legit. Of course, this was even easier to sell than my assassin service because we had the monopoly.

"Well, Saint Cypher…" Uno began.

"Excuse me for a moment, did you say Saint Cypher?" I asked.

"I believe he did," replied the Bramapoo known as Dos from here on out.

"I would tend to agree," the Bramapoo now known as Tres concurred.

"Why, 'Saint'?" I asked.

"As you have been told, those with names are either gods or saints where we come from and you, Saint Cypher, are certainly not a god," Uno smiled.

"Certainly not," Dos and Tres agreed simultaneously.

"Not much of a saint either," Bristol snickered. Everyone including myself shot him a potent glance and he quickly returned to a state of seriousness. I was flattered by the title but insulted by my low rank in the eyes of the Bramapoos. Of course then I considered the fact that I had secretly named them after Spanish numerals for lack of a more creative notion and all was once again copacetic in my head.

"Sorry for the interruption, please proceed," I smiled with professionalism.

"As Mr. Bristol may have told you the resources of our country are quite rich," Uno continued.

"Literally," said Dos and Tres.

"And as a result our people have become very rich themselves. But with any fortune comes an *un-fortune*. Our unfortunate status is that obtaining our rich resources comes with a very high price," Uno explained.

"The ultimate price," insisted Dos.

"Priceless even," said Tres.

"And what would that price be?" I asked, though I knew the answer already.

"Death!" replied the three in synchronicity. I didn't respond immediately. I let the word hang in the air to let them know I was absorbing the seriousness of the situation. Their eyes grew wider by the second as they awaited my response and they fidgeted in their chairs, anxious for the reply of the newly great Saint Cypher.

"If you are already rich, why do you need more?" I asked.

"Whatever do you mean?" Uno responded with a bit of agitation in his voice, as the other two crossed their arms.

"I'm not trying to insult you my friend. I'm simply saying if your population is suffering and you are already extremely wealthy, why not just stop harvesting the treasures of your island and live your lives?" I could sense that Bristol wanted to kick me in the leg for making such a suggestion. But little did he know that I knew greed had no reason or sense of self-satisfaction. This overpowering sin consumes the minds of all that indulge in it and a suggestion of simple rationality was simply irrational to those engorged with overindulgence.

"This is certainly an absurd notion coming from a man who lives in a casino," Uno laughed, joined by the others.

"Perhaps, but neither Bristol here nor I have to die to get wealthy. We feed off the dreams, hopes, bad luck, and eventual misery of strangers from all over the world. I guess you could say our money comes from those who are 'slaves to desire.'"

"An interesting point you make and perhaps we too desire some slaves to gain our wealth," Uno leaned forward as he spoke with definite interest in his eyes. I knew I had him and the rest would follow suit.

"Well then, we just might be able to help you," I grinned wide with capitalist pride and everyone in the room returned it.

CHAPTER 27

Coffee is for Closers (Who Can't Drink)

The next few hours were spent discussing the details of our operation. I explained that despite our business the organization had nothing but the utmost regards for humanity and would never think of selling someone's actual child into slavery. Instead we had a secret lab in North Dakota where sperm and embryos were donated by a vast number of supporters. The embryos were fertilized and incubated in the lab, and nine months later the product was born, having no prior knowledge of its mother or father and thus subject to any type of brainwashing we wished to induce. This was all complete bullshit, of course, but let's be realistic, if you look up *sales* in your thesaurus, *bullshit* is the first synonym you'll see. Besides, what they didn't know wouldn't hurt them and it would certainly benefit me and therefore it was a win-win situation. Having gained their acceptance of our moral and ethical practice, it was time to discuss the product itself in more detail.

I explained that it was an investment and they would not see the benefits immediately but within five years their people would never have to work in the perilous mines of Bramapudha again.

"But why babies?" Uno asked, "Don't you have any adolescent children available?" As it was a fair question, I answered honestly. Describing the idea of a caste system and how when individuals are born into a plot in life they are less likely to attempt to change it, especially when they know of nothing else.

"As our products are bred for servitude, from birth they are under the impression that it is their sole purpose in life; otherwise they would rebel and want freedom," the Bramapoos nodded in understanding and so I continued, "Plus, if you train a child to work from its birth you can maximize its productive years in the workforce. Think about it, a child born and bred into typical middle-class society doesn't even understand the concept of labor until its later adolescence, these slave children on the other hand can be given a shovel as a toy instead of a rattle and begin digging ditches before they can walk." I then reminded them of the United States' own history in relation to child labor laws and how children were once permitted to work as soon as they could stand. The bottom line being that these white babies had it in their blood to work in the mines and fields instead of attending school. Furthermore, I pointed out that a little discipline and a gallon of sweat in exchange for dinner is the recipe today's kids are in desperate need of anyway, especially spoiled, white American children. The Bramapoos agreed that things like Nintendo and singing puppets had made their children and for that matter, the world's children, soft and that there was no harm in putting the next generation of newborns to work if only to preserve the silver spoon life for the others. And to make an example out of heartland born, American, white-bread brats was the most ingenious plan the Bramapoos had ever come across.

"This business of yours could change the world," Uno said to Bristol and me.

"Maybe even for the better," Dos and Tres added. Bristol and I shot each other glances of proud excitement and though we remained silent, an air of unprecedented self-satisfaction filled the room with fumes so thick our egos had to apply deodorant before the stench of arrogance overwhelmed the entire casino. We nodded modestly to our clients and Bristol walked over to the bar. He poured a round for everyone and passed out the glasses.

"I would like to make a toast," Bristol declared.

"Wait a minute, gents. Despite our obvious interest the deal is not yet done. Do you always celebrate before negotiations are complete?" Uno asked shrewdly. Dos and Tres sat silently in agreement. I was interested to see how Bristol would react to such a question as he was, in fact, caught celebrating before business was concluded.

"No, sir," Bristol replied, "but I do drink at the beginning of any friendship." Bristol raised his glass and the rest of the room followed in a joyous "SPAM!" which coincidentally also means "cheers" in Bramapudha. Bristol had impressed me with his smoothness and I could see how he became the man that he was. He had that "guy-everyone-likes" thing down like no other. He was truly the perfect mentor and manager for a fast-talking, loose cannon hotshot like me. We could make an uncertain amount of money together; that was now very apparent. I knew he had the trillion-dollar enterprise, and I had the million-dollar mouth; between us I figured, we could make billions a year. It was a combination of wits, pride, and riches so potent that most planets had declared it illegal. Of course, Earth as always, was the last to know and in turn, the last to react.

Some nights I lie awake wondering if we've really got if figured out or if we're just so fucking far behind that any progress seems revolutionary. I stare out my window, above the pitiless glow of street lamps and all-night sin sanctuaries, looking out at the expired light of deceased stars wondering if perhaps, we're just the last to go. The other planets in our solar system allow for no life to exist; they remain barren deserts, empty graveyards for astronomy's wet dreams. They are homes only hurricanes and cyclones could love and yet every decade, someone has new evidence, new reasons, new guesses for why there's life out there. To the dreamer, its hope for something wondrous, something not yet written about in a textbook, a new twist to that old and overused plot; but to the realist, and to those of us that know why these projects get funded, it's just another attempt at finding a new home for humanity once we fuck this place up beyond all distraction. Which gets me back to the original question, what if we're just the last to know? What if there were other civilizations on all these other planets that were destroyed long before we began exploring them? What if these "signs of life" scientists claim to find aren't signs of life, but signs of death? Not new wave, space alien links but archeological artifacts meant to remind us that just because we think we're the high and mighty brilliant minds of the universe, some other arrogant species already thought the same way and they have since become extinct.

We claim to be so brave and curious, products of the greater good, a mass of noble scholars, but it is really fear that drives our exploration of everything. We're a high society of bed-wetting schoolchildren afraid of changing seasons and the cryptic text of tinker toy instructions, all the while trading scripted prayers for an extra sip of soup from God's own silver spoon. If we could simply sit back and let the world work itself out without the fear of death, I think you would soon see a society of happy idiots and deadbeat prodigies, and a healthy society at that. The fact is, we as people have complicated the world past any point of return and now each moment is forever fleeting. You can't turn your back on the daylight and you might as well not sleep at night until the Japanese invent a camcorder for your dreams, and America makes a poorly constructed competitive model that will only sell during Christmas when choice is limited and patriotism is an excuse.

It's certainly not the world it was when it first began, and it's highly doubtful that this is the world it was intended to be. No matter what you believe though, the undeniable reality is science, war, and business are the global religions we have become accustomed to. Because of this we have left a path of destruction so wide with error that the only solution is to use more of our science to find a place to start over, fight more wars so that peace may forever reign, and if nothing else, for god sakes, buy low and sell high!

But I digress and remain biased at the same time. I'm a self-confessed despiser of humanity and thus a cold-blooded killer more barren of remorse than Saturn is of retirement property. And still I must say, for all the things we as people have done wrong in our hunt for purpose, we still have a conscience and therefore, we accept responsibility for the problems we have created by searching for other things to blame them on. There is always another link in the chain that can further distance us from the blame; the problem is that the search for each new one is perpetual and kinetic.

Me and Bobby McGee

Wisdom draws pain from a well as deep as our potential, and knowledge is a brawler always hungry for a fight. Every time you think you know better you end up knocked out, face swelling with the pain of pursuit, because each punch you throw is always countered by a universe of abstraction and half-baked thoughts waiting for their chance to rise to the challenge of possibility. Of course this is a tragedy of science that perpetuates war and business.

"How?" is often the question and the answer is simple; war is fought over religion, and nothing pisses off religious radicals more than science. Meanwhile, the rest of us need a distraction from the sadness of science and the violence of war, and what mirage is better to provide that than money. These simple truths are the keys to the free world or so it would seem. But if you look closely enough, the way I do these days, in that layer between the stars and strip-club billboards, you see a people bored with these ideas as well. A world so tired of worrying about science, war, and business that it just wants to be free to remember its youth, its renaissance, its ages of exploration. It's a world on trial, hungry for laziness, before it finally finds out about its hidden, but inevitable fate...

And yet for all these gracious, self-indulgent remarks, I hope I haven't lost my point. Past, present, or future, it's a universe of doom. The more you think about anything, the less sense it makes. So be sure that you don't get too caught up in the formalities of morality and the intrepid lies of the people that say they have embraced them, especially when all you're really trying to do is be all that you can be. Spray paint "Fuck You NASA, Armstrong was a fag" in mile-high letters on the side of the moon and take what you can from this life, chances are you aren't getting out alive; you just want to make sure you don't spend the rest of eternity wondering why. With all this in mind, I can draw my shades each night after only a few moments of silent reflection and I can then sleep soundly, knowing that I can give people the opportunity they so silently desire and then, even if Earth is the last planet to know that life isn't meant to be, at least people can find new ways to waste their existence before the bad news is printed on a small corner of the fifth page of the Sunday paper, just after the latest celebrity divorce articles and used car ads.

"You gonna drink that?" Bristol asked, "I know it's just Coke but it's still refreshing." I smiled, tipped my glass back, and regained my focus as there was still plenty of work to be done. Verbal commitments as most anyone knows are as valuable as the gum in a pack of baseball cards. That's why no deal is ever done on a handshake alone because the reality is, no matter how much you trust someone, unless you have it in writing, you don't have it.

When everyone finished their drinks we sat back down and Bristol buzzed Bobby on the intercom. We were to negotiate the details of the order with the Bramapoos and she would then draw up the paperwork. I assumed this was done in parallel so the transaction could be completed that day and the client would have no time for second-guessing or snooping around for further information on the organization, or any of a number of scenarios that could delay the deal. These were the tactics of a seasoned professional, and though I was convinced I knew everything there was to know, there was obviously still plenty for me to learn.

The next thing I learned was that putting a massive deal together makes one salivate out of every orifice. Your body is covered in moisture at the thought of a signature on that dotted line. The problem is one has to maintain composure through all the bullshit in order to ever reach that point. As we discussed the Bramapoos' purchase of their first three hundred babies at twenty grand apiece, I nearly had to take my suit off and wring it out. The feeling of success had been banished from my heart and mind long ago and I was not fully prepared for its return. But when Bristol read back the final details of the agreement that Bobby had put together and brought to us, I felt a sense of security and accomplishment I hadn't known since my last sanctioned kill so many years prior. It's truly amazing how comparable ink and blood can be; I handed Uno a red pen to help further illustrate the similarities.

The three Bramapoos read over the contract several times. First just Uno read it, then Dos and Tres read it together, then they all three read it, made notes, discussed them, and then Uno read it again.

"This all looks good, but what is the return policy?" Uno asked.

"Well, there is no return policy but each product does come with a three-month warranty as you'll see right here," Bristol pointed out the warranty and the Bramapoos read through it.

"Pretty standard stuff," said Bristol, "just says if any of them arrive on yer doorstep sick or dead or have any defects that render them incapable of working, et cetera, we will send you a replacement and/or perform corrective surgery or other necessary medical treatment on the inferior product. If after that three-month period you still desire support from our organization we can send you staff nurses or whatever else you need for an additional fee. Hell, we can even send you some with lactating titties if you need them but we recommend you don't breastfeed the babies as it causes them to form bonds with other human beings, which is strongly discouraged. The goal for a successful investment is to have the little ones as withdrawn from personal relationships as possible. Just an added tip, free of charge," Bristol winked at the Bramapoos, "does this satisfy you gentlemen?"

I could tell he was ready for that signature too, he knew he had disarmed any doubt in their minds and now it was time for the big payday. While the Bramapoos discussed the warranty policy, I made a mental note to find out about the nursing support staff offering Bristol had mentioned. This was news to me and I wanted to familiarize myself with it as quick as possible as it appeared to be a good way to make some extra margin on the order.

"Give us six months on the warranty and you have a deal," Uno proclaimed. Dos and Tres nodded in agreement. Bristol didn't answer immediately; he just stared at the Bramapoos. I thought he was seconds away from one of his PCP-induced visions of impending terror and slowly made my way under the table. Lucky for the entire room, he was just working his magic.

"I'll give you the six months," he finally said, "but then I want you to take a look at the documentation on our support program. If you think you need six months to get started, you may find you need even more help down the road and we just wouldn't want you to be unhappy with yer investment." The Bramapoos agreed and Uno picked up the pen to sign the document. Then he stopped and looked at Bristol and I sadly.

"Alas, my friends, I cannot sign this document," Uno stated.

"But why?" I asked, "Didn't we give you everything you wanted?"

"Yes, and more," Uno replied, "But even so, I do not have a name, how can I sign this contract?" Dos and Tres looked at us inquisitively. This was certainly a scenario I had not prepared myself for but luckily it left only one question to be answered.

"How do people make deals in Bramapudha?" I asked, "I mean you guys deal in precious stones and gold; surely it is not just a handshake that closes business."

"But there you are wrong, Saint Cypher," Uno replied, "the handshake of blood brothers is our custom." Uno showed me his palm as he answered. It was covered in scars from the many "deals" he had made. The tortured hand of the Bramapoo businessman gave me an idea.

"Another question for you," I began, "'Spam' is like the universal word in Bramapudha, right? It can mean just about anything, right?"

"This is true," Uno nodded, as did Dos and Tres.

"Then here is our solution," I nodded back, "you sign the word 'Spam' in blood at the bottom of this contract and we can get the process started." Everyone was terrified by my suggestion until it began to make sense. Uno agreed that such an act would be seen as a binding contract and he extended his hand in my direction. I quickly grabbed my red pen back and stabbed him in his pointer finger aggressively enough to break the skin and draw blood.

"AAHHH!!" Uno screamed.

"Shit!" screeched Dos and Tres. I waited proudly as everyone collected themselves.

"I was just looking to shake your hand," Uno gasped, "but I suppose this is painfully convenient." Uno pressed his bleeding finger to the paper and wrote out the word, "SPAM," in big red letters. All circumstances aside, the deal was done and now everyone could enjoy the finer Las Vegas attributes, like gambling, hookers, and all-night clinics that specialized in tetanus shots. I apologized to Uno for catching him off-guard but he told me to think nothing of it as his hand had suffered far worse pain making deals in Bramapudha.

"It must be tough and self-mutilating, being a politician and businessman in your country," I said as we stepped into the elevator.

"Saint Cypher, it doesn't matter how you sign an agreement," Uno patted me on the back, "Ink and blood are very closely related."

CHAPTER 28

Forget What You Think

It was nearly 2:00 in the afternoon when we finished the business with the Bramapoos. Bristol had the casino's private doctor tend to the gash on Uno's finger and a handshake and a hydrocodone later, the wound was completely forgotten. Bristol explained to the Bramapoos that from this point on his direct communication with them would be extremely limited and that I was to be their primary point of contact. To further ensure the security of everyone involved, the Bramapoos would receive a special untraceable cell phone that they could use to reach me and only me. If there was anything they needed I would be the one to get it for them. Trust was an essential component in this deal and I was sure I had earned theirs; perhaps they would choose to stand out of my reach while I held sharp objects such as razor blades, chainsaws, and fountain pens but when it came to the well-being of their investment, they knew it would be a relationship of effortless pleasure. I was sure it would be as these were good people and I was as dedicated to their satisfaction as I was to making my money.

The Bramapoos were eager to enjoy the many delights of the Bogota Casino and I was equally eager to join in until Bristol informed them that we had further business to attend to. Of course, everything they desired was on the house and they were to indulge as if our spirits were by their sides. The Bramapoos were an understanding people and they left us with a bow, a firm handshake, and a respectful "Spam."

Bristol shut the door and walked over to the bar. As he poured himself a scotch and me a soda, I threw my feet up on the table to recline in the glow of success. I knew I had done well and I wasn't opposed to showing it; after all, if I couldn't indulge in alcohol's induced sense of self-confidence I might as well enjoy the real thing. Bristol handed me a Coke and I snickered at the irony of commercialism.

"Do you know why they say that?" Dan asked. I looked at him puzzled as one was never sure where Bristol was going with his thought process. He could tell I had no idea what he was talking about and came over and sat on the table next to my feet. "Do you know why they say 'spam?'"

"No, Dan, I didn't even know there was a country called the People's Republic of Bramapudha until 7 this morning."

"Interesting place, Bramapudha; one of the oldest civilizations in the world. The secret to its longevity is that it's also one of the most unknown civilizations in the world, and the reason it's so unknown is because it's a nation of secrets, and secrets make you powerful," Dan began looking deep into my pupils to make sure I was interested. The absence of any smart-ass remarks assured him that he had my attention and so he continued. "The Bramapoos are a peaceful people. That's not to say they don't wage war, that's just to say they don't wage war with violence. They use their minds to conquer their enemies yet they have no enemies because they remain peaceful by only claiming what is theirs and sharing the things others want with them. Do you follow?" Dan asked.

"In all honesty, Dan, I have no idea what you're talking about," I replied, more full of truth than ever.

"What's so hard to understand? Stop thinking, and start listening, you might learn something you thought you already knew," Dan said as he pushed my feet off of the table forcing me to sit upright, "Let's take a step back for the feeble-minded individuals in the room." I looked around the room and saw no one else and wondered who he could be talking to. I resolved to listen despite the man's hallucinations. "What are the primary exports of Bramapudha?"

"Gold, diamonds, and opal," I replied.

"Oh, so you did take yer head out of yer ass long enough to listen to me at least once today, I'm pleased by that," Dan said with an awkward smirk tossing and turning on his mutilated, insomniac lips, "But moving on, those items are priceless but are obviously treacherous to obtain; this of course is a statement that is clearly supported by the very issue that has driven the Bramapoos to inquire about our services. Agreed?"

"Agreed…"

"That was a rhetorical question, Cypher. Learn to talk when it's necessary, not just because someone simply poses a question and you feel compelled to respond to it because that is what society has conditioned you to do. Sometimes you can pick a man apart just by making him uncomfortable with silence and sometimes you can gain great admiration from yer superiors by not interrupting them to answer questions with obvious answers. Understood?" Bristol asked in all his bug-eyed glory. I didn't say a word, I just stared at the fucker, and not because he told me to. I paused because I had to decide whether I wanted to give in to my disregard and lack of respect for authority and knock the bastard out cold or to give into my greed and agree without protest to take his advice. Needless to say, the latter won out and I nodded.

"To put things into a more attainable perspective, think for me if you will about the American Indians or Native Americans or more so, the many tribes of native peoples that lived on this continent before European settlers arrived and gave everything a politically incorrect name. No matter which semantics you prefer, these people were a flourishing nation, kind to the Earth and thankful for its resources, but they were blessed with one fatal flaw: the ignorance of generosity."

"The ignorance of generosity?" I repeated perplexed.

"Yes. They gave away their secrets instead of trading them. When the Europeans, or 'white people,' as I like to call them, arrived here, they were sick and starving. A pack of helpless, pale-skinned, funny-dressing refugees that were so damn annoying their own countries didn't want them. That's why they were sent on what was presumed to be a suicide mission. European royalty didn't believe in exploration; they believed in power and population control. They didn't fund discovery, they wrote off potential rebellion by silently persecuting curiosity."

"I don't know if that's all true, Dan. I mean history tells us…"

"Haven't you stopped thinking and started listening yet? Books, teachers, preachers, *reachers*, even the goddamn signs over the stadium bleachers, only tell you what they think you should think. I'd be lying if I told you I wasn't doing the same thing but the difference is that I wouldn't lie to you. To do what we do it is important to understand the reality, not the history," Dan glared hard at me. Like a third grader I zipped my lips and gave Bristol my full attention. "As I was saying, those explorers and settlers were sent here, to this continent, to die. And they damn sure would have if the kindly natives didn't generously show them how to farm, and hunt, and how to be self-sustaining. The Europeans needed the natives and were grateful for their assistance and rewarded them with peace. Now I don't for a minute believe there was a big Thanksgiving dinner where everyone sat around passing plates of turkey and pumpkin pie and playing footsie under the table, but I do believe there was harmony between everyone to such a degree that it inspired such a story and probably an orgy or two with them damn kinky French sashaying about. All porno aside though, it was work for both the whites and the natives to get the relationship to that point and to sustain it as long as they did."

"Weren't there several wars fought between the colonists and the Indians? I don't think they simply sat down and taught the…" I began but was cut off by the tomahawk glance of Dan's failing patience. I nodded to let him know that I was finished and he continued.

"The problem with the white man is he's always thinking of ways to do less work. It was work to maintain a relationship with the natives and once they had given up all of their secrets they lost their value in the eyes of the Europeans and so they were slaughtered and enslaved and ultimately pushed out to the desert. Their land and the life they knew vanished with their secrets. Had they simply sold the white people their produce instead of teaching them how to farm, they would have maintained power and control. You know that old saying: 'give a man a fish feed him for a day, teach a man to fish and he'll steal yer land and rape yer women.' These mistakes are what the Bramapoos have managed to avoid."

"So you're saying the Bramapoos have never let white people settle on their land and that's why they say 'spam.'"

"No, you idiot, I'm saying the Bramapoos have maintained power and control by keeping secrets such that no one would ever think of invading their land. Being one of the oldest civilizations in the world, the Bramapoos have grown wise through prolonged existence. They have seen the world grow and expand and though they are seemingly isolated, they are dialed into the powers that run the planet," Bristol proclaimed. I wasn't sure whether I was supposed to laugh at his lunacy or be amazed by the peculiar depth of his knowledge of classified global politics. I resolved to be firmly inquisitive and a bit suspicious without being rude.

"Dan, what the fuck are you talking about?" I asked in my most sophisticated tone. He was not amused by my ignorance as he was positive that he was making sense.

"Cypher, forget what you think you know about world trade and economics; the truth is the Bramapoos are responsible for supplying the world with seventy percent of its diamonds, eighty percent of its gold, and ninety-five percent of its opal among other gems. The country has more precious stones and minerals than it has fucking grass. The many mines of the islands are so precious to the world that if the country were to be swallowed by the sea the global economy would collapse and international chaos would certainly ensue. The small number of countries you think export these types of riches are simply middlemen buying their shit wholesale from the Bramapoos."

"If that's the case how come no one has attempted to invade the Bramapoos as they did the Native Americans?" I interjected, attempting to add something besides a dumbfounded look to the conversation.

Me and Bobby McGee

"Now yer listening. That is where the Bramapoos were smart. First you have to understand that the discovery of Bramapudha by any nation was completely accidental and as such, occurred quite rarely. On top of that, the country is made up of nearly thirty small islands and it is impossible to know where all of the mines are without a vast knowledge of the land. The Bramapoos made sure never to draw maps and instead verbally passed on the location of the mines from generation to generation. Being a civilization that had been witness to the very first attempts at exploration and international trade, the Bramapoos became very keen to the greed of man and thus very protective of their treasures. A wise society, though, they soon figured out that if people were willing to take sea voyages that had the strong possibility of ending fatally to obtain goods from other lands, then surely the people valued the items more than their own lives. If they would die for the items, they would certainly fight for the items. With this in mind, the Bramapoos drew up treaties with each of the few nations that ventured onto their soil. The treaties stated that no citizen of any foreign nation was permitted to step onto their lands and in turn, they would supply the foreign country with an adequate amount of precious treasures in exchange for peace, defense, and secrecy. These treaties were agreed upon by the handshake of blood brothers and are 're-signed' with every new generation of leaders, hence the reason our friend had so many scars on his hand besides the one you added," Dan giggled a bit. I was at a loss for words, he could tell, and took full advantage of the situation, "As time went on and the world advanced, the gray areas of the map were all filled in and early forms of global communication were established. Lucky for the Bramapoos, the nations they had signed treaties with were many of the most powerful and advanced in the world as they had prospered from the trade of gold and gems. Though many of these countries considered a hostile takeover of Bramapudha, knowledge of the island nation's other allies, coupled with their lack of knowledge with respect to the gem mines, prevented them from doing so. The powers-that-be soon resolved to remove the People's Republic of Bramapudha from the map and thus it became a secret known only to the most powerful nations in the world. Funny enough, its concealment is consequently the only thing the most powerful nations in the world have agreed upon in nearly two centuries," Bristol paused to make sure he still had my attention and admittedly he did. I thought I was privy to some pretty intense shit but Bristol somehow knew the secrets of the world. Either that or his bullshit was so extravagant that you either had to force yourself to believe it or feel guilty about not having the guy committed.

"How do you know all this, Dan?" was the only response I could think of.

"I read a lot, I listen when people speak, and I am forever willing to believe that I'm being lied to," Dan winked and sipped his scotch, "the fact is I know because I know and I'm telling you because I want you to be able to say the same. Whether you want to believe me or not is up to you but either way, I hope I've made my point."

"Actually you haven't made your point at all. You were going to tell me why the Bramapoos say 'spam.'" He looked at me with a bit of concern in his eyes and then shook his head.

"Cypher, you better get yer head in the game," Dan smiled, "the Bramapoos say 'spam' because they can do whatever the fuck they want and they don't have to explain themselves to anyone. Their way of life is a secret, their power is immense, and they are completely removed from the rest of the world's bullshit. They knew, from the beginning of their civilization, not to trust pale-faced foreigners bearing nothing but disease and the selfish intentions of God-selling missionaries."

"But then why would they want to deal with us now?"

"Because now we have something they want. We have the secret to the preservation of their society. With our product they will no longer be forced to kill themselves in the mines, they will be free to enjoy the beauty of their islands and the perseverance of their culture. Plus, it helps that the babies are white," Dan stopped and then extended his hand to me. I shook it firmly and he grinned, "you did a good thing for us today, kid. You got us a customer for life. Once they see how much easier their existence is, they won't ever want to work again. Their only problem is that the slave children will perish in the mines just as their own people have. The good news for us is that when they notice this happening they will certainly want to purchase even more product! Talk about reoccurring revenue, it's six million today but in five years this account will be worth six hundred million. Not only that but as the Bramapoos are a powerful nation they are also influential. Rest assured boy, the word will spread somehow or another and we could get very busy very fast. I hope you are ready. Take the rest of the day off and relax." Dan patted me on the shoulder and exited the room.

As he left and I collected my thoughts, I quickly resolved that Bristol was equally full of both wisdom and shit. This made it hard to decipher which components of his ramblings were actually true and which were just lies left behind to make me wonder if they were true or not.

CHAPTER 29

This Way to Your New Life

The world is forever a mystery and clichés are always an adequate cover up for limited insight. Beyond that there are just assumptions; assumptions about life, living, and the pursuit of escape, assumptions about death, doom, and the days after. The curse of humanity is an overactive mind, the need to always fill in the blanks. The uncomfortable shadows of doubt loom just outside the protective glow of constant analysis just waiting for the chance to darken the picture. But embracing ignorance would leave us with nothing to do so even I tend to keep the light on as much as possible, regardless of the electric bill.

And then there is routine, the fine line between ignorance and analysis. A living daze filled with predictable events, redundant conversations, and an ending you've seen a thousand times. A slow poison, but at least it's orderly and in America, at least it's an identity. What would we be without our careers, without our accomplishments on paper? If you were forced to tell people about yourself without giving your resumé, what would you say? Would you know where to begin or simply dance around the point by discussing the weather and how it affects your mood? Would you recite out-of-context lines from the six o'clock news to appear worldly or would you simply be honest and say that you just don't know, that despite all the years you've lived with yourself you are still not sure who you are and every time you think you get a handle on it, the disruptive wink of change forces you to once again reinvent yourself, this time wiser, older, less motivated, and inevitably apathetic. Do this enough times and it too becomes nothing more than a sadistic routine that fools you into thinking things are going to be different; it leaves you to wait instead of actively searching for yourself.

Of course, from nine in the morning to five at night there are limitless employed distractions and those mystifying concepts regarding existence and interplanetary alignment are pushed aside for deadlines and coffee machine indulgences. Television shows and sports statistics are what matters when people are in public, they're safe topics, common ground. Essential tools used to hide the fact that we're all crazy and not quite ready for primetime. But what if you had to tell people what you were really thinking about? What if you were paid to be honest? I'll tell you what; they'd lock me up ten minutes into the project, pray to heaven for forgiveness, and then give anyone within fifty feet a lobotomy in an effort to help them forget the terrible alien utterances that had bounded off my tongue. But that's why we have weather, so we don't have to talk about politics or religion with people we hardly know. That way the routine can continue and so can the clichés. It's just another day at the office, if you know what I mean.

But there is always another side to it. There's always

that .001% of the population that goes against the grain and says fuck the office, the company, the executives, and the board. Fuck the stock market, and Wall Street, and even fuck Montgomery Ward. Fuck taxes, social security, and caring about what your boss has to say, dim the lights Uncle Sam, now I get to fuck you for a day. This is an elite group of individuals and in essence you can break the whole workforce down into two groups of people, artists and panhandlers aside; there are those that sell white babies to foreign countries and those that have normal, *Leave-It-to-Beaver* lives with the addition of booze, drugs, teenage pregnancy, and divorce. I guess my point is, I can't live typical, I now know that for sure. There is this defect in my circuitry that just won't allow me to live that cardboard-cutout life. I'm a skewed prototype, a negative, I'm everything they wish they could throw away...and they've tried to before.

The government doesn't give a shit about the environment but there are certain pollutants they make sure to keep out of the air. I believe the code internally is "hecklers." People that disagree with *the common one* and defy the unified front, the germs that don't flow with the gene pool, the stains on the carpet you can't remove, you know, the ones you put furniture or Persian rugs over, it's the only way to cover that type of spill, that type of mistake. But sometimes it's not in a place where you can cover it up and you just cross your fingers and pray that no one notices, especially if you're the decorator.

I hate being alone sometimes; it makes me think too much about things I keep trying to forget, ghosts in the machine. Maybe it's just the echoes of silence in an empty room that brings me back to the past, it reminds me of those moments and hours before a target was neutralized. I always wanted someone to talk too, someone to tell me I was doing the right thing or the wrong thing, not that it mattered. TV did nothing for me and the radio was always too much of a distraction. I'd get a song caught in my head and it would throw off my aim and alertness. Sometimes I'd just talk to myself in the mirror so I could at least look myself in the eye before I blinked another being out of existence. Funny enough, my code name was "Mouth." And even funnier, but ultimately predictable, it was my mouth that got me fired and almost got me killed. And it wasn't just from running my mouth, no, I hold my mouth accountable for swallowing all that booze too, especially because it lubricated my tongue and allowed it to wiggle loose from its typical restraints; it also made me a little trigger happy and less tolerant of ignorance but that didn't matter now, the past was left there for a reason. Like lost pirate treasure, it's not meant to be found by the person that originally buried it.

"What are you doing staring at yourself like that in the mirror?" Bobby said as she burst through the door. I hadn't realized I had drifted so deeply into my daze of soul searching, which is mainly an exercise in futility, being that I don't believe I even have a soul. Nevertheless, it was an ample way to occupy the hours in a day off from work and I would have been content to continue had she not begun undressing herself in front of me. I had to hand it to her though, she was the only woman I knew that could do something extremely sexy right in front of me while giving me a death look for being myself. That resulted in a feeling of inferiority and borderline insecurity instead of primal desire. In the end she was really just hurting herself by slowly making me impotent.

"What am I doing that is bothering you?" I asked trying

to sound annoyed despite the fleshy landscape of perfection that stood before me.

"You're just fucking weird, Cypher," she snapped back, "I mean, how long have you just been sitting here by yourself?"

"Not long," I replied, not quite sure if it was true or not but positive she would correct me if I was wrong.

"Bullshit!" she barked. I raised my hand to my mouth and pretended to cough as a means for hiding my smile; it seemed I could predict her every move now too. "I just went looking for you in Bristol's office. After I convinced him I wasn't a space monkey trying to eat his beehive head, he told me he let you off three hours ago!"

"Spider monkey," I replied.

"What was that?"

"Spider monkey. He sees spider monkeys not space monkeys," I corrected her.

"Excuse me, Keesey, how long have you known Dan for?" she put her hands on her hips.

"Feels like I've known him my whole life," I answered confidently.

"Your whole…It's been what, two days? Maybe three at the most?" she was bitter angry and sweetly naked all at the same time. It was a beautiful sight to behold if you're into fine dining and S&M.

"What's your point?" I asked just to keep the show going. There are certain things in life I can't resist and those things, well, they're the natural love triangle of full frontal female nudity, the classic trio laying down my favorite jazz compositions in a furious fusion of flexes and bounces that hit notes beyond conventional scales.

"My point is that I have been working for Bristol for longer than I like to admit and he sees spider monkeys, space monkeys, brass monkeys, even flying blue monkeys with tails for heads and soup bowls for feet. Pick a type of crazy fucking monkey and he has seen it. Do you understand?" she took a deep breath and waited for me to reply. I gave the appearance of nodding as I scanned her body up and down. Though she could clearly see I was not looking at her face she chose to accept the gesture as a plausible answer and sighed.

She came around behind me and began to rub my shoulders. All the world's tension and grief could be wrung out of even the soggiest towel with those two angel tools, the eighth and ninth wonder of the world, Bobby's magic hands. The massage was hypnotic and like a cobra opting to dance rather than kill I wiggled back and forth in her grasp. She had me so that I would confess to the Kennedy assassination if she so desired but she remained silent and so I did as well, perfectly cocooned in our bizarre relationship, waiting for the silk to unravel.

And thus my day off in Vegas was not spent milling around in the casinos, tempting myself with alcohol and other pay-as-you-go pleasures, but was instead spent in the arms of my lover. I will add that I felt this to be the strangest twist in the adventure so far. I mean, selling white babies into slavery to secret world powers was certainly not something I ever dreamed I'd do in my life, but neither was coming to Vegas and missing a day of drinking and gambling. In fact, I'll go as far as to say that before all this began, if someone had asked me which I thought would be more likely to happen, I would have certainly said the former.

But weird shit seemed to be the motif in this life as of late and so I chose to go with the flow. And I was rewarded for it as Bobby and I shared intimacy like we hadn't before. I told her about the Bramapoos and the details of the conversation that ultimately closed the deal. I told her how it would likely start a world trend that we would get fat and rich off of. She asked me if she could skip the fat part, adding that she didn't even want to have kids as she was so afraid of gaining weight. I told her it was just a figure of speech and not a speech about her figure and she laughed and then asked me if I thought her lingerie made her look fat.

I'll never understand the female *Homo sapiens'* obsession with asking this question especially when they know they are not. Women need to realize that no man who has the privilege of putting his penis inside of you will ever admit that you look fat. If he is dumb enough to do so it will haunt him like a tainted apparition and linger like a cattle brand, forever, until he is sent to the sanctuary of the slaughterhouse.

But alien behavior from the planet Venus aside, it turned into a truly beautiful encounter. And as the conversation faded and the night brought forth the irresistible silence of contentment we fell asleep with a sense of oneness that we would never know again. Had I known what the future had in store, I might have stapled my eyes shut and thankfully never seen another day.

Part Two

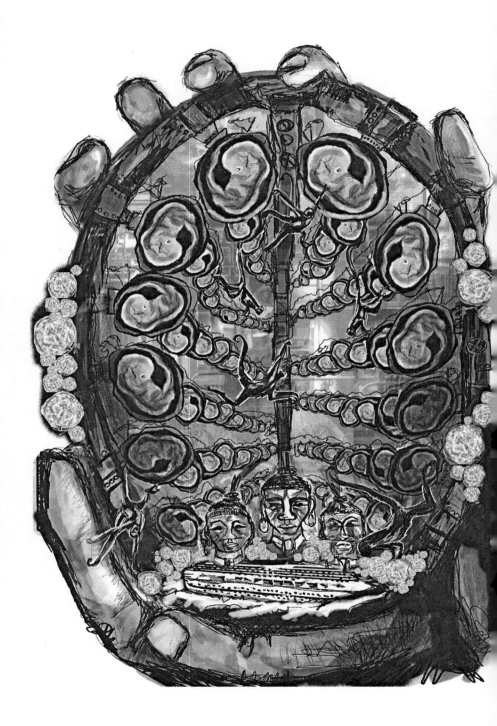

CHAPTER 30

Seven Years of Luck, Some Good, Some Bad

The phone is a savage tool. A modern-day leash for mankind that keeps you plugged into the grid regardless of your own personal desires for peace and isolation. As the damn thing blurted in my ear for the 2555th day in a row, once again waking me from my well-earned rest, I debated ripping it out of the wall, marching up to Bristol's office, and placing it snugly up his ass, though I doubted there would be room for it with his head already lodged so far up it. But nonetheless I had resolved to be a semi-respectable citizen, career oriented, driven, heading for the top and so was my plot in life. Our little organization was busier and hungrier than a cannibal in a leper colony.

The Bramapoos turned out to be the real deal and the word spread quickly to the proper international investors that an innovative solution to certain issues related to both economics and laziness was readily available via a young man in the US they called "Saint Cypher." The nickname gave our little corporation a very positive marketing spin, as I was the face of our international dealings and I was not seen as a slave merchant at all; I was "the Saint of Siesta." I was blessing people with the opportunity to invest in one or many servants (or "labor-waivers" as we like to call them) for life. Best of all, I was selling the only race of baby no one really seemed to be uncomfortable enslaving. In all honesty if I didn't have to live in the Bogota casino and I could've gotten the house I kept dreaming about up in those Northern California woods I would have bought myself a few of the little spuds without thinking twice.

But back to the point, we grew up fast. I spent the first couple of years flying only to Asia, Africa, and South America and then later added Australia and most of Europe, and eventually even Canada was added to the route. It seemed even Caucasians didn't mind investing in these *born-for-work* specimens and frankly, I was happy to sell them to anyone regardless of nationality or race. It seemed we had found a service that inspired a strange sort of global unity and brought together people of all kinds in a shared disregard for human rights, a wholly unified appreciation for a permanent paid vacation.

The only problem was the orders were coming in faster than we could fill them. Between the Mexi-Zona Desert trade route and the People's Republic of Bramapudha, a good amount of our supply was already spoken for. We knew we could not delay our first shipments to the new clients for too long as the investment itself already took three to five years to even begin showing a major return. Therefore we had to find a way to increase the supply quickly and significantly. You've heard the expression, "there's a bun in the oven," well, you could say we needed the microwavable version.

On top of that we had to develop some strategic and evasive overseas trade routes. It seemed air travel was out of the question as no pilot or crew could stand to listen to that many crying babies for such long periods of time. We could not risk any suicide-related delays of our shipments so we opted not to reinvent the wheel. Instead we took a page from history, which led of course to the creation of Saint Pierre's Missionary Fleet for God and all his Blessed Children. This was a rather brilliant initiative dreamed up by Dan and me in which we dressed the slave ships up as members of a missionary cruise company, "sailing the globe to bring the word of the lord to the many 'Neo-Barbarians.'" The crew dressed as kindly priests and nuns and born-agains so if they were ever questioned the story would stick. And if one of the ships were to ever be boarded by suspicious Coast Guard officials it would be explained that the lower quarters acted as a sort of marine orphanage for abandoned children the Missionaries happened to find along the way. As the crew was primarily made up of Dan's own slaves, we dressed the younger ones up as altar boys, which we felt was the perfect touch. I'll point out that there were never any reported acts of sodomy on the voyages but that we did ask the crew to keep the whole charade as true to life as possible.

I should also note at this point that I had come to find out that all the employees of the Bogota were at one time slave babies and even though they were now full-fledged adults they had not attempted to escape their indentured plight. The entire staff had their own separate quarters in the basement of the hotel and they were perfectly content to stay there especially since they were terribly afraid of the swarm of horrific creatures they encountered in Las Vegas and thus preferred their secret chamber to the many menaces of freedom. And who could blame them? I would have been afraid of all the creatures in Vegas myself, if I wasn't their self-appointed grand leader. Dan referred to the building's bowels as "the Plantation" and called all the men his "Cracker-Jacks" and all of the women his "Cracker-Janes."

Anyhow, the missionary cover was working great and we had already dispatched two successful fleets across the globe before the shortage of product became very apparent. And this shortage was certainly the reason for Dan's call this morning as I had no other appointments scheduled until the afternoon and my travels were completed for at least the time being.

Not that my location ever prevented Dan from calling me. I firmly believe he enjoyed waking me up extremely early more than he loved PCP as he managed to do so no matter what continent I was on. For all my past hangovers, none of them compared to the pain, sickness, and irreparable psychological damage caused by waking up to Dan Bristol's voice every day.

"Hello," I said, coughing loudly into the phone in hopes that the bastard would end up deaf. I quickly changed my mind though, realizing that if Bristol went deaf it would just make him speak louder.

"Cypher!" Bristol screamed, "Do you know what time it is?"

"Looks like 4:55 am on my clock, yours must be broken. That would explain…"

"Shut up, Cypher, as per usual, yer wrong!" Dan continued to scream, "First off, that was not the answer I was looking for and had it been, you would have been wrong anyways, as it is 4:56 am!"

"Well, it was four…"

"I wasn't finished, besides, we don't need any more of yer wrong answers; they are hindering progress. We need right answers! You know, the kind of answers other people besides you come up with!" his voice got louder, "And that is a perfect segue back to the original question. The 'time,' Mr. Cypher, is now. And it is now time for you to get yer lazy ass in gear and find a solution to our supply chain issues. In fact, you should have started three minutes ago! Why are you always late?!"

I hung up the phone as I was sure I would kill him if I had to listen to him ramble for another second. I had already begun to boil a solution for our inventory stocking issue and that was the 1 pm lunch appointment I had scheduled. Bristol never trusted the fact that I had things under control but there are just some parts of people's personalities you can't change. Like with Bristol, a large part of him was a giant asshole and not even a plastic surgeon with a spool of steel string and a needle of gold could change that about him. I resolved to accept his shortcomings with cordial open arms while secretly waiting around for him to die.

And then there was Bobby. She had become resentful of my traveling and exhausted with the business. She wanted to settle down and get away from the madness but most of all she was ready to get away from me. Not that she would ever say it but her eyes didn't look at me the same and though they did their best not to sweat under the lights, I could tell they were lying to me.

She didn't bother to roll over and say good morning to me as I swung my feet from the bed to the floor. Hotel carpet never feels good beneath my toes. It is full of lies and transgressions and stories you don't want to hear. That's why they have to vacuum it every day, suck away its memories so it smiles sheepishly at its new guests, freshly lobotomized. They have to vacuum it every day, but even though the dirt is gone, a hotel carpet is never clean. And let me tell you something about the Bogota Hotel and Casino, as an added amenity, every room is serviced twice daily. Who needs a priest when the maid is the person that truly forgives your sins?

    I readied myself for the day despite the hour but I guess it's always "that time of day" in Las Vegas. You can invent your own definitions for the moments you spend with your eyes open as night and day are only relevant in the real world. And if ever there was a living world of fiction it would be that neon Nevada oasis; every motivation a dream, every story a half truth, every guarantee with a guaranteed catch, every glow joyously tainted, and every humble person with an equally humble price. It's a gangster's fantasy at all angles.

CHAPTER 31

Bigger Picture Partners

I left the room without saying goodbye to Bobby and spent the morning drinking coffee and sketching out a solution for the problem so that by the time my afternoon meeting rolled around I had a full-on plan to present to my potential investors. As I greeted them in the conference room they each requested a glass of wine and I had two of the house's finest reds brought in. The men thanked me graciously and asked that we delay any talk of business until after their first glass was finished. This was how my first meeting with Jean-Paul Flehflahflu and Fritz Danish began. Jean-Paul, as many know, was France's most prominent and well respected pimp and Fritz was the well-to-do super for most of the apartments in Amsterdam's red light district. I needed foreign allies that could produce an abundance of unwanted, illegitimate, white children and these two high-class hustlers were the best I could think of, at least to start.

Jean-Paul looked like the pudgy clown prince of Mardi Gras in his velvet green suit and frilly shirt. He walked as if he had his ass replaced with a horse's; his Riviera barnyard scent confirmed my suspicions. Fritz wore dark sunglasses and an open leather jacket with a flesh colored t-shirt that I would have mistaken for his bare chest had it not had the words, "**FLESH COLORED**," written in bold black letters across it. He had gold teeth that looked as if they had been hammered into his crooked jaw. This caused him to spit whenever he spoke, charitably donating his 14-karat saliva to anyone he conversed with.

We chatted casually about all manners of worldly subjects as they sipped their wine and I a spiteful glass of mineral water. We discussed world politics and the cultural differences in our societies, as well as the current state of prostitutional economics, which is in fact a very rousing subject as you may well have gathered.

As the polite chit-chat dwindled I decided to cut right to the chase. "So my friends, you understand what it is we do here, correct?"

"Certainly," giggled Jean-Paul, "I am zhe proud ownare of a few of your fine pro-ducts." Fritz nodded as well but didn't say anything. He was a man of few words, and those he spoke I could hardly understand with that damn Dutch accent anyways.

"Fine, fine," I said. "We appreciate your business of course and stand by our product and such. But let me cut right to the chase here, boys. You know that we are a respectable underground corporation doing the world a grand service by recycling unwanted human life, giving it a purposeful existence, while at the same time curing the laziness of another more important person," I paused and looked in all four of their eyes simultaneously to make sure our value proposition had resonated clearly in their minds.

"Ex-zactlee," Jean-Paul smiled. Fritz continued to nod with silent indifference.

"Well then," I continued, "as you know, every corporation has to grow at some point, add new, larger investors and increase the supply chain by opening up 'factories,' per se, on foreign soil."

"Cut zhe bullshiit," Jean-Paul grinned and giggled, he was the only hyena native to France, "wha do you want wit us?"

"I need more white babies."

"Huh?" Fritz interjected. He didn't speak much but when he did it was certainly insightful.

"I need more white babies, gentlemen. We've got every possible avenue tapped here already and we can't produce the little fuckers fast enough. I need your help and partnership to continue to supply the world with 'the ultimate solution.'" The words filled the room with a gas as pleasing as nitrous oxide and as souring as methane all at once. The hot air I had learned to spew almost made me feel like I was ready to go legit and work on Wall Street. Every sentence was a lead-in to a marketing ploy, every intention a closure, and every smile made of the finest imitation fiberglass.

The two said nothing at first but at least they didn't say, "No." It seemed the reality that had just presented itself before them was a bit too overwhelming for an immediate reply. And I could fully understand their shock; one day you're a high-rolling prince-of-the-street-snatch, the next you have the opportunity to be a major part of the world's fastest growing corporation. Of course that corporation isn't exactly sanctioned by the official world trade commission and the price for getting caught, well, not sure such a thing has ever been brought before a modern grand jury but if I had to guess I'd assume crucifixion as the most likely and deliberately cruel punishment.

Jean-Paul tapped his fingers rapidly against the table as he devised his reply. Fritz's eyes seemed to spin around in his head like a malfunctioning slot machine; it seemed that thinking about difficult matters, and probably thinking in general, were hard things for him to do. But nonetheless he was the first to reply.

"Bitz vot eeez inite fur oos, in-divay oof carantsee?" Fritz asked.

"Well, my friend, I'm glad you decided to join the conversation," I replied, "Of course, with no offense intended, if you could refrain from speaking again it will make this whole meeting a bit less confusing." He looked at me, seemingly angry at first, but then nodded in agreement and leaned back in his chair with his arms folded. There are few people in the world that can recognize their limitation in value and shut the fuck up once in a while. Fritz was one of these rare souls and therefore I liked him most of all.

"Anyhow, continuing on, you are set to make big money on this. We're talking at least ten times what you guys are making now, and think about it logically. This partnership would certainly resolve what I see to be a pimp's biggest general issue..."

"And hwatt myght that be Monsieur Cypher? You seem oofly shere of your assumshawns," Jean-Paul croaked in an attempt to boast of the complicated life of a whore's chauffeur. Now I'm not claiming pimpin' is easy but the inherent challenges are very clearly defined.

"Well, to give you the long answer with a short point, had you been from one of many states here in the US, excluding this one of course, or many other more civilized nations than the ones you both are from, I would certainly sympathize that 'the law' is the most common obstacle. Bearing in mind that said such demon is equally as menacing to an operation such as ours and perhaps with far deeper consequences," the two nodded incessantly as I began to deliver my impromptu dissertation on the frustrations of pussy peddling, "But luck has dealt us both a card on many levels with reference to our occupations. I am no pimp nor have I ever claimed to be. But I am a pimp sympathizer and that is one of the many notions that led me to my business. I get to work first-hand with all of the high-end hustlers to help resolve challenges that in turn lead to our mutual success. I need them in business to keep producing unwanted illegitimate children and likewise they need me to turn these 'accidents' into a profit center. I will note that a lot more of these 'accidents' started happening when my partners saw how much cash they could pull in. The purchase price of a single baby far exceeds the average revenue a whore brings in for any three-month period, even around the holiday season."

"Pardon me monsieur," Jean-Paul interjected, "wot is dees 'tre months' you are referring to?"

"Well, Jean-Paul, we figure that the third trimester is the proper amount of time to allow the 'expecting mother' to get some rest prior to giving birth."

"Abzurd!" Jean-Paul shouted, "Zhat is complete cruelty and inhumane at best!"

"Okay," I began, a little agitated, "well, if you think they need a longer rest period than…"

"Longer?" Jean-Paul gasped loudly, "I am zhinking shorter. Maybe one month give or take."

"But you just said three months was cruel and inhumane?" I responded.

"Yes, to us and our wallets," he nudged Fritz and the two giggled. I didn't do it in front of them but I made a mental note to let out a sigh of relief as soon as I had the chance. These Europeans had begun to make me sweat with their arrogant questioning and accented English; I was beginning to wonder whether or not the alliance was going to happen until Jean-Paul showed his cards.

And he had shown them; whether he meant to or not, his motivations were out in the open. There was no need to deliver a human interest message to these guys, they were coin operated like a street corner Laundromat, eager to give you their time and attention, as long as you kept pumping quarters in – regardless of race or creed. But I found this to be true of most of my clients so it didn't really surprise me that personal gain was their primary and in fact only interest. What did throw me off was their utter disregard for the rights of their employees. Certainly I had a strange moral stance on existence but these guys didn't even want to let a pregnant woman stop turning tricks for more than thirty days. Sick as it seems, I suppose everyone has their principles and all you can ask for these days is someone that will stick to them.

"So money is the first question that pops up..." I scratched my chin for an air of drama and pretended that I didn't hope the question was coming. As if I was standing on the mound in the midst of the World Series, I wiped the sweat from my brow and took a breath, knowing it was time to play hardball.

"Well, I have already guaranteed you an increase in your overall revenue, isn't that enough?" I knew it wasn't enough but I figured I'd ask just in case. The two laughed in perfect synch without even looking at each other. I wiped a little more sweat from my brow realizing that women's fast-pitch softball was probably more my game.

"All right, I figured that would be your answer so why don't we make this easy," I smiled, "name your price." Women's fast-pitch is actually a pretty difficult game, so I decided co-ed youth Tee-ball would be the best way to go with these two. The fact was they were the only solution I could think of to our problems, at least in the short timeframe I was allotted by both the forces of nature and Dan Bristol, and they had all but signed on the dotted line. Plus, they were now privy to more information than we generally like to give our clients and that of course meant they were not leaving here without signing up in the first place. I didn't want to have to kill them...well, I didn't want to have to kill Fritz, so I figured I would just rollover and get it done. Which I'll add is a very easy thing to do when you are negotiating without boundaries, and with someone else's money.

To my surprise they came back with a very modest number; it seemed they were not as greedy as they were cruel. I pretended to squirm for a few minutes but then made a phone call up to Bristol who agreed to the deal without hesitation. I could hear relief in that insanely loud and purposely obnoxious voice of his, and for that matter, I'm sure my new companions and perhaps the rest of the Bogota Casino could as well.

Bristol then put me on hold and phoned down to Bobby to have the contracts drawn up. To his dismay she informed him that it would take longer than a few hours to put such a detailed proposition down on paper. Three days would be necessary for it to be done properly. When Dan returned to the line to tell me all of this, I in turn passed the info on to my two soon-to-be partners, who asked if we could do the follow-up meeting in Amsterdam. This was instantaneously agreed upon by everyone and thus the resolution to our problem was very near at last.

Upon coming to this agreement the two stood up hastily, shook my hand, and departed without so much as another word. The customs of Europeans have always baffled me. I mean seriously think about it. They stand too close to people when they're talking, the men wear fuckin' Speedos, the chicks don't shave their pits, they don't tip, and they don't speak a gracious or even semi-kind word to a new major business partner at the close of a deal. And the more I thought about it, the more something didn't feel right. It was my stomach and thus I quickly ran to the restroom.

CHAPTER 32

The King on the Throne

I once heard someone say that a man's most honest moments in life are the ones he spends on the toilet. And though that sounds like crude, two-dollar-beer-night logic, it does have an odd truth to it. And I'm not talking about taking a seat amongst your humble peers in some stadium-style public lavatory; I'm talking about one's own private throne room. A place of reflection and humility, pretty much a church, without all the bullshit, just actual shit.

In any case, as I took my relief I did take the time to reflect on the situation and it began to dawn on me that perhaps I was being set up. These foreign characters, these prestigious merchants of VD, had been rather easy to deal with as if they were fully prepared for the conversation already, as if they knew where it was going to go, or more, where they wanted it to go. And when I handed those greedy bastards that wouldn't even allow pregnant whores to go on disability-leave a blank check, they came back with a modest seven figure number; a number far lower than the salary of a decent pro athlete, probably even lower than a decent Canadian pro athlete. Something stank.

After giving myself a courtesy flush I resolved that it wasn't me, or at least just me, the whole deal smelt like shit. I would have to proceed with caution and continue to not trust anyone; at least not much had changed. I had been doing too well and growing this thing too fast, and I'm pretty sure Bristol felt like he didn't need me anymore.

It made sense, just like in any large corporation; once you become big enough you can get rid of the high-paid people who got you there. That's the golden rule of business: *everyone's expendable.* The only problem was I knew a lay-off didn't come with severance and there was certainly no 401(k) plan as retirement was futile. The sad truth was that despite my nose for treason, I really didn't care.

You live fast, you die young, that's just the way it goes; no one can save you, when nobody knows. Is it just that *the rejected, the forgotten,* the unappreciated living, are often ironically rewarded for putting up with everyone's shit by immortality in death? It seems all you can hope for is that the folks that knew you remember your contributions to the world and turn you into a legend, or a myth, or perhaps a myth amongst legends. If not, than the world is probably better off without you anyways.

All that being said, I was not going down without a fight and there was still an outside shot that these morbid conclusions I was jumping to were just the products of longstanding sobriety, the source of all true paranoia. There was certainly a chance of that but one thing I learned from all my time in the Bogota was that I like gambling a lot more when I know I'm going to win…or when I'm drunk.

Point being, games of chance were no longer my style; I

had a newfound affinity for the cool confidence of *the fix*. In any case, I had to stay alert and on my toes for the next few days and if I made it that long, I would have to be even more alert and possibly grow a second set of feet. But for the time being, it would probably be best to cut off my feet and even my legs, in order to keep the lowest of profiles.

This of course meant I needed an alternative plan of departure in case something seemed suspicious at the Las Vegas airport, which is where I assumed they would try and take me out. If the slightest thing was off, if the wind changed directions suddenly, if too many people were wearing sunglasses, I was going to head for the hills and not look back.

The lingering issue was that I still wasn't sure if anything was up or if I was just flipping out needlessly, and flying on assumption alone is like falling from a plane without a parachute. If perchance I was just turning into a paranoid lunatic and creating a false reality I wanted to make sure I made the trip to Amsterdam as planned and avoided jeopardizing my relationship with Bristol or, more importantly, my professional reputation. But alas, the two were really just one and the same because if I pissed off Bristol needlessly, I'd likely end up without *a reputation* altogether as I decomposed at the bottom of some Laughlin sinkhole, perpendicular to the sewer line. Knowing Dan, if he had the slightest inclination of my distrust he would likely flip his rapidly rotting lid, accuse me of breeding venomous snake monkeys or some other figment of his hallucination, and try to toss me out of his bulletproof glass window. Though I would not plummet to my death having been saved by the glass, Bristol's repetitive attempts to break through it with my head would be a far more painful and unsightly way to go. It was a delicate matter to say the least.

For some reason my dreams of Northern California floated back into my mind as I pondered all the possibilities of both peril and prestige that the coming days presented. And suddenly the purpose of this recurring image became very clear to me. It was not where I was going to retire to, not just yet at least, it was where I would seek my safe passage to Amsterdam or wherever else the circumstances lead me too. After all, California is the land of a thousand airports, big and small, and the one I knew of in Monterey would be just right for this excursion. I would book myself two tickets, one to Amsterdam and one to Tasmania, Australia, and thus be prepared to flee if necessary or continue the course with the most minute of detours.

It felt relieving to have some sort of plan in mind, now it was just a question of survival. I hoped it was all in my head. I truly did want to believe that after all this time Dan and his associates were my friends and colleagues and not just typical cutthroat businessmen, the worst breed of criminal. It was sink or swim time for sure, either rise from these self-imposed depths and reach the top or be pulled down by the current and forever lost at sea, another victim of aquatic narcolepsy. Whatever the case, I was relieved. *FLUSH.*

CHAPTER 33

Plan for the Worst, Hope for Anything Else

So as To best prepare for this latest suicide mission I spent the next few days in a haze of mental downward spirals and self-loathing. I figure if you hate yourself enough and can clearly articulate to your conscience the reasons why your life sucks, it is much easier to embrace the possibility of death, and to be more specific, self-perpetuated, reckless, premature death as was the suspected flavor in my case. But clarification aside, it can be quite therapeutic to disown yourself for a while unless of course you are expected to be just the opposite – fully in control and confident. This complicates matters because you essentially have to lie to yourself twice in the same second, yet remain wholly dedicated to the proper external mood appearance, while still remaining true to yourself inside your own mind. If you are not careful in this ballet of internal distrust you can end up fucking up all of your plans and simultaneously forgetting your motives… as I have just done. In any case I had to tread carefully and be prepared for anything, especially the inevitable.

Bristol on the other hand was all smiles, as cheerful as

ever, getting fatter and crazier each day from the forbidden fruits of my labor. For a second I considered the dependence he might have on me as I was like a pair of sterile latex gloves for him; I kept his hands clean no matter how thick the shit got. I pondered this notion rather deeply every time I saw Bristol prior to the day of my flight and though it was a joyous fantasy, I came to the conclusion that a man with an addiction such as Dan's does not do things out of logic or reason, but more through pensive spells of temporary insanity. Thus, the only thing to do was bury any remaining sense of optimism in a lonely hole in the Nevada desert, next to the rest of the rats and liars, and continue forward without thinking any further on the subject.

Bobby was in a self-manifested cave somewhere preparing the necessary documentation. It seemed a bit extensive for an illegal syndicate but Bristol figured if our record-keeping was solid than we would always have the opportunity to convince a court that our corporation was run in accordance with the *Nevada Code of Business Ethics and Standards*, and furthermore that we were prepared to pay all back taxes on the spot. In any other state it was more of a punch line than a plan, but in this test site for genocide, it could prove to be a valid defense. This notion was the reason Bobby was so integral to the organization, she kept all the books in order and made sure records were stored and destroyed as necessary. She was the only one who was disciplined enough for such a job amongst our crew and the only person Dan trusted to keep things organized; therefore, she was the only one who had a key to the Bogota's *special-information-vault*.

The day finally came for my flight to Europe and Bobby decided to accompany me to the airport. I thought it was a sweet gesture, her wanting to see me off, but then I recalled how this whole mess began. My genitals cringed at the partially repressed memories of my first encounter with this beautiful chaperone and for a fleeting moment, it all but confirmed my suspicions that Bristol was disposing of me. Who better to do such a deed than the only person more bitter and hateful and wonderful than the beast called "Cypher?" If I were to at least catch a tear in her eye before the scene went dark I'd forgive her venomous nature knowing she might mourn me secretly, the blackest of widows.

The dark clouds of woe were certainly threatening, but in my heart I knew there had to be some bit of humanity I had gained from my time with Bobby, no matter how sadistic our relationship. And with that in mind, I resolved that it was time to at least trust someone and for once, follow the convincing beats of my heart. In the same instant I realized that my heartbeat mimicked the bass line to Marvin Gaye's, "Let's Get it On," or maybe it was all in my head. Either way I figured that with at least two of my three *truly vital organs* pulling for trust, I might as well give the vote to the majority. My crotch shook its head subtly with disapproval but alas, it was a true anatomical democracy, and he was outnumbered. This of course meant that Bobby was now going to have to trust me if I peeled out of the airport like a maniac instead of exiting the vehicle at the terminal. The verdict on that case was left solely to my gut, as he is a drunken dictator that creates his own realities and vanquishes all who oppose him. Not a truly vital organ like my brain, heart, and genitals, but certainly useful in times of quick decision making.

So to the airport we went. I had already mentally prepared myself for the potential of unadulterated retreat. If one person looked at me wrong, one car seemed out of place, or if one goddamn dog barked a little too goddamn loud my "flee impulse" would be ready to assume control of my mind. Bobby being stuck in the car with me was a mere afterthought that I would have to think about...well, after, should I need to abort the mission. I could not afford anyone else controlling this backwards bent, twisted knot in my fate. Without really asking, I offered to drive and though I could see the protest in her eyes, she agreed and sat down in the passenger seat.

So often in life we come to that obligatory crossroad, the mandatory intersection of all things ambiguous and life altering. Be it the lyrics from your favorite blues song or a mental collision that happens every time you make a choice, we've all been to "the crossroads." Or maybe we haven't. Maybe the metaphorical crossroad is only a conceivable abomination for those of us who constantly make bad decisions. All my life I've been trying to find a place to call home and it finally dawned on me. My address, home sweet home, the place I hang my head because I don't wear hats, is "the *Crossroads.*" It's the place where the sun stops shining just long enough for the devil to get his due. It is truly the lost settlement of indecision, a place devoid of reason, like a giant scale that never lies or tells the truth. And yet, I find solace in this purgatory for consequence, because despite its infinite indifference, the next step is always clearly defined: *heaven or hell.*

CHAPTER 34

Why I Hate Public Transportation

There is no place on earth more savagely confusing than an airport. Boastful, iron death traps spew fuel and smoke in every direction while hordes of confused lemmings chatter in yet-to-be discovered dialects, each more inaudible and confusing than the next. And to further complicate things, airports employ the only two animals more devoid of intellect than fucking lemmings. These lowly creatures are hired to "keep the peace," or more eloquently put, "to shepherd all the dumb, little rodents to their *flying doom-cans*." You guessed it, these are, "cops" and their inbred nephews, "rent-a-cops." Of course, these *mascots of law* are a necessary evil, due to the fact that most of the airline ticketing personnel are so dreadfully rude and incompetent that the peacefully confused lemmings are often driven to potential violence and momentary fits of deserving rage. Yet, one can't help but empathize with the airport personnel, because after all, lemmings are the stupidest fucking animal on the planet, next to cops and rent-a-cops, and the ticketing agents are surrounded by all of these species of ultimate ignorance from the moment they start their day. Thus, the overall mood of airports can best be categorized as, "indefinitely pissed off," a state of being generally only attributed to rabid animals and people from Boston.

And on this particular day the airport was a place of familiar strangers and rabid paranoia. The blistering desert sky-fire burned through clouds, heating the pavement to a thousand degrees above normal. I was in the midst of a temperate abnormality, standing in the doorway of a desperate funhouse, run by diabolical carnies and rejected circus midgets. I had no friends here, just a series of one-liner-punch-lines fluttering in the air; they had no beginning and no build-up, just fleeting humor I couldn't catch. *Knock, knock…the joke's on you.*

A cop with a cruel-eyed German shepherd trotted slowly past our car as we stopped at a crosswalk. The stare in the dog's eyes, complemented only by the grin on the cop's lips, suggested the beast had been recently sodomized by its master and was inevitably looking for something to kill. A group of businessmen in black suits, all matching by accident, scurried by in dark sunglasses and glanced blankly towards our car. Old women, all disguised as wax figurines of my dead grandmother, waited for taxis in the wrong location as we neared the terminal. Traffic lights flashed in backwards patterns sometimes turning blue, sometimes forgetting to turn. The dog barked in the distance as a group of people whirled by in a wind of foreign dialects, none of which I could recognize but all of which seemed suspicious. One of the sun's rays tried to reach for the pavement but was repelled by the black lenses of a random pair of sunglasses, which rested snugly on the nose of a not-so-random face. But there were so many of those these days…those faces. But this one I believed I knew from the casino and I believed it enough to begin to fear the possibilities, just like a religious fanatic...*fuckin' heat.*

We reached the terminal and I could feel eyes on me, poking into my every pore. It was like street corner acupuncture treatment, which is mainly just waking up in an alleyway on top of a bunch of used hypodermic needles. The question was who was watching me? The familiar face with the sunglasses, the dead grandmothers, the matching businessmen, the foreign cyclone, the carnies and circus midgets, or maybe it was that goddamn dog. Perhaps they were all conspiring at the same time and for different reasons. Reasons that weren't even connected to the slave-trade business; it dawned on me that perhaps here in the airport some vortex had opened up and pitted me against every sin I had ever committed. Of course, then I realized how big the airport was and figured that it could only house my major sins at most.

In any case, it was a head full of those types of thoughts that forced my foot to reestablish its position on the gas pedal and rocket off the curb just before Bobby could exit the car in an attempt to switch seats with me. No Vegas vermin dodging for me today, no cops, no unconfirmed conspiracies and potentially imagined setups, and especially no fucking rent-a-cops. It was life in the fast lane for sure. Or at least life in the fastest lane at the Las Vegas airport, which is more like life in a slow cruise, behind the lucky and the doomed in their tainted hotel caravans, taxis, and rent-a-car shuttle buses that subtly advertise all of the best Nevada lies.

Bobby, keeping with her ever-puzzling approach to almost every situation, remained silent and still until we were well out of sight of the Strip, and on the highway headed towards California. The adrenaline I had spawned by the *escape event* had subsided and I was ready to relax. Apparently Bobby's silence was her way of giving her approval. I knew that she would never turn on me. Her love had been the guiding light in this late phase of my life, especially when I needed it most, and this gesture of sanctuary confirmed it. And yet she did not confess her love for me as we continued down the highway, against the winds of emancipation and other Death Valley mirages. I gathered that perhaps Bristol had made her wear a wire and she didn't want to say anything that would give us away, and that she didn't want to tamper with it because it was probably rigged to set off an alarm or bomb or who knows. There was certainly a bit of lingering uncertainty, but at least all of my suspicions were confirmed: Bristol wanted me dead, Bobby was my true love, and most important of all – no one can ever trust the fucking French.

CHAPTER 35

Double-Cross Squared

One thing I've learned from living a life Hollywood makes bad suspense movies about is that always being on "the edge of your seat" can really make your ass sore. We had been on the road for nearly five hours, and it had been a very tense edge-of-your-teeth, skin-of-your-seat type ride. Every high-pitched noise was the howl of some crooked cop's squad car and the hairs on the back of my neck were constantly trimmed by the blades of a fast-approaching helicopter; the same exact one that was never there when I looked back.

Knowing that it was only a matter of time before we reached Monterey, where I would board my flight to Tasmania and then vanish from this sideways-sucked society with my true love on my arm, I allowed myself to relax to the whimsical music of daydreams, until I heard the familiar click of God's own steel in my right ear. The glare of the barrel caught my eye like a shiny meteor headed straight for earth. Just think, in a blink, it could all be gone.

The thing that surprised me most was that I hadn't counted

on this happening. In my heart, the stupidest part of me, I truly believed the bitch was on my side. My crotch had never grown to trust her after that first attack and it had proved to be far wiser than both my dimwitted chest pump and my mind, which is coincidentally, the same flavor. Of course, only the strong survive and knowing that she would likely put a bullet in my brain and/or my chest, it would leave my cock to be my only *truly vital organ* left intact. It felt good to realize the true essence of science versus creationism in what I thought would be my dying moment. It gave me hope that there was in fact, no life after death, because that is in fact what I believe hell is. At least for someone like me anyway. It's thinking the noise is going to stop, and that you're finally going to catch up on all the sleep you've missed while dreaming and trying to live just enough to make it all worthwhile. It's getting beyond this beautiful abyss and having closure, only to find out that it's not over, and that it never will be. Put that notion in a book…and I'll read it religiously.

"Wipe the fucking smirk off your face darling," she whispered with piercing hatred into my ear, "Put on your blinker, and then your flashers, and pull over to the side of the road."

"Or what, you'll blow my brains out?" I asked, half hoping she would.

"No," she said, and pointed the gun towards my already sweat-soaked lap. Fate had turned on me once again and thus it was once again time to say, "fuck Darwin," and start praying.

"Hey there," I smiled calmly and turned on the blinker, "Relax, I'm on your side." She didn't say a word so I obeyed, and quickly made my way to the side of the road, almost forgetting to flip on my flashers; **almost.** There are few *pure* forces in the world more commanding than the scornful silence of the one you think you love.

Me and Bobby McGee

As I put the car in park, she slithered close to me and in a single seductive motion she straddled me and placed her knees firmly on my corresponding hands. She let her breasts surround my face and then put the gun between them and against my chin, hiding its ever judgmental existence from curious motorists and rape-crazed hitchhikers. The few cars that passed by were obvious representatives of some lost West Coast mutant race of immature assholes as they whizzed by honking like sex-deprived jack-offs, thinking I was in the process of getting lucky. And in the darkest of ways, no matter how you see the piss in your cup, perhaps I was.

"Now Cypher, my love," she snarled like a rabid prostitute forced to work while pregnant, "Please start by giving me one good reason not to kill you." I thought I was fucked because I honestly couldn't think of one. My mind went blank, like in a fit of stage fright, or abusive electro-therapy, I was void of saying anything compelling or audible. Of course, then I snapped back like a good little bastard and answered with confidence.

"Well, it really depends on why exactly you want to kill me?" I replied. I've learned a lot from hating politicians; and one of the most annoying, yet effective, tactics those vultures use to buy time with when caught off-guard is to answer a question with a question, so that they don't have to think of a real answer right on the spot. I had become all the things I hated already, so I figured I might as well take it one step further with a scholarly nod to the White House.

"What sort of dumb question is that?" she hissed, each snake-bitten word laced with Venus-grade reptilian venom, "You're fucking us over and I'm taking you out!" her breaths were short as if she were ready to hyperventilate and I could tell that killing me did bother her at least slightly. Of course, adrenaline can have a similar effect on the respiratory system, whether or not you actually feel remorse. This I know, from years of experience.

"Bristol had a feeling you had turned on us and I honestly can't believe he was right!" She shouted, more like an angry mother than an assailant. But despite her varying degrees of personality, she was excellent at relaying information.

"Wait one second, Bobby! You are the one packing heat. You fuckers turned on me…" I attempted to declare, only to find myself being smacked square in the chest with the butt of the gun.

"Wait a second, Cypher! You're the one ditching the trip to Europe, only to run off with…" she was silenced by her own lack of purpose. I could see the moment of realization in her eyes. What did I have to gain from running away from the only occupation that had ever made me a decent, trusted, well-respected, upstanding citizen? I could tell she felt stupid and thus I didn't feel *the need* to point it out, though I did feel *the want*. Nevertheless I resolved that I still wasn't quite ready to die and would therefore take a raincheck on telling her she was an idiot; I'd save that comment for when I was truly "ready."

"Listen, Bobby, there seems to be a bit of confusion here…you're confused too, aren't you?" I questioned. She nodded in somber agreement.

"Okay then, let's get this cleared up right now. Is Bristol trying to set me up?"

"Bristol?! Set you up?! Are you kidding, he loves you like a son. In fact, he truly thinks you are his next of kin. I believe in his mind you have fully replaced that nephew of his you killed. You remember, right? The one with the girl's name…"

"Vaguely, but I guess that's more than his uncle can say,"

I tried to let a chuckle escape but her gaze held me hostage just as she held me at gunpoint. It was romantic and psychotic, there by the side of the road, very much a living metaphor for my entire relationship with Bobby. Nevertheless, I can only say, in a melee of dyslexic clichés, that it is better to have loved and driven each other fucking nuts than to have never even tried to play the game.

"So what's the deal, Cypher, where are you headed?"

"Anywhere except for this land of espionage and treason, just not by way of any departing Las Vegas flight; my trip begins in Monterey. You know, just in case."

"Just in case what?" she asked.

"Just in case Bristol wanted to have me rubbed out," I confided in her, she was always good for that. A man doesn't need a maid; he needs a twenty-four-seven, life sentence psychiatrist. I wondered for a moment if Bobby would be mine and then remembered she was still ready to shoot me. More car horns honked as they raced past, I wondered how long before they would turn into sirens. I could hear the faint buzz of a helicopter in the distance and waited for it to be hovering over our heads, ready to detail our car with its special brand of, "lead-based paint." But in those next seconds the sounds vanished and only the hum of the highway and Bobby's dissipating patience were left audible. It seemed I was becoming as paranoid as Dan; perhaps soon the spider monkeys would finally show their ugly fucking faces.

Mammals from beyond the imagination aside, I proceeded to further explain myself to Bobby. I could sense the relief running through her veins though her face remained stern. When I finished relaying my conspiracy theory to her she replied with a similar story but from Bristol's point of view. It seemed that we had both become so cautious that we didn't even trust each other...or ourselves. The good news was I could in fact still make it to Europe in time since we were already so close to the Monterey airport, and that meant I could still close the deal.

"Hey Bobby," I said as I turned the blinkers off and the motor back on, "Why did you let me get this far before you pulled the gun out?"

"Why do you think?" she asked with a grin.

"Well, I kind of had this idea that you were wearing a wire or something and didn't want Bristol to know where we were headed, so instead you just decided to be silent...I mean...basically...that you wanted to help me get away," I felt like a bashful twelve-year-old who was just selected to do a math problem on the blackboard in the midst of "high noon." She grabbed my arm and laid her head on it, smiling in obvious amusement.

"Well, Cypher, you are half right," she replied.

"I knew it," I said joyously, "you did want to help me escape." She kissed my neck and moved her hand with delicate precision across the inside of my thigh. With the other hand she began to unbutton her blouse and I, in plain English, was very aroused, but only for a moment.

"No," she kissed me again, "I was wearing a wire though." She opened her blouse to reveal her hot tits...I mean the little voice transmitter she was wearing.

"But don't worry. At least now you won't have to explain all of this to Bristol again."

"That's great," I said with very little enthusiasm, "but you didn't really answer my question."

"About the wire?" she asked.

"No! Why did you let me get this far out of town before you pulled out the gun?"

"Cypher, were you in the fucking CIA or not? I let you drive all the way out here because no one would come looking for your body here. I figured you'd be heading to some log cabin or whatever in Northern California. I mean, for Christ sakes, you talk about it in your sleep!" she snapped while batting her eyelashes at me. I made a mental note to cut out my own tongue before ever sleeping again but shortly after I reconsidered as the odds had actually worked out in my favor this time.

Falsely accused, would-be-traitors and conspiracy theories aside, I set the compass for the lower lip of the luscious Pacific Northwest. It was good to know we were all still on the same team. And I'll add that it was especially good to know that my once-again-beautiful Bobby was in for the trip to Monterey. It had been a day full of deceit, fear, and resolution; a short and exhausting venture to the undetermined boundaries of trust, love, and lust. The only thing left on my mind was the sophisticated pleasure of "road-head."

CHAPTER 36

Where Do We Go From Here?

Time on the road tends to move like an asthmatic fat kid in the last leg of a junior varsity cross-country race. It wheezes and moans in the distance, painfully plodding along in a state of bitter slow motion until you have almost forgotten about it altogether. Then, after several hours of avoiding even checking on it, time all of a sudden seems to sprint forward, leaving you surprised at how fast it has gone by. The only difference is you don't have to congratulate "time" on a job well done in order to preserve its self-esteem; time has no feelings unless you count indifference.

And despite my perspective on "time," I can never help but behave like that same asthmatic fat kid, just after the race, as his parents promise to reward his embarrassing efforts with a bucket of ice cream. The impatience and the eagerness that obese little bastard must feel is the same way I feel on the way to anywhere…unless I'm drunk. And as such, perhaps this anticipation is something I have rediscovered within myself having been sober for what seems like decades now.

But there is no reason to wallow in self-pity nor to loathe

self-inflicted torture; that is something that alcoholics do. That is why they have meetings for recovering drunks; so they can commiserate and complain together and then collectively mourn the loss of their identities. It is more like a wake than a meeting except that there is far less religious bullshit at wakes. In fact, a wake symbolizes the end of the bullshit, at least for the person who died. Not such a bad party in my opinion, at least for the guest of honor who doesn't even have to give a speech.

One thing about being born-again-sober is that it tends to make you wish you were dead. And one thing about wishing you were dead is that wishes rarely come true. I've gazed up at the same fucking star for years with that one simple wish and you know what I've found out, both Walt Disney and talking crickets are full of shit and always have been. When you wish upon a star you don't get what your heart desires, you get the fucking shaft.

And perhaps that is life's greatest lesson: *it makes no difference who you are*, life sucks and your dreams are better off being wiped away with the dust from your eyes every morning. They are simply a means of escape, not a wish waiting to come true. The sooner we all learn this, the less likely we are to find ourselves selling white babies into slavery, though I must say, I think long ago perhaps I did dream about doing just that…but still, good, kindly, God-fearing wishes never come true; only horrible, menacing evil, and greedy corruption can be manifested out of thin air and stargazing, just look at what Walt Disney achieved.

But I suppose it is far too late for any sort of real regret and just the notion of it makes me a bit queasy, primarily because I have done things that merit such feelings and yet have never experienced the emotion of self-doubt or remorse in its most basic sense. As I have watched bullets pierce through the past and future of people, riddling their chest and/or foreheads with crimson letters that spell "The End," no matter how you look at them, never once have I felt bad about it. I suppose the closest I've come is that fateful day that ended my official career that has continued to plague my nightmares ever since…

    But fuck growing feelings in the midst of stressful times. They only slow you down and make you lose sight of your goals. The past could find better timing if it so desired to be rehashed. For now it was all about the moment.

CHAPTER 37

The Inevitable I Told You So

Somewhere near Salinas, we pulled the car over at a gas station to fuel the tank and grab what Bobby called, "the last necessities," before finishing the long cruise to Monterey. We had been on the road for somewhere close to eight hours not counting our little gun-point discussion in the middle of the desert. The shit stains in my shorts will forever remind me of that quasi-beautiful moment. But the trials of the day were now draped in darkness and thus forgotten until the morrow.

Everyone is a different person at night, down to the very core of their being and so much so that the *nighttime* "YOU" follows a parallel timeline and thus assumes a different history and future than the *daytime* version. Strange creatures, we humans, both cursed and blessed with a constant identity crisis forcing us to forever juggle the state of our spirits. The night grants a higher degree of freedom than the day and the monster within can show itself beneath the guise of darkness; midnight's shadows are for far more than sleeping… And so we embrace this as if we are all the lost lineage of a race of semi-evolved and severely mutated werewolves waiting out the redundancy and the boredom of each day with apathetic patience, just to enjoy the simple pleasures of howling at the moon.

I must admit, as I sat in the empty parking lot of the fueling station, waiting for Bobby and staring up at the hollow California sky, I had the notion to rip my clothes to shreds and scamper off into darkness in search of decadence and a good place to begin baying at the full moon. I thought about it long and hard until I realized I had been waiting for Bobby for nearly twenty minutes. The hairs on the back of my neck tickled my spinal cord in an unpleasant but familiar way, reminding me that something wasn't right.

The pumps were located on the side of the gas station so I really couldn't see into the little store. I got out of the car slowly and made my way around the corner to the front entrance of the place only to find the door was locked and most of the lights inside were turned off. According to the door the store closed at 9:30 pm; a wall clock inside the place confirmed that it was now 9:42 pm. This only further confirmed my original suspicions that something wasn't right and the rapid tickling of the hairs on my spine once again brought the whole thing full circle.

But of course the brief magic of *symmetrical being* was interrupted when the questions really began to mount, bubbling up from the depths of my brain; the expected byproducts of too much spinal tickling. *What had happened exactly? Did she run or was she kidnapped? Was she still inside on the toilet and unaware that the place had closed down? Was she carried off to Oz by flying monkeys?* Anything was possible.

The wind began to pick up as I glanced around feverishly in every direction. I couldn't tell exactly what I was more worried about, the fact that Bobby had vanished, or the possibility of me being next. Perhaps I'm a narcissistic prick to even think that way but in the grip of desperation, everyone can find a way to justify self-righteousness, and I wasn't going to be responsible for changing that trend. But still I searched for her instead of doing what I should've done so many years ago, even before all of this began – cut my losses and move on. Unfortunately, I have a nasty habit of hanging on to bad habits, collecting new ones like baseball cards, and only trading out my doubles.

The wind seemed to be displeased with me as I searched for Bobby; it became constant and ferocious, whooping and bellowing loudly, in attempts to tear down everything around me. It seemed as though some sort of divine miracle was about to occur right in front of me until I looked in the only direction I had yet to search; up.

As my eyes became enlightened, the sounds surrounding me became even more familiar. The samurai slice of the blades through the air, the churning and moaning of tax-payer-purchased overpriced steel, and the rippled retreat of the Earth's top layer of dust. A helicopter can never land in secret; it is a boastful machine, proud of its engineered abilities, so much so that it makes sure to announce its presence long before it settles on the ground.

My mind raced back to the paranoia I had been feeling and ignoring for several hours. I began to wonder exactly when I had stopped trusting my instincts, and began to tune out my fear. I couldn't pinpoint the moment, though I tried, but nevertheless if I made it out of this mess alive, I'd resolve to stop avoiding my impulses, start avoiding other people, and perhaps dig myself a hole to live in somewhere in the middle of Siberia, where no one would come looking for me.

It is important to note that anytime one finds oneself fantasizing about life in Siberia, it is because everything has officially and clinically gone to shit.

I thought about running for a moment, but then a voice from the sky spoke graciously and outlined my options for me.

"You there!" the voice barked through a megaphone, "don't move or we will blow your fucking head off!" Knowing the noise from the chopper was too loud for them to hear any response I had, I put my arms in the sky, got down on my knees, and smiled up at them.

"You've got me, here I am!" I shouted into the wind, "I know you were just down on your knees a few minutes ago sucking the pilot's dick, so please don't get the wrong idea from my surrender..." they continued their descent to the Earth and so I continued to communicate all my inner thoughts and feelings. "Hurry up already, I've got to call your wives and mothers and tell them that the orgy is off for this evening. I am not usually into fat girls but those sluts really know how to make a man happy; you both must be so proud." I figured if I was open with my thoughts they wouldn't shoot me for hiding any secrets.

"That's right asshole, do as you're told," the megaphone voice continued as they brought the flying machine to rest. I looked in through the helicopter's windshield and saw only two men and no Bobby. Maybe my beautiful and resourceful lady sensed trouble and took off or maybe that bitch was working with this pair of morons and had slipped away to avoid having to explain herself.

As the blades came to a complete halt the two men inside readied their very visible weapons, Tec-9s with silencers on the barrels. Locked and loaded, they exited the chopper and made their way towards me. They both wore black hoods and masks as they moved swiftly in my direction. I had no idea who they were or what they wanted from me; all I knew was that I hadn't been in a situation like this since the last time I was in New Orleans and that situation had certainly not ended up in my favor...at least in the conventional sense. I did however make it out of that situation alive so I did my best to recall my exact approach. As the two came within arms' length of me I took a deep breath and prepared my explanation.

My shoulder almost snapped with the force of the punch I released right into the knee cap of the guy on the left. No protective armor can protect against the power and pain of pure hatred, especially when it is ignorant and unfounded. I felt the bones give way beneath my knuckles and tear through his tendons and ligaments as my fist pushed forward with no sense of ever slowing. And as I suspected, the bastard fell straight to the ground giving me the opportunity to look directly into his watery eyes before I snapped his neck with the force and speed of primal instinct.

His partner was paralyzed by shock but only for a moment. The instant I turned my wrath towards him I felt the agonizing pain of steel against my lips and teeth. The bastard hit me three times in the face with his gun. The world slowed down as I swished the warm blood around in my mouth as if it were Listerine. As I spat some of it out a few of my teeth followed; I hoped they weren't my front teeth and more so, I hoped Bristol had some sort of dental plan in place as the out-of-pocket cost of any medical procedure these days is far more expensive than buying black-market, white slave babies.

I tried to stand but a deafening sound brought me quickly back to my knees. I tried to figure out exactly what it was and then it hit me. Well, it had actually already hit me, I just didn't notice until I consciously acknowledged it. The son-of-a-bitch had shot me in the shoulder, just to the left of my heart. Not a kill-shot by any means but certainly enough to make even the most stubborn criminal behave like a frightened altar boy tied to a priest's bedpost. Whoever these fuckers were, they weren't trying to kill me; from a moral standpoint, I wish I could've said the same.

The fight had exhausted me and the wound made it hard to keep my eyes open. As the crimson liquid trickled out of me I began to tremble before my body forced me to lie still on the ground. My eye lids growing heavier, I took one last look up at my assailant just in time to see him remove his mask. Beneath it was the face I'd thought I had recognized from the airport several hours earlier. It wasn't a face from the casino though like I had originally assumed; it was a face from my past, and an ugly fucking face at that. But I didn't have the strength for further investigation. My eyes shut and my body gave in to its weariness; with any real luck I'd be dead before I woke up.

CHAPTER 38

Memories, Like a Bullet Through My Mind...

The lack of originality in the world often depresses me. It seems as if almost everything has been done before and all you can hope for is to put enough of a twist on the subject to fool people into believing that you have an inventive nature. The thing about that is that there are plenty of ideas and concepts that are just plain cliché, and if you can avoid those altogether you are pretty much on the right track. But there is just something about being abducted unconscious and waking up to freezing cold water in the face…it happens far too goddamn often and people need to think of better ways to rouse a hostage. How about really loud, horrible disco music in your ear or a fucking tiger that roars right next to your face? Anything but cold water; it is just not comfortable to have to sit there soggy and shivering while some asshole explains to you "why you're here." I'm sure you know what I'm talking about, who hasn't been woken up that way before? Frankly I'm tired of it and will likely write a letter if I can find someone who cares.

That being said, there's something about the classics that

makes you miss them when they're gone. As in this instance, during which I was not in fact awakened by the familiar sting of cold water; this time I was abruptly startled by the recently reminiscent burn of hot lead. And let me tell you, there is nothing worse than being roused from a pain-induced coma by the infliction of additional torment. I made a mental note to never again bitch about the sound my alarm clock makes or the insane wake-up calls I get daily from Bristol before the alarm clock ever has a chance to make a sound. Anything was better than this and the only thing that could possibly make it worse was if my captor fired off a second shot…

…Which of course he did. The pleasant armor of fear and shock had worn thin and now I was consciously in severe pain. Both my knees had been blown out but not in places that wouldn't heal. These were warning wounds, cautioning me to stay honest, while constantly reminding me it could all be a lot worse; they're what the CIA calls "compass wounds," three inches in any direction from the initial shots and the victim is severely fucked for life. This guy was trained by someone but the question as always was, "Why the fuck are you shooting at me asshole?" which I didn't mean to blurt aloud but ironically did anyway. I once read that it's important to get things off your chest when you perceive that you are in your dying moment; I figured this was as good a time as any.

He looked at me perplexed as if he didn't understand my language; it was either that, or he had randomly shit his pants. A closer look revealed that neither was likely the case but I chose to believe he had shit his pants anyways, primarily because he had put three bullets in me already and all I had to show for it was my overactive imagination. Dumbfounded look and all, his face was very familiar to me, even with the scattered drops of my blood on it. They highlighted the pale and awkward blues and browns of his eyes; familiar, hateful eyes. They were like sea stones, faded and formed by the battering of ever-changing tides, their smooth exterior hiding the wear of a thousand salty years. He grinned slyly at me through his slightly crooked jaw, filled proudly with a well-balanced mix of real and false teeth, which he gritted as he reloaded his gun. It was now my turn to shit my pants.

"You…" he began slowly and then trailed off as his eyes seemed to follow the splinters of dim light reflecting off of the weapon's barrel. He then held it beneath his nose and breathed in the lingering fumes of guilt-laden gun smoke.

"I can do that for you if you don't want a guilty conscience," I said, interrupting his most special of little moments. I gathered he was likely one of those gun-loving cowboy wannabes who signed up for the job simply so he could legally fire weapons at other human beings and then go home and jerk-off to the NRA's centerfold of the month, just before he proceeds to gang-fuck his younger siblings and any other farm animals within a fifty-foot radius. There is only one terrorist organization in the world that I can think of that is foolish enough to employ these types of individuals: the U.S. government.

"You can do what?" the prick responded without even looking at me.

"I can blow your fucking brains out for you," I smiled, "I just figure anyone stupid enough to point a loaded gun at their own face is likely contemplating suicide. I've also heard that 'guilt' is in fact the number one reason people have for choosing not to go through with it. Therefore, I figure if I'm the one who shoots you in the face, you won't change your mind."

"Still a smart-ass," he snickered, "actually I'm just admiring the weapon that has so graciously assisted in the capture of the illustrious Keesey Cypher...or do you prefer 'Saint Cypher' these days?"

"Who the fuck are you?" I asked as politely as possible.

"You don't recognize me?"

"I think I do. It's just that I've been having so much promiscuous anal sex these days that every asshole I meet is starting to look alike," I smiled proudly with a sense of self-satisfaction that he tried to disrupt with another coarse gaze. He held onto it for a second and then began to chuckle to himself.

"I must admit," he snickered, "that was a good one. You always could lighten up any moment with that vivaciously viscous tongue of yours. It would be a crying shame if I had to cut it out of your mouth," he said wiping a tear from his eye.

"I would have to agree with you there," I gulped.

"I'm sure you would," he answered.

"It's not a question, I do agree."

"Yes, I understand that, but..." he began before I cut him off.

"There is no 'but' in this situation, I agree with you."

"Yes, but, what I meant was..."

"I don't care what you meant. That's not the point."

"Well then what is your point, Cypher?!" he shouted confused and mildly enraged.

"The point is that I agree with you, dumbass, isn't that enough for you?" I figured I could get into his head a bit by using special tactics that I had learned on the elementary school playground. People underestimate the power of pure, adolescent annoyance but I have found it to be a very effective tool. Don't believe me? The next time you are around a little kid and they start playing that game, you know, the one where they keep asking you, "Why?" after everything you say. Acknowledge it beyond your trained subconscious and then see how hard you have to work mentally to avoid punting that little brat fifty yards down the street. Children are simplistic in their manner but their methodology consists of evil wisdom; they are relentless and have all day to break you. Their strategies of interrogation are developed far beyond that of any federal intelligence organization and I think we can all agree on that. Furthermore, little kids carry pinkeye, and I hate fucking pinkeye mainly because it essentially means you have shit in your eye, and despite the *conventional* horrors these eyes have seen, pinkeye is still the worst chaos they've ever absorbed. Thinking about it makes me feel even more comfortable with my life's decisions especially in reference to my occupation; this is the *Zen of White Baby Smuggling*, detachment and constant reassurance are the first steps towards enlightenment.

"Cypher," my captor began in a hushed voice just loud enough for me to hear, "I would agree with you if you didn't have all that shit on your face."

"What shit on my fa..." my response was interrupted by the rudeness of hard knuckles crashing directly into my nose. Pain and blood eagerly erupted from the point of impact and raced across and through my face, hot and rapid, like newly blooming lava during volcano spring, the most feared of all island seasons. The horror of the instance was countered only by the immediate resurgence of my memory and a strange sense of long-forgotten camaraderie.

"Dingoe!" I shouted as a truly familiar face slithered into view from behind the scars, faded eyes, and those false fucking teeth that the bastard now wore proudly, like cub-scout merit badges.

CHAPTER 39

A Real Bad Guy

The cruelty of Jones Dingoe is most closely compared to the fresh scent of mustard gas just before one's eyes explode. It has no sense of stopping its destructive path, tearing its victims apart from inside-out and outside-in all at the same time. It's a menacing cloud of peril, the acid rain on your doomsday parade; it knows no shame and one can be certain that it continues to kill the body long after the soul is dead.

He was young and pretty the last time I saw him; now he wore his work on his face and all the women he dated turned out to be rape victims. But fancy introductions aside, the guy was a real asshole, since the first day I'd met him. In fact, I think he may have been born out of his own father's asshole amidst the debris of yesterday's meatloaf, wrapped in a placenta of methane gas; some of sort of scientific fecal anomaly meant to have been flushed instead of nurtured. How lucky was I to be his mark? Not lucky at all...in case you were wondering.

His presence alone was alarming for certain, but what

bothered me more was the fact that he was after me in the first place, primarily because I didn't fully know why. That's probably the biggest residual problem one can have after working for a deep-cover government spook operation; once they're done with you, which they never are, they may come looking for you again, and you'll never know the reason until they tell you, and most of the time, when they tell you, you'll wish you hadn't asked. That's why I promised myself a long time ago if the past ever came back to haunt me, I'd just shut my mouth and act like I'd seen a ghost. The problem with asking questions is it usually means you're guilty of something and you are trying to find out if that is what you are in fact in trouble for. Therefore, if you simply act scared and shocked, silently trying to rationalize your situation, it is less likely that you will reveal anything you didn't intend to. It's a lot like poker; the cards don't really matter, it's how you hold them.

"What the fuck is this, Dingoe? Why the fuck am I being targeted and who the fuck gave you permission to shoot me so many goddamn times? I'm going to fucking bleed to death!" I've never been good at following my own advice and frankly, I never thought I would have to worry about it anyways. The reality is that everything is easy to contemplate and hypothetically resolve when you're not being tortured and beaten, but in the thick of despair you've got to go with your instincts. Plus, he had called me, "Saint Cypher," which meant I was definitely in deep shit.

"This ain't my show, Cypher. I just wanted the chance to shoot you," he said with a grin.

CHAPTER 40

Send in the Superiors

Ambiguity can easily be more frightening than definition depending on the situation. For example, if you commit a criminal act such as murder in the US, there is a good chance that with enough money, a top-producing lawyer with limited morals, and enough press coverage, you will not get the death penalty or even serve life in jail. The worst possible penalty is clearly defined but rarely applied and thus, an accused defendant doesn't sweat as much as he should. Now let's take that same offender to another country, how about Syria or Singapore for argument's sake, where punishments range from limb removal to crucifixion, and often don't fit the crime, at least in the conventional American sense. With those types of potentially horrible possibilities you can almost guarantee that someone gets paid to clean up the urine stains from the defendant's chair after every trial. The fact is, what we don't know or don't understand has always frightened us as people; we seek out definition like backwoods bounty hunters with a one-syllable nickname and the brain-cell count to match.

"Who the hell is running this carnival of ambiguity and relative pain?" I thought to myself for a change. There I was, doing what little I could to avoid bleeding to death while my former ally turned scar-ridden-date-rapist chuckled to himself while stroking his weapon in some sort of demented ritual known only by Charlton Heston's closest inner circle, and other people who like the feeling of a cold gun barrel up their ass. It sickened me to think of what Dingoe did in the privacy of his own home.

This of course raised a red flag for my inner hypochondriac; if Dingoe stuck that thing up his ass as often as I thought he did then the gun was certainly a carrier of pinkeye, just like the smelly kid in any given kindergarten class. Furthermore, it was highly likely that there were fecal particles inside the barrel of the gun from which the bullets that were now lodged inside of my skin had been fired. Therefore, if a kid with a little shit on his fingers could cause a pinkeye epidemic, what could shit-covered bullets do to a man already infected with paranoia? I decided it was best to ask Dingoe outright, before my wounds turned any pinker.

"Do you clean the shit out of your gun before each use?" I inquired.

"What?" he replied as if he didn't know what I was referring to.

"Do you clean the shit out of your gun?" I hate having to repeat myself, especially when I know the other person heard me the first time. He stared at me blankly so I clarified my question.

"You know, after you're done tickling your prostate with it?" his semi-playful countenance turned to pure anger in seconds and he pushed the gun against my face, just under my left eye. Now, I'm not proud to admit it, but in that instant I began to scream like a little girl.

"Ewwwww! Get that thing away from my eye you sick son-of-a-bitch!" He laughed like a bully on the playground as he beats the weakest kid in the schoolyard to tears. In all honesty I probably would have joined in and giggled a bit at my own expense if my eye wasn't already beginning to itch.

"That's enough for now, Dingoe," a sinister yet familiar type of voice interjected. And if the sinister aspect of it wasn't frightening enough, the voice also had the wear of many years wrinkled all over it. This increased my fear level significantly since there is nothing more horrible, evil, and desensitized than a government agent with seniority. It's true; senior officers for government-sponsored-murders-R-us firms got to that position by agreeing with and/or overlooking everything that happened around them for the last X-amount of years. Promotions in "the business" are not really based around performance; it is more of an endurance and tolerance (or lack of tolerance for people that disagree with your political agenda) test that one must pass in order to become a commanding officer. Judging by the crotchety yet poised voice that had just called off the undomesticated Dingoe, pinkeye was likely the least of my worries.

The voice had the stench of a thousand rotting corpses billowing off of every word. The legacy of a hundred revolutionaries vanished with each breath he expelled as if he were some sort of fantastic dragon from deep within the lower intestine of the Pentagon. The problem with this type of monster is that no matter what you do, they keep coming, in one form or another. Cut off the head, the body splits into three so that it can not only destroy you, but your two closest friends as well. Cut off its legs, it sprouts tentacles and chases you to the depths of the sea. Call it an asshole, and well...

"Hey, thanks for stopping that from getting ugly, asshole," I said out of the side of my mouth, attempting to get a peek at the beast. He didn't respond, but I heard slow footsteps edging closer to me as if I were about to be the next contrived victim in some B-grade Hollywood horror movie such as *The English Patient*. And as my luck would have it the guy took forever to come into sight. What first started out as an adrenaline-fueled anticipation session, colored in with all manners of potential doom, soon relaxed into a boring and prolonged waiting-around-to-die moment, even more so like *The English Patient*. And for the record, the only movie worse than *The English Patient* is the unreleased sequel which will be showcased in theaters worldwide the day after the growing Antarctic Neo-Nazi regime of Cooks Island takes over the world. They figure that enough people will end up killing themselves halfway through this reported eight-hour opus (which includes a prequel, a pre-prequel, and sequel all wrapped into one) and therefore, they won't be responsible for the resulting mass genocide. But that is another story altogether...

Finally the bad guy was close enough for me to smell moth balls and stale urine, the signature scent of almost any senior citizen. He put his hand on my shoulder as if we were friends and then he must have signaled for Dingoe to leave us alone because the crazy bastard quickly backed away into the shadows without any protest or even a kiss goodbye. The air in the room grew thick, making it hard to breathe and had there been a clock on the wall, I'm sure that it would have stopped or at least broken under the pressure of the moment. In any case, all signs indicated that time had finally run out.

CHAPTER 41

The Truth, The Whole Truth, and a Little Extra

What amazes me most about life is its lack of preference for anyone. No matter how kindly you behave or how poorly you treat your neighbor, or how ugly you are or how much plastic surgery you get to fix the aforementioned condition, life still doesn't care. And believe it or not, everyone knows this is true. That is why we as human beings spend so much time preparing for death. We want to make sure we are good natured and well mannered in the midst of all the horrific trials and tribulations we experience on a daily basis, not because it's the right thing to do, but because we don't want to think that this life is as good as it gets. We want to believe that this is merely a test, and those who pass it get to move on to the next level. The reality of this is that you end up with a lot of jackasses smiling widely and saying, "It's God's will," while their world is crumbling in all directions.

As I have never been partial to this mode of thinking, shitty situations typically cause me to devise a plan for improvement as opposed to accepting the plight and hoping for paradise. And this is perhaps a semi-scientific explanation for why the good die young and assholes live forever. "The good" passively accept woe and doom and pray that heaven awaits them, while the "the bad" willingly refuse it, plot their revenge, and then buy an island and call it "Heaven." The point is that life doesn't care and maybe we shouldn't either.

"Thinking of a way to escape?" the frail but yet seemingly fierce voice asked. He still had his hand on my shoulder but now he began to change his position. As he rotated around he placed his other hand on my opposite shoulder and looked me squarely in the eye. The pressure being applied by his hands indicated that he still had plenty of strength hidden behind the withered looks and nursing home–smell that disguised him on the surface. Aside from early-bird dinner specials and discount matinees, it was clear that the bastard had no use for his age. His jaw drooped slightly to the left, as if one side had been used more than the other, and his rebellion against dentures was evident by the scattered remains of rotting teeth that protruded like melting glaciers through the tundra of his gums. His face was wrapped in the comfort of a full beard in which, it appeared, he kept a collection of leftovers from *all* of his previous meals. He was bald, but his bushy eyebrows gave the illusion of a forward-parted comb-over as they rested very high upon his head. I gathered that they were as afraid of his eyes as I was. His cold and menacing gaze revealed only one thing: the cruel possibility of anything.

"Are we in Europe?" was the first response I could muster.

"Why?" he asked, "Is that where you were headed?"

"I was just wondering why you are talking so close to my fucking face," I replied. He stood back, a little abashed by my impoliteness but still tickled by my obvious disdain for European culture. A man does not get to have a long career in government-related affairs without first knowing that true patriotism is only achieved by the rejection of everything even seemingly un-American; chances were that this guy had probably invented that requirement.

"Your file said you were 'a little rough around the edges,' so I suppose I should have expected that kind of disrespect."

"Good, then my continued lack of respect won't come as a shock to you either."

He smiled oddly at me and then reached behind his back and pulled out a gun. He pointed it at my forehead and looked deeply into my eyes. Then, in a single swift motion, he flipped the barrel around so that he was holding it in his hand and pistol-whipped me across the face with the butt of the gun. The pain was severe and crippling, and swallowing my own blood was all I could do to keep from crying.

"Let's make a deal," he grinned, obviously proud of himself, "you watch your tongue and I'll try not to hurt you again. Sound good?" Out of strength and too rattled to be a smart ass, I nodded without a word and stared forward like a good pawn should. This was far more perilous than my previous perils; this was the beginning of the end with limited possibility for a sequel or even an unsuccessful spin-off.

"That's a good boy," he continued, satisfied with my silence, "Well you are an interesting character to say the very least. I know you started out as one of us and perhaps that has been what has kept you alive and useful for so long. I suppose the question is: are you willing to work for us again?"

I had been waiting for what seemed like my entire life for someone from "the inside" to ask me that question, someone who could truly understand the reasons for both my actions and other related decisions that ultimately led to the end of my former career. Finally, I was going to have the opportunity to tell the story to the correct set of ears and perhaps get my derailed life back on the right track.

"Well, Sir," I began, "as I am sure you have full clearance, I would estimate that you have read even the classified sections of my file. In that, I am sure it discusses the details of my last mission and the relatively horrific events that occurred. The part it doesn't tell you is…"

"Enough," he cut me off, "that is not relevant nor is it important at this juncture. I am not here to interview you for a job or to reconcile past mistakes. My current focus is only on current events and even more so, my current focus as of this current moment is on the organization that you work for now, currently!"

"So no talk of the past or future, I'm presuming?" I prepared myself for another blow to the face but it didn't come. Instead he just expelled steam from his ears and eyes and glared at me with utter distaste. Regaining what little composure he had, he stood back a bit and decided to rethink his strategy.

"Perhaps I have been going about this wrong," the old man stated, "let me tell you why you're here and then maybe you can use all of your wits to determine your next course of action."

"Sounds fair enough," I responded, though I could tell I had no other option. He ignored me and then took a deep breath before continuing.

"Have you ever heard of a little chain of islands called 'Bramapudha'?" I was hesitant at first but then nodded cautiously, indicating that I was aware of such a place.

"Well that in itself is awfully interesting since the place is not on any maps and only the most powerful of world powers have any inkling of its existence," he paused as if he was waiting for me to say something but I refused to incriminate myself any further by speaking as I figured that there were plenty of other ways to fuck myself over and thus I wanted to diversify. Knowing he now had my full attention, he continued.

"In any case, as you are likely aware, Bramapudha is the world's primary supplier of gold, diamonds, and other precious gems. As you can imagine, many have thought about and even tried to invade this territory but both the geographical complications associated with obtaining all of its treasures as well as the World Power Protection Alliance have prevented this from occurring."

"Holy shit!" I shouted, "All of that nonsense is true?" I was honestly shocked by the reality that had just been revealed to me once again by a completely different and equally credible source. What amazed me the most was the lack of American greed for a change; the fact that we had actually protected these people, as opposed to making them the 52nd or 53rd state or whatever number we are currently at, made me want to change my opinions of patriotism a bit…but only for a moment.

"Yes," he replied, "all of that cryptic, legend-sounding stuff I'm assuming you have heard is true. But therein lies the conflict that has recently developed. You see, the US only agreed to this alliance because the eventual extinction of the Bramapoos was quite evident. The deadly mines consumed at least one or two of them a week and though they once had a large population, our original calculations indicated that the native inhabitants would be almost fully depleted within this current decade."

"That's very interesting and all, but where do I fit in?"

I asked, trying to discern how much they really knew about our operation.

"Oh, Mr. Cypher, or should I say, Saint Cypher, don't you dare play games with me. You see, in recent years the decline in population has become somewhat stagnant, as opposed to the exciting high mortality rates we have seen in the past. This, as you can gather, set off several internal alarms, raised red, bright red and even maroon flags, and forced us to examine the situation. As we pulled back the covers we found that the Bramapoos had somehow gotten their hands on hundreds of servants, all of which were children, that they now had working in the mines for them. At first we thought, 'good for them, this will just delay the inevitable for a few extra years,' but then we realized that all of their servants were white children and we then had to act accordingly.

"We began to research the origin of these white servants and all roads lead back to the Bogota Casino in Las Vegas. We inserted undercover agents to work as waiters and dealers in the Casino but didn't find anything. That is, until we found something, and then found something else. At first the only real issue we could identify, with regards to the Bogota, was that it was an unequal opportunity employer that appeared to hire only white people. Soon, however, our boys found out that all of the employees of the Bogota chose to stay there as well and not keep a residence of their own. As our agents further mingled with these folks, blending in unnoticed, they discovered their "living quarters" in the bowels of the Casino. It was then that we knew something wasn't quite kosher. We launched a full-on, classified, triple-undercover investigation and found out the truth: The Bogota casino is home to an underground corporation that specializes in international cures for laziness, also known as "slave trade." Furthermore, as opposed to capturing fully grown, foreign adults and taking them from their homeland to be sold in an auction like decent slave merchants would, this organization prides itself on only selling white babies that are typically orphaned, unwanted, or stolen. This of course seemed preposterous to us at first because after all, infants can't really add any value with their constant crying and tiny little hands. Hell, we even tried it in this country a hundred years or so ago, and as creative as we got, it still never worked out. But then we realized that they were being sold as long-term investments as opposed to something that produces an immediate return...Are you understanding all of this?" He looked at me sternly, expecting some sort of answer.

"Understanding what exactly?" I asked sheepishly.

"Are you understanding exactly how much fucking trouble you are in, son?" the bastard kind of smiled as he said it and all I could do was nod silently in acknowledgment of my own defeat. Apparently it was an acceptable answer as he continued on without hesitation. He proceeded to accurately describe many of the details of the operation and the only one he really missed was the, "Mexico Exchange." The silence and lack of communication between Koetay and Bristol had certainly paid off as it seemed at the very least, my tequila-swilling friend was going to get out of this mess unburned while the rest of us went down in red, white, and blue flames.

"Good for him," I thought to myself. He was a high-caliber individual who took care of his people and thus his life was filled with purpose. And my life...well, I never had much use for it anyway.

CHAPTER 42

Oh, and One More Thing

"**So you see,** Mr. Cypher, we've got you by the balls. We know all the ins and outs of your operation. We know about Dan Bristol and we know about his affinity for PCP. We know about your attempts to increase your supply chain and we know about your little 'Missionary Cruise Ship.' Essentially, we know enough to publicly crucify you and all of your affiliates and with the help of the media we could perhaps turn this into the biggest crime against humanity ever!" He finally shouted after two hours of telling me things that I already knew. I stared at him blankly, too exhausted and short on blood to respond any other way; like paralyzed, last-breath, desert road-kill, all I could do was hope that death came before the vultures picked my bones apart.

"Not very talkative are we? That's all right, there's not a whole lot you can say at this point and this of course brings us to the turning point in our little conversation. You see, for all the evil you have helped bring back into the world with the rebirth of slavery and the endorsement of sloth, you have also opened the eyes of our own national treasury department," he grinned. Thoroughly lost and bewildered, I shifted from my blank stare to one of utter confusion but remained silent. Knowing he at least had a portion of my attention, the old fart continued.

"As you know this great land of ours is in deep debt and has been for many years. Because of this, we have been searching for a way to stimulate the economy so that the nation can once again be the richest and most opportunistic in the world, a land of milk and money, just like our forefathers intended."

"Don't you mean 'honey?'" I wheezed, trying my best to join the discussion.

"Ha!" he croaked, "That phrase was edited decades ago to mask the true values that this country was founded on. Now stop talking, and listen!" I returned to the comfort of my confused stare and shut my mouth.

"Good boy," he said and patted my head, "I guess you can be broken. Anyhow, the point is this: There is a lot of money in this wholly immoral venture of yours and Uncle Sam, fat, covetous, brilliant bastard that he is, wants his piece of the pie. Consider it your own voluntary, infinitely honorable, and awfully generous contribution to the glorious land of the free. And just maybe, if you help us make this an easy transition, I may find a way to let you slip through the grubby, red fingers of your favorite dirty uncle," he said and stood in a full salute staring off into some distant memory of napalm and repressed cannibalism as the air filled with the scent of his favorite type of barbecue; another candid pre–fourth of July celebration, another great *Un-birthday* at the white-bearded, finger-pointing, Mad Hatter's tea party, "God bless him."

I didn't reply at first as the shock of what I was hearing

shot through me like fifty million death row volts of abashed electricity. After all of the years of running and hiding, all of these secret meetings, shootings, crooked deals, disguises, fake names, complicated fronts, world secrets, and elaborate diversions to keep the US government from discovering our organization, shutting us down, and executing us, the sons-of-bitches wanted an exclusive partnership!

I guess I would have been even more shocked if I didn't secretly smuggle white babies into foreign countries to be sold into slavery for a living, but given the nature of my occupation, this new twist only caught me off guard momentarily. I think the most insane aspect of the whole thing was the fact that Bristol was really spot on after all. And I don't mean with regards to the Bramapoos and the secrets of the world; I mean in his views of Western European human nature (antecedent and descendant). If it meant more money and less work, the pricks were willing to sell their own children and in parallel, the rest of the world was more than happy to purchase them at a fair and profitable price. Somewhere deep inside of me my stomach began to turn and for the first time in seven years I began to question my occupation. Now that it had the potential to be a government-sanctioned project, the cruel and inhumane aspects of the whole thing started to become evident to me. But what the fuck was I going to do? I was down to my last few pints of blood and they already knew enough to blow the cover on the whole operation and turn it into a media-sponsored stoning for all involved. We would be publicly bludgeoned to death by the cast stones of a thousand hypocritical sinners; one nation under God.

As the decision to cooperate became a reality I finally succumbed to being physically sick and vomited all over the shoes of my geriatric interrogator. He scowled at me with absolute intolerance and then kneeled down and untied one of his shoes. As he rose back upwards he placed it under his nose and inhaled the scent as if my stomach was laced with rose petals and bath oils; I nearly puked a second time.

"Aha, the scent of surrender," he smiled, "Was it your nerves or your principles that got the best of you? Smells like a bit of both to me."

"It was, along with the sight of you in general," I replied.

"Does that mean you will cooperate?" he asked gleefully.

"Does that mean I have a choice?"

"Son, the beauty of freewill is that you always have a choice," he grinned, "But not in this case." And with that he pulled a syringe from out of his pocket, uncapped it, and plunged it into my arm. The prick of the needle only resonated for a moment as the room began to spiral in a fitting downward fashion as if someone had pulled the drain clog from the black hole in the middle of the floor and every particle within a thirty-mile radius was being sucked into the sewers of a perpendicular universe; the lowest point possible, all-star leagues below sea level, beyond the deltas of the River Styx to a one-room-mosquito-shack in Hell's own bayou. Finally I would have a chance to rest as the waking world melted into memories.

Chapter 43

In This Corner, "The Shit." In That Corner, "The Fan."

I awoke...on my own accord, slightly disoriented but in a pleasantly sunlit room in what appeared to be a hospital. No cold water, no gunshots, no telephone, just pure, instinctive desire to wake from the deepest of dreamless sleeps. I was dressed in doctor-grade hospital scrubs, not the typical patient gowns with the open air ass flap the nurses use as an excuse to check you out and if you're really lucky, molest you in your sleep. I lifted my arms and found that they were not bound, nor were my feet handcuffed to the bedpost. Despite the strange location, this was in fact the most normal awakening I had had in almost a decade.

I began to wonder if perhaps I had dreamed the whole thing and if I had simply been in a coma the entire time, or maybe I had just gotten severe alcohol poisoning at Mardi Gras. The fact that I was not in a holding cell or seemingly under any sort of guard only added additional support to my suspicions. Was it all just the byproduct of my overactive imagination? Could a dream be that vivid and frightening, and lengthy for that matter?

Me and Bobby McGee

Still in a mild daze, I decided to further explore my surroundings and thus I made my way to the room's only exit. As I stepped through the doorway the shocking reality of the situation surged through me like the menacing revenge of an electric fence on an unsuspecting public pisser. If only it had been in the figurative sense.

I fell to my knees in a fog of pain and disillusionment. In my dazed state I had failed to notice the collar that was locked around my neck, which I found out the hard way was apparently set to produce a massive shock if I attempted to exit the room. I quickly concluded that I was not a lap dog in any way, I was officially their bitch. Furthermore, after pulling up the sleeves of my scrubs and seeing the bandaged wound on my shoulder, as well as the matching ones on my legs, I realized this was certainly not a dream – it was merely a continuation of the nightmare already in progress.

As I lay on the floor recovering from my unexpected encounter with electricity, several sets of shoes suddenly walked into the room; one of the pairs was crusted with the lingering legacy of my last lunch.

"I see you are feeling better," the crusty voice that matched the shoes pronounced.

"Well, I was until…" I began.

"Enough!" he snapped, "We have no time for your whining and complaining; you should be thankful that you are still alive. Now get up!" The guy was a demanding asshole but at least he didn't mince words or waste any time. I stood up slowly as not to cause any panic and made my way back over to the bed. I sat down and found that my new pal was joined by five other individuals, one guy in an expensive silver suit and a prep-school issued hairdo, and four others in white medical coats. The four "Med Coats" all had the same glasses, the same conservative gel-drowned haircuts, and basically the same face; plain. I assumed they were also sharing a brain, be it a very large and deviously intelligent brain, but it was surely quad-community property nonetheless. The old bastard hadn't changed; not even his shoes.

"So how do I get out of here?" I asked, trying to be as concise and to the point as they were.

"We just need you to answer a couple of questions for us," the man in the silver suit said with a golden grin and then extended his hand in my direction, "Dick Richardhed, liaison to the liaison of the executive branch of foreign and domestic trade; pleased to meet you." I felt a sneeze coming on and quickly released it, allowing its slimy residue to take sanctuary in the center of my palm. I then of course used the same hand to shake Mr. Richardhed's, who politely cringed but still proceeded with the standard ritual of introductions without protest.

And with that he launched into the purpose of our discussion without any further hesitation. He explained to me how excited he was about the opportunity and how beneficial it was going to be, *"Not only for a bunch of lazy foreign countries, but for the American way of life as well, from both an economic and social standpoint."* He told me that he personally truly believed that I *"was a saint of some sort, sent by Jesus to save us all from the pains and trials of manual, as well as white-collar, labor."* There were only two major issues with the whole thing in his opinion. He added that there would have been three major issues but it appeared that the rest of the world already seemed to be generally acceptant of the white-baby-slave-trade or, "labor waiver," as it had come to be known. With that out of the way the two hurdles that remained in his opinion were the supply chain methods and the *"Goddamn Religious Right."*

As I had singlehandedly gotten most of the world to endorse and invest in our organization, Mr. Richardhed was hoping I could assist in devising a strategy to overcome the predicted objection from these Christian radicals. When I asked how they planned to convince the rest of the country, he responded by saying that the government figured that the rest of America would just wait for Hollywood to decide if the whole thing was morally objectionable or not and then simply follow suit like *"good little lambs."* They had therefore already gathered a crack team of celebrities, actors, and athletes, to endorse the venture. To my best estimation, they had pretty much thought of everything.

"Well, Dick," I chuckled, "the Religious Right thing is actually an easy one."

"Please enlighten us, Mr. Cypher," he said eagerly. The four Med Coats raised the four clipboards that they had been holding at their sides and prepared to take notes. The old bastard looked at me sternly, hoping whole-heartedly that he was going to have another chance to hurt me.

"Think about it like this, what does the Religious Right hate more than anything?" I asked. The Med Coats all raised their hands but then decided that blurting was a better strategy.

"Jews!" shouted Med Coat One.
"Muslims!" shouted Med Coat Two.
"Catholics!" shouted Med Coat Three.
"Gays!" shouted Med Coat Four.

For a moment I was caught off guard by their responses as I had not originally considered the open-ended aspects of my question. Upon second thought I laughed aloud and it spread contagiously through the room. As the moment of unified hysteria passed I regained my semi-serious composure and continued on.

"I suppose that is all true as well but I was thinking more along the lines of 'Abortion' for this particular discussion." My entire audience nodded in agreement and the Med Coats frantically began to scribble notes on their clipboards. As they did I proceeded with my explanation.

"Since we all agree that this is the thing they hate most, the trick to gaining their acceptance, or blessing, if you will, is to play into that." They all looked at me confused but seemingly still intrigued so I pushed on, "What I am saying is that you should position the selling of white babies into slavery as a solution to the long-debated abortion issue. Instead of killing the unborn fetus, the mother of the unwanted child has the option to give it to us so that it can then be refurbished and sold at a fair market value." It took a second but the wave of nods began and I could tell they were in fact liking my idea, and then of course the old bastard spoke up.

"I think that is a pretty damn good idea, the only part of it I don't understand is the 'us,'" he barked.

"What do you mean?" I questioned, not quite accepting his comment though I was fairly certain I knew exactly what it meant.

"I mean, there is no 'us.' You are not a partner in this and I apologize if you thought for a minute that that was the case. This is more of a hostile takeover and not a merger of any sort, Mr. Cypher."

It was a little disheartening to hear the truth but I suppose I should have known all along that this ride wasn't going to last forever. If it wasn't the government that was muscling us out it would have eventually been the mob, or some other two-bit, organized crime syndicate such as Ticketmaster. But perhaps it was for the best; the only lingering question in my mind was what was going to happen to Bristol and his minions. I decided to wait and discover my own fate before I began to ponder that of others and thus resolved to not ask questions just yet.

"That is a brilliant idea, Mr. Cypher," Richardhed said trying his best to soften the blow, "we will certainly be using that spin." The four Med Coats continued to scribble their notes, never once looking up.

"Yeah, whatever," I said, "what is your issue with the supply chain?"

"That really wasn't the second problem, I just threw that in there," Richardhed replied, "You see that's where our four friends here fit in. We've decided that we need a more predictable 'manufacturing strategy,' if we truly want to make this venture a success. Therefore we have already constructed a new and improved specialty facility dedicated to the continued success of this new program. It's sort of a NASA for white-baby-slave-trade, if you will."

"I don't understand," was my only response.

"Well Cypher, as you know from your own recent supply chain issues, these babies don't grow on trees…at least they didn't before," his enthusiasm was evident with each sickening word, "but with the help of these four geniuses we have created the first indoor white-baby-orchard, if you will. Through the wonders of genetic research and the power of artificial intelligence we have developed synthetic trees to which we can attach fertilized embryos. The branches of these trees have internal tubes that carry all of the essential vitamins and nutrients these embryos need in order to grow into full-fledged babies or 'product,' if you will. This process is sustainable and repeatable and the best part is that it does not require the employment of prostitutes and/or orphanage robbers. And now, with your ideas on how to overcome the Religious Right, we will also have a secondary supply chain that will not only assist with unwanted pregnancies in this country but will also be endorsed by the Lord and all his goddamn modern apostles as a means for eliminating abortion!"

As he finished speaking, the sunlight that had been illuminating the room seemed to retreat in shame. I sat, appalled and abashed, and strangely comfortable with the whole thing. As a businessman I had to hand it to them, they had thought it out pretty well and had the chance to really take the whole project to the next level. As a real human being, all I could think about was my own ass.

"So then that's that and I can go on my way, right?" I asked.

"Not quite," Richardhed replied, "I said that the supply chain was not the second issue; that doesn't mean there isn't still a second mountain we need to climb."

"What's the other issue?"

"Well, you are of course," his golden grin turned into a demonic smirk made of mica, "You see, we can't have you messing things up by blabbing to the press or signing a book deal or going on a daytime talk show. We need to make sure this transition is smooth and as such, we need to make sure you continue to behave yourself."

"So what, does that mean you're going to kill me?"

"Well, Mr. Cypher, that has certainly been a consideration," he said, looking over at the old bastard, "but because of your years of service to this country we figure utter exile and identity abandonment is a more fitting sentence for you."

"How about I promise to behave myself and you just let

me the fuck out of here?" I offered my word but it apparently wasn't enough to soothe their swelling, infected paranoia.

"Oh, we know you will behave yourself, Mr. Cypher. But just to be sure, we're also going to hold onto your friend Dan Bristol for a while in one of our most luxurious padded cells. If you so much as send out a message in a bottle that even references your connection to any of this, we will kill him, revive him, and then kill him again. Do you understand?"

I couldn't believe that they were using Bristol as leverage against me. And yet, despite his relentless phone calls and temporary fits of insanity, the guy had been like a father to me and I would forever be in his debt. The strangeness of the moment was enhanced by my own feelings of disappointment that it wasn't Bobby whom they planned to take into custody. And not because I wished any real harm to befall her (though one or two kicks to the groin wouldn't be such a bad thing), but just so I knew she was still out there. And I suppose she probably is, burning up more matchstick miles on the ever flammable highway to nowhere, searching for a home…I hope she finds it.

CHAPTER 44

Which Way Back to Nowhere?

Freedom is just another word for...a lot of things. It is both the essence of humanity and the empty promises of ten thousand pages of scripture. It is the pledge of a nation to its people and the favorite hostage of a tyrant. It is the cryptic poetry of the oppressed and the windswept caution of the rich and powerful dancing away happily on the breeze it was thrown into. It is the isolated lament of the incarcerated and the pale, moonlit ballad of the wanderer. It is the mantra of the militant, a cause worth fighting for, a hope on the horizon, a fleeting and forgotten dream; it is the way nature intended it.

And perhaps this is the central flaw in the concept of freedom. When a word has too many variances in its meaning, it becomes the constant victim of misconstrued interpretation and its value ultimately begins to decline. The term itself becomes broad and ambiguous, leaving it open to be redefined by anyone who has some lingering notion of its original definition. And then, suddenly, something simple and beautiful is washed in a bathtub filled with high-stakes arrogance and toxic waste and it melts and mutates into a weapon, or a bribe, or a myth.

Yet it has been said that "freedom comes with a price." I believe wholeheartedly that this phrase should be changed to "YOUR freedom comes at a price," because that is the honest truth. As far as I can tell, everything that seems to be free is either lying, ignorant, or rich enough to appear that way. The only real freedom we have is in our own minds, which is conversely the reason why the world is so fucked in the first place. The freedom to imagine the possibilities of progress, the choice to dream of a better tomorrow, and the liberty to take as many liberties as we so desire is the molten core of both prosperity and demise; we're just left to hope we pick the right type of crust to stand on. Unfortunately satisfaction is only guaranteed in commercials and the grass is always greener on the other side of the fence…unless of course you let your dog piss and shit on your next-door neighbor's lawn.

And isn't that really what happens in this world? We just find ways to constantly provoke each other by sending the proverbial hounds out to piss on our neighbor's lawn in order to make our own *seem* better, greener; the envy of the planned, residential subdivision. The reason for this constant defacing of figurative property is simply that destruction is easier than creation and in parallel, history (along with the people who write the history books) helps to heal all wounds. Of course time, like a scratched record, skips ahead and then inevitably repeats itself over and over again until someone either changes the track or turns off the music altogether. Then there is a silent lull, until the album is remastered and repackaged and sold to a brand new generation of soon-to-be-deaf ears with their own pack of dogs primed and ready to do their bidding.

And if that's how it is, if it is all just a big government-sponsored piss party, what more can we do as bystanders than attempt to enjoy our existence by doing whatever makes us happy all of the time? And more so, if our freedom has boundaries, how can we ever expect to be personally satisfied? These questions are as open-ended as the ingredients in fast food and as such, will probably never be truthfully answered by anyone until high-priced lawyers and Supreme Court Justices are involved...okay, you're right; they will *never* be truthfully answered.

My mind wanders like this on a daily basis, celebrating its freedom, even if it's only in my head. Luckily my own days of wandering appear to be over though I must say from time to time I miss the game. But I suppose even if I wanted to play again and was allotted infinite rolls of the dice it'd be awfully tough to come up with an idea as cunning and lucrative as Dan Bristol's white-baby-slave-trade.

And even if I did there would be no one to fund it as the last of the insane venture capitalists was dead and gone, and finding another would take luck that I've never had. I still wish to this day that Bristol had just gone quietly but anyone who ever knew him knows that wasn't his way. The way I'd heard it was that they actually managed to detain him, handcuffs and all, for about 30 seconds. Somewhere within that short window his pupils swelled and I'm sure the agents shifted shape before his eyes, becoming uniformed spider monkeys with loaded shotguns and the ability to multiply when exposed to oxygen or something of that nature. He broke free of the handcuffs by using all the PCP-induced might that he had but the struggle itself shattered both of his frail wrists. He had no methods of defense other than his hands and his potentially lethal insanity, and still they fired upon him. Of course, he didn't go down from that and so they fired upon him again and again until he fell to his knees. As the life trickled from his body onto the foam floors of the Bogota penthouse, Dan looked up one last time and smiled at the agents. Then he lifted his hands and extended both of his middle fingers and shouted, "You're all a bunch of germs and apes, soulless creatures made to kill and rape, go sell all of your children like recycled trash, my last words are spoken, KISS MY ASS." And with that, the master of vision, real, imagined, and all points in between, fell to the floor never to move again. Well, except for about thirty minutes or so of twitching, which often happens when one's body is shredded to pieces by bullets but that would just be too gross to mention.

But vile, unnecessary details aside, the man was gone and so were his visions. And so we come to me. First off, after what happened to Bristol I guess I can revel in the fact that I killed a bunch of people for the government; murder for hire did have its perks and a sort of 401(k) plan after all. And besides, I could never come up with a hallucination as vivid as Bristol's and perhaps that was the real reason they let me go and took him. They were afraid if he ever got the opportunity to come up with another idea, it might not work out as much in their favor as the selling of white babies into slavery did, and I would tend to agree.

Anyhow, I was given an ultimatum. I was told I had two days to vanish and never be heard from again. The caveat being if they ever found me or discovered my whereabouts, I would be shot on sight. This seemed to be about the fairest deal I had gotten from anyone since I first met up with that

Absinthe bottle and its associated thugs in New Orleans some seven or eight years ago now…I can't believe it lasted that long and that it is still perpetuating itself with a whole new and even more sinister crew leading the way, so sinister in fact that they took all of Bristol's assets including the casino and all of its "employees." And since all of my money was essentially dispersed from that big pot of gold, I was left with nothing but the thousand dollars I had in my wallet. Everything else, including my social security number and grocery-store-club-card memberships, was erased. I was less than a ghost; I was an untold urban legend that no one but the best secret keepers in the world had ever heard of. Anyhow, I took the hint and high-tailed it to the one place I knew I could find sanctuary, forgiveness, and most importantly, forgetfulness.

It is a scientific fact that the Mexican desert has no long-term memory; it is a region of amnesia. It forgets all it has seen just as quickly as the wind shifts the sand; no footprints, no fossils, no past, no questions. Basically, if you have been quasi-convicted of a major crime against humanity that the government is looking to cover up and you need a place to hide out so they don't kill you, the Mexican desert will do nicely. And so I drifted down below the borderline and hitched a cab that I asked to drop me off by a statue of the Virgin Mary that seemed a bit out of place.

I walked slowly in the direction of Koetay's hacienda, hoping I was in fact going the right way. I hadn't gotten more than a mile when I heard the sound of an engine in the distance. It got closer as I stood still and began to think perhaps I wasn't going to make it after all, but soon a sigh of relief, along with a cloud of sand and dust, washed over me and there sat Koetay on an old motorcycle, sidecar and all.

"It is about time you stumbled back down here. Get in, Mr. Villalopez, or are you not going my way?" he grinned.

"That depends, which way is that?"

"The opposite of the one you came from," he replied.

"I am definitely going that way," I said and jumped into the sidecar. As we approached the plantation only one thing came to my mind. It was something I hadn't thought about in a very long time, my long-lost love…

"Hey, Koetay," I began.

"Yes, Mr. Villalopez?"

"Can I have a drink?"

"Anytime my friend, anytime."

And that is how it went for Koetay and me. He had been informed a few days before I arrived that the organization had been taken over by the greediest corporation in the free and not-so-free world and, therefore, he expected that I would come to find him if I got out alive.

We lived well with plenty of servants to take care of us. They built me my own little house on the property and took care of virtually everything for me, which made it much easier to stay drunk all of the time. If nothing else, it felt good to be me again, even though I had a new identity and technically wasn't really me at all, but that's beside the point. Just know that even though I am drinking heavily again, I haven't lost my ambition. If I get around to it, I plan to start an opal farm sometime next year and have already ordered a team of our strongest white slaves to begin digging a hole down towards the Earth's core where the best opal grows.

But enough about me; as for the rest of the world, they continued to show their support for the white-baby-slave-trade and after just a little bit of protest, a smidge of help from Hollywood, and the eventual overturning of Roe *vs.* Wade, *all* of the citizens of the United States of America began to embrace the idea of "labor-waivers," and in time (a month or so from the unveiling) began to purchase their very own. Soon the major celebrity endorsements and advertisements began to surface all over television and in magazines and the whole thing went prime-time global, and will probably end up being intergalactic at some point. Needless to say, the US economy reached a new high and people became generally nicer to each other since they didn't have the pressure of their jobs to worry about anymore and there were no unplanned pregnancies, or at least no "unplanned parents." Meanwhile, the government eagerly produced the bulk of its product from their indoor white-baby orchard, which soon became several indoor white-baby orchards and eventually, full-on farms that even offered festivities and hay-rides in the fall for the non-slave kiddies. In short, the best way to describe this brave new world is with simplicity and concise elegance – it is fucked.

    I suppose at the end of the day all one can really do is smile up at the calming pastels of poisonous gases on the sunset horizon of any urban empire, and marvel at our own copacetic comfort level. There is nothing fleeting about indifference, it will likely outlast even the cockroaches. It will remain as some omnipotent force, forever altering the path of gravity, and not caring about the possibility of life on Earth ever again. Yes, it seems the whole world is going to hell in a recycled hand-basket; I'm just glad I could do my part.

THE END

About the Author

CHAD COENSON was born in Orlando, FL, but he can barely remember that and pretty much spent most of the years following his birth in a nomadic state of perpetual motion until finally finding a home in the Pacific Northwest with his wife and two dogs. He has a degree in creative writing from the University of Arizona and spends his time "trying" not to take life too seriously. Despite his generally adventurous nature and willingness to attempt almost anything, he has never had the opportunity to cast the first stone.

CPSIA information can be obtained at www.ICGtesting.com
Printed in the USA
LVOW11s2240071114

412630LV00001B/11/P